Prelude To A
Certain Midnight

Prelude To A
Certain Midnight
Gerald Kersh

With an introduction by Paul Duncan

LONDON BOOKS CLASSICS

LONDON BOOKS
39 Lavender Gardens
London SW11 1DJ
www.london-books.co.uk

First published 1947
This edition published by London Books 2017

A catalogue record for this book
is available from the British Library

ISBN 978-0-9568155-4-5

Printed and bound in Great Britain by
CPI Group (UK) Ltd, Croydon, CR0 4YY

Typeset by Octavo Smith Publishing Services in Plantin 9.75/12.5
www.octavosmith.com

FOR

MY MOTHER

INTRODUCTION:
ONE MURDER MAKES MANY

> I loved that desperate period when black was black and white
> was white, and light was light and darkness was darkness. Now
> comes Blind Man's Holiday. I hate this dismal rat-grey twilight.
> I hate this little hour. I hate the squeaking and the scraping behind
> the wainscot. This is the hour of the mice – damn their beady
> eyes...
>
> – *Gerald Kersh*

Guardsman Gerald Kersh was unhappy. He had enlisted on August
13, 1940, to fight for his country against the Germans. After being
buried alive during one of the many German bombing raids on
London he returned to his barracks with a wonky leg – a cartilage
had to be removed, and he was invalided out of active service.
Unable to fight on the battlefields of Europe, North Africa or the
Orient, or on the high seas or in the air, Kersh mounted a concerted
campaign on newsprint, over the airwaves and on the silver screen.

Unofficially, Kersh wrote propaganda pieces, under the name
Piers England, on the horrors of war and the stiff upper lips of
the Brits for *The People*; he was read by five million every Sunday
morning over a late breakfast. These provocative articles tapped
into current news, speculated about the future and exposed war
crimes using eyewitness accounts, headed with confrontational
titles like 'Hell-Hounds Of Poland', 'Love Thief Of The Gestapo!',
'A Slight Case Of Atrocity', 'A Daughter Of France Strikes Back'
and 'Britain Under The Swastika'. In response, the Nazis put 'Piers
England' on their death list.

However, Kersh was best known for his novels and short stories.
Novelist John Brophy wrote of Kersh in the *Sunday Graphic*:

> Whether or not war poets are in short supply, the war has produced
> one outstanding prose writer, a novelist with a sharp and distinct

individuality of his own who nevertheless contrives to express a considerable amount of those common national characteristics we lump together as British. He is Gerald Kersh.

His stories about the Coldstream Guards, *They Die With Their Boots Clean* and *The Nine Lives Of Bill Nelson*, revealed a style as vigorous and racy as Kipling's, and a comparable gift for spellbinding the reader by the deft resourcefulness of his storytelling.

He is that rare combination, a master craftsman with the popular touch; he can satisfy highbrow and lowbrow alike.[1]

After the publication of *They Die With Their Boots Clean*, Kersh published novels and short-story collections every six months. Although he had corresponded with the BBC since the 1930s, hoping to capitalise on the publication of *Night And The City*, it was only after his enormous success as a war novelist that they decided to make use of his talents for their radio broadcasts. Kersh wrote accounts of bravery on the field of combat for *Into Battle* and *For Gallantry*, a series of comedy sketches featuring Joe Twist on an anti-aircraft battery for *Ack-Ack Beer-Beer* and a number of stories told by kindly suburban newsagent Mr Chickery in *At Home To The Forces*. Kersh was never credited.

For his day job, the Ministry of Information allocated Kersh to the Army Film Unit, writing commentaries for *Malta GC*, *Street-fighting* and *The Ship King George V*, but he was thrown out when he did not pass officer training at Sandhurst – becoming an officer was a requirement of the post. Retained as a specialist, he was assigned to the Films Division and used as a roaming author without portfolio, writing treatments and stories (for *Nine Men*), polishing existing scripts (*The Gentle Sex*) and spitballing with producers and directors in story conferences. He rarely sought or received credit:

The Ministry was not sorry to lend me to Sir Alexander Korda, to work with him and Wesley Ruggles on a picture called *The Perfect Strangers* – another piece of nonsense, starring Robert Donat in a bowler hat and Deborah Kerr in an apron, or some such frippery.

The less said about this the better.

I liked Korda. But there was a war on. We were, it is true, ducking every five minutes as the V1s came down. In France the armies of democracy were smashing to Paris, Germany was beginning to fall back. Heads were rolling, blood was flowing, desperate legions were joining battle on the torn-up plains.

I behaved improperly. Having talked Colonel Morrow Krum into getting me accredited as an American war correspondent (Brigadier Turner had said that as far as I was concerned accreditation as a British correspondent was neither necessary nor possible), I got a uniform, put it on, and made contact with a man I knew and said that I wanted to get to France without any chi-chi, as soon as possible.

The nameless man said: 'We take off after dawn tomorrow. Will you be ready?'

I was ready.

I had not flown before. I cannot say that I enjoyed it, but it was more exhilarating than story conferences.

I ought to make it clear that I was not hunting news. The newsmen – the professional hunters – are better at that kind of thing than I can ever be, and I should never dare to tread upon their stalking grounds.

I was watching the emotional, the human side of things. I am only a teller of stories, not a historian; that is to say, I glean in the wake of reporters who record events.

I covered a great deal of territory between Heston, Mont Saint-Michel, Rennes, Saint-Jacques, Le Mans, Chartres, the four corners of Paris, Houdan, Dreux, Verneuil, Mortagne, Alençon, Mayenne, Fougères and Paddington – but operated as a kisser of babies, an embracer of sobbing women, and a slapper of backs in a friendly kind of way among liberated men.[2]

Kersh wrote about 'His Paris Pilgrimage' for *The People*, detailing his banter with farmers, café owners and the Parisian lowlife that worked with the Resistance to kill Nazis. In true Kershian fashion, he regards his travels as an epic comedy of errors:

I am demonstrably guilty of sneaking out of the British Isles without a permit, travelling as an unauthorised person in a military aircraft, landing in a Certain Zone, flying over Forbidden Territory in another military aircraft, landing without authority on a Military Airfield, misdirecting a Colonel, travelling without authority in an Army Transport, insinuating myself into a Theatre of Operations, carrying arms as a Non-Combatant, firing a couple of shots as such, stealing a Jeep, kidnapping a Courier, immobilising another Jeep, stealing oil and petrol, falsifying Orders, misappropriating bandages, stowing away on a military aircraft, entering Great Britain without a permit, slinking past Camp Guards, riding as an Unauthorised Person in a Military Vehicle, and misbehaving in general.

I am informed that I cannot legally be hanged or shot, but that I may consider myself lucky if I get off with three hundred years in San Quentin. My record being what it is, I may be paroled after two hundred years; and then the British Authorities will get me.

Nothing much happens: the War Department withdraws my accreditation. (They re-accredit me later, and gave me the blue card of the Supreme Headquarters of the Allied Expeditionary Forces.) I have got off lightly – I have got away with worse than murder.[3]

But what was the real reason for Kersh's dangerous and unauthorised trip?

***

When I get to a place I smell out the people I know. Soon after I arrived in Paris I went to see if the Simon family still lived in their old flat in Montmartre.

The Simons are Jews by origin and have lived in Paris for about forty years. It occurred to me that the Simons might be in, or at least near, their old block.

Why? Because they have two children who have been missing for a long time: therefore it was reasonable to suppose that they would have left word as to their whereabouts just in case somebody ever chanced to come back.

By good fortune I found them.[4]

Kersh does not reveal that the 'Simons' are the Kershenblatts – his uncle's family. When his father Hyman Kershenblatt, and Hyman's brother Simon, both born in Poland, escaped service in the Czar's army and walked across Europe to make a new life for themselves, Simon remained in Paris while Hyman fulfilled his destiny in London as a tailor. The families stayed close. In 1929, the eighteen-year-old Gerald Kersh stayed with the Kershenblatts for more than six months, became fluent in the language, and, some say, fell in love with his cousin Anna.

When Simon and wife Berthe visited London for a family wedding the following year, they brought Anna and her brother Maurice with them – Anna stayed with Gerald's family for six months.

Now Kersh had found Berthe in liberated Paris:

She began to cry. I hate to see women crying: there is nothing I can do about it. I did not even have a spare handkerchief.

She stopped soon after and said: 'One would have said that it was a hundred years. I have been so lonely and miserable. I have not known what to do.'

She wept a little again.

Then, lacking conversation at this point, I pulled out of my pocket a tin of steak and kidney pudding, and offered it to her. It was one of those moments of embarrassment in which one finds nothing in the world to say.

She looked at the tin and asked what it was. I said that I did not know because I had not yet opened it.

'Maurice, my son, he left Paris shortly after the Germans got in and went to the Midi. From there he went, I hear, to Corsica. I have heard nothing from him for three years.'

I was able to tell her that Maurice had got to North Africa, and was a brigadier in the Fighting French Forces. This made her cry again. He seemed so young for all that... Her little Mimi, a brigadier!

'And Annie... I do not know where she is. You remember my daughter Annie? It is several years. I know she has two sons. For the rest I must wait and see.'[5]

After the fall of France, the Nazis systematically rounded up the French, Polish and German Jews of Paris, held them in Drancy internment camp, formerly La Cité De La Muette (The City Of The Silent), a failed modernist social housing project built in the early 1930s, and shipped more than 67,000 souls to Auschwitz extermination camp in Poland.

'Ah, God, [the Germans] have wrought us infinite woe... infinite woe! What is there left for us? Ashes. Dust. Broken stones. Ruin and also loneliness. Only one thing remains for us to be thankful for. The Germans are gone.

'But... Gerald... can you bring back a tree out of the ashes of the wood with which you made the fire? Or a life out of this filth with which they have smothered us? Nothing you do or say will ever bring anything back that they have taken away!'[6]

***

Towards the end of 1944, as the war in Europe was being won, both Kersh and Piers England wrote of the social and psychological repercussions of the conflict. They campaigned against the profiteering of black marketeers ('Men Who Thank Heaven For The War'), extolled the virtues of the British spirit ('Of Such Stuff Are Britons Made'), and repeatedly called for the protection and well-being of children ('But No Tears For Children').

Many of the articles were generated by correspondence from the readers, including 'Piety And Charity', published January 7, 1945, which detailed the treatment of women with unwanted pregnancies by an unnamed organisation. Mrs X, who became pregnant while her husband was serving overseas for several years, paid the Home, handed over all her monies and papers and was 'confined' for three months after the birth – the child was given up for adoption.

> She was not allowed out of the Home except under supervision, and both her incoming and outgoing mail was censored. The reason given for their refusal to release Mrs X and the baby was that a *Repentance* period was necessary for these mothers, and that all of them had to stay and work for a while after their babies were born.[7]

Odhams Press, the newspaper owners, would not allow Piers England to state that the Salvation Army was the organisation in question.

A few weeks later Kersh wanted to highlight complaints about conditions at Duncarse Children's Home in Dundee. The article was not published. Kersh wrote to editor Harry Ainsworth, also his close friend, on February 28, 1945:

> It was nice to see you again but let's get the position clear. My only inducement to write under the Piers England pseudonym was the hope of doing a certain amount of good by writing from time to time on subjects about which I felt deeply. Piers England wasn't materially advantageous to Gerald Kersh who got no publicity and little money out of it. Well, as far as I'm concerned, Piers England died when his article on the Duncarse affair was killed. The lawyers objected. But did they or anybody else, before killing the story, take a look at the documentary evidence in my possession concerning the matter? Again, the Salvation Army article lost all this effect by the suppression of the name of the organisation concerned because Odhams Press was afraid of losing a few Salvationist readers. What incentive have I, therefore, to go on writing stories under a proprietary nom de plume for an organisation which fears the slightest possibility of controversy? I see, of course, their point of view. Why risk losing a few readers for the vague hope of making life a little less miserable for a few helpless brats whom nobody gives a damn about anyway? But I

can't look at things in that way. No personal aspersion, pal, and no ill feeling. I'll write a weekly Gerald Kersh article if you like, but Piers England pays no dividends.[8]

***

In the 1930s, Kersh had desperately haunted the bars of Fleet Street to pick up crumbs of work for the *Daily Mirror*, willing to write about anything for a few kopeks. Now, in 1945, Kersh was a bestselling author of war fiction, and he was free to express himself on any subjects he chose. As the war came to an end, Kersh's articles for *The People* were reflective, philosophical and angry:

> While the victory fever was burning up to its crisis, and the public pulse-rate was bounding somewhere near the danger mark, I went emotionally flat, and found myself thinking of all the wrong things. The night before [Victory in Europe Day, May 8, 1945] I had run into a grim-faced young man with one leg who had hailed me with a melancholy kind of pleasure and asked me if I remembered him. There was something familiar about his face, but for the life of me I could not place him.
>
> Then he told me his name and it all came back to me in a kind of sick gush of recollection. In September 1939, I taught him the right way to sharpen a Scout knife and gave him for his birthday *The Big Book For Boys*.
>
> He was fifteen then; one of those bright-eyed, strong-limbed, wholesome bounding boys, with a round red face which expressed nothing but an enthusiastic appetite for life.
>
> And here he was, a veteran soldier, crippled for life and shaken by suffering. His light was quenched. There were too many things he needed to forget. I felt a dreadful impulse to burst into tears.
>
> He seemed, just then, to symbolise all the sadness and ruin of the war; all the wastage of the years that have leaked away and left us so grey and tired.
>
> He went away singing, and came back silent; to hop and hobble through the hard years yet to come.

14

This has been an expensive war, and a dangerously high-priced victory, I thought; and I said so to my young friend, who replied: 'You're right. We have paid pretty dearly for it. But we couldn't afford to lose.'⁹

As the victory celebrations overtook London that night, Kersh witnessed it from a rooftop, drinking beer, lost in contemplation:

This war has hurt us more than we know. The visible wounds of London will be easier to heal than its internal injuries.

We have lived too long in the Valley of the Shadow of Death. We have learned bad habits. Too many of us, in petty ways, have lost some of our pride. In begging for little favours and stooping to meanness for the sake of a little extra something to put in our bellies.

We have become cadgers, opportunists, bribers-and-corruptors, belly-worshippers, spendthrifts, boot-lickers and bullies. We have forgotten our manners.

We have perhaps lost our morals, and prostituted ourselves for an extra bit of fish. We have perhaps thrown away restraint and deceived husbands and wives. We have, in smashing the tyranny of Germany, fallen under the dictatorship of our flesh appetites, and come under the domination of the 'stomach god'.

We have lost much and, between ourselves, maybe we are not much to boast about. In point of fact, I would go so far as to say that we are an undeserving lot of cases – if we had lost the only two things which, as it happens, we have never lost. I mean courage and honour.

We still have these, thank God, and, therefore (with care and patience) things will turn out well for us in the end.

Now that the European war is over, let us get down to some real fighting.

The war against Fascism and Nazi Oppression was only one fall in a larger combat: I mean the unending tussle of good and evil, wrestling desperately, tooth and nail, all-in and nothing barred, in the ring of eternity.

Good and Evil mix only in combat. The slightest concession to Evil is collaboration with the enemy. If you do not resist Evil, you become – with all the goodwill in the world – the accomplice of Jack The Ripper, the Beast Of Belsen, Charlie Peace, the man who manslaughtered the little boy and got six years for it, and every murderer at large.[10]

A fortnight later, Kersh's anger is palpable as he surveys the damage wrought by the Nazis:

Several members of my own family, it is established, were taken away in one of the death trains to one of the gas chambers for scientific examination, and no doubt their calcined bones, distributed as fertiliser, are helping to grow cabbages to feed the Germans.[11]

He reached the following conclusion:

It will take more than our lifetime to tidy up the filthy mess the Germans left behind. Whole peoples have gone to ruin. A hundred years must pass before the starved and vitiated Greeks breed good, ordinary healthy children again, for example. And the marrow has been sucked out of the bones of Holland, Hungary, Yugoslavia, Czechoslovakia, Italy and Poland.

If you could see the whole of Europe from a height it would resemble a washed-out old patchwork quilt spoiled by cigarette burns.

I mean to say that we are not likely to see the ripe, sweet final fruits of the Victory. It's all right; I'm not being pessimistic. It is a law of life; no man may live to see a full harvesting of all the seeds he has sown.

He sweats for his children, and his children's children, as his grandfathers sweated for him before he was born.

This is what makes man Man, this blind and patient striving for an unknown object; this sublime and beautiful love for the unborn; this very gallant planting of trees in whose shade he is destined never to sit; this wonderful, unalterable faith in the buried mysteries of the good earth which, properly cherished, replenishes itself and grows sweet and gracious.[12]

***

If this were a slush story about a horse, you would hand it around until your sentimental tears had made pulp of the paper. But you will pay little attention to this. For I write of the Dead. The Dead don't make circulation. The Dead have no sex appeal, win no beauty competitions, ride no Derby winners, and pay no dividends. The Dead tell no tales.

Death is not news, unless it happens to come sensationally by – for example – a knot in a silk stocking in a Soho bedroom; or the slash of a bread knife at one of the three sordid corners of some Eternal Triangle.

The fact is, that while one corpse makes you think, 10,000 corpses in heaps stun you and lead your mind away from the agonies of death.

You are stimulated by a lunatic running amok with a jackknife on Clapham Common. But the cool, calculated butchery of a myriad of men, women and children is something you brush away like fluff off the sleeve of your Sunday suit.

I have been privileged to see several thousand feet of film shot in the horror camps of Germany; especially Belsen.[13]

The British 11th Armoured Division liberated Belsen concentration camp on April 15, 1945, and discovered over 60,000 prisoners inside, most of them half starved and seriously ill. There were also 13,000 corpses lying around the camp, unburied. Sidney Bernstein of the Ministry of Information ensured that the horrors were fully documented on camera. Kersh wrote about it on June 17 in *The People*:

> Sergei Nolbandov, who is editing the 10,000 horrid inches of filth that our cameramen photographed in Belsen, told me that he had much to contend with. He showed the moving picture

of the Belsen horrors to one of those silly men who maintain that the reporting of atrocity is ninety per cent propaganda, because people simply don't do such things to their fellow men.

For example: among the tens of thousands of pictures taken, roll upon roll in Belsen, there is a picture of something that looks very much like a wax dummy.

It is a photograph of the attenuated body of a young girl who has died of sickness and of hunger. Her flesh has the appearance of candle grease; and her face, which is composed of dead, shiny white skin upon hungry bone, doesn't look real. At the same time, in a weird and deathly way, the girl looks beautiful.

'I don't believe it,' says the silly man. 'She looks like wax.'

'What can one say to such people?' I was asked.

There is nothing to say to such people, because they're rigid in their determination to apologise for the Germans, and will not believe that it is possible for human beings standing upright on their hind legs and having nice blue eyes and shorts and trousers to behave really outrageously, like people in horror stories. It occurs to me that a dead weight of obstinate stupidity is going to hang on the heels of Peace.

The sentimental Old Believers in the reconcilability of Good and Evil are coming back. They are going to maintain that the abominations of places like Belsen were, so to speak, merely local phenomena; that the Germans in general were not responsible for the torturing, starving and neglect of hundreds of thousands of men, women and children.

It will be argued that a Camp is a Camp, and that the people of the surrounding country knew nothing of what went on behind the barbed wire; and that even the Belsen guards knew not what they did.

Crime, you will be told, is a disease; a disorder of the nerves, to be dealt with by the psychologist rather than the policeman and the judge.

I don't believe that the people – the fat, well-dressed, placid people passing along the road on the safe side of the barbed wire fences – failed to observe the desolation within – the filth and the wretchedness that, even in two dimensions on a screen, will get at your nostrils.[14]

An edited version of the atrocities film was screened for Kersh on September 25, and the following week he was sent all the dope sheets and other documents he needed for him to write the commentary.

The film, which was formally titled *German Concentration Camps Factual Survey*, was never completed and released – it was deemed too controversial and confrontational. The Allies were trying to rebuild Germany, and a reminder of the brutal crimes of the Nazis that, by association, were also the crimes of the German people, would do more harm than good to the nation's collective psyche:

> The outbreak of sentimental pity for conquered Germany disgusts and frightens me. Beware of pity! That which you pity is dangerous; by pitying it, you give it a stranglehold on your throat.[15]

Some footage from the film was used in short documentaries, and extracts were presented at the Nuremberg trials of twenty-three prominent leaders of the Third Reich that ran from November 20, 1945, to October 1, 1946.

Although Kersh was relieved to find out that his cousin Anna had escaped capture and was alive and well, it was with the Nazi atrocities and the Nuremberg trials fresh in his mind that Kersh began writing *Prelude To A Certain Midnight* during the autumn of 1946.

***

A remarkable novel, which has been ignored for more than fifty years, *Prelude To A Certain Midnight* follows the hunt for a child-murderer in Soho.

Almost absentmindedly, we are introduced to the denizens of the Bar Bacchus, beginning with Amy Dory, known as 'Catchy', a degenerated beauty whose eyes have become like 'a couple of cockroaches desperately swimming in two saucers of boiled rhubarb'.[16] Through her we meet her landlady Mrs Sabbatani, widow of tailor Sam Sabbatani, and learn that fifteen years earlier their eleven-year-old daughter Sonia 'had been gagged and bound, raped and strangled, and thrown into the cellar of an empty house'.[17] The Sabbatanis were destroyed by the murder. They never recovered. Sam died soon after, from grief as much as from his ulcer.

The story continues to drift from character to character, jumping back and forth in time and place, ignoring the rules of conventional narrative. It is also a deconstruction of the crime and mystery genre.

The police investigation is in the hands of Detective Inspector 'Dick' Turpin, who understands the psychology of his prey and explains it while having a drink at the Bar Bacchus:

> Say, for the sake of example, I am a timid sort of man. I am as quiet as a mouse. Why am I timid? I'm timid because I am afraid. What I really want to do is show myself to the world as a great big hairy creature with a pair of fists on me like hammers and the courage of the devil. I'd be a real thug, a tough guy, if I could. But I can't. I'm always, if the truth must be told, one of those shrinkers-back full of all sorts of hate. You see, I'm dead yellow. And what happens is, I cover it all up by pretending to be sweet and soft and gentle. But underneath I'm waiting for just one chance to get at someone.
>
> How does it break out? You can mark my words, somebody's got to help it. The person that helps is always the willing victim. You know what I mean; somebody who gets a thrill out of suffering. This willing victim is all that he needs to make him feel powerful. He never felt powerful before. You give him a feeling of self-confidence because you lie down and let yourself be ill-treated by him.
>
> And so there comes a certain night when somebody falls into his arms. More often than not it's a child. All of a sudden he feels that he's something like a man of power; and he rapes that child. After he has raped that child he knows that if she lives she'll recognise him; and her identification together with the medical

evidence will make things hard for him. So what does he do? With a child it's easy. Get hold of her throat and hold on tight.[18]

Where the motive and trail of a theft can easily be deducted and traced, there are no such concrete clues to work with on a sex murder. Turpin can progress no further.

Miss Asta Thundersley, a habitué of Bar Bacchus and a formidable do-gooder, pokes her nose into the investigation. She is in the mould of Gladys Mitchell's character Beatrice Adela Lestrange Bradley, or, more precisely, the antithesis of Mrs Bradley. Where Mrs Bradley is stick-figure thin, Miss Thundersley 'resembles a man, a man to be reckoned with. Imagine a retired middleweight boxer, turned gentleman farmer, impersonating his aunt'.[19] Where Mrs Bradley is a distinguished psychiatrist, pre-eminent in her field, and a woman of commanding intellect and erudition, Miss Thundersley is simply a blundering, loud-mouthed battleaxe. Where Mrs Bradley is seemingly omniscient with her deductions and confrontations with the criminal classes, Miss Thundersley is at a loss and without a clue how to root out the murderer.

However, Miss Thundersley believes that 'whosoever kicks a dog kicks a man by proxy', because 'if you tear the wings off a fly, then you'll graduate from fly to mouse, mouse to rat, rat to cat, cat to dog, dog to child'.[20] Asta gathers everyone she suspects – the denizens of Bar Bacchus – at a party, and learns nothing. Yet, she is right – the murderer is present.

***

In January 1945, Kersh was at Number 1 Court of the Old Bailey to witness Karl Gustav Hulten, an American soldier aged twenty-two years, and Elizabeth Maude Jones, an eighteen-year-old dancer from Wales, being sentenced to death for the murder of George Edward Heath – the Man With The Cleft Chin. Writing as Piers England, Kersh presented Hulten as a symptom of the times:

> There is nothing more pathetic than the credulity of the crook. It is childlike. But I have observed that a remarkably large number

of criminals, especially criminals of the violent kind, haven't progressed beyond the infancy of ambition – the stage at which little boys want to be outlaws and yearn for the day when they can drink, swear, spit, smoke, stay out all night, back horses and lark about with girls.

Retarded adolescence is the disease of the age. The false ideals of men and women who will not grow up pollute our civilisation. The undeveloped soul of a naughty little boy, in the body of a grown man, becomes damnably dangerous.

The swaggering self-assertion of the child, hanging over into adult years, breeds the terribly touchy vanity of the gunman... the gunman who descends from infamy to infamy in order to prove that he is not afraid, and who will shoot a man in the back in the dark to win the good opinion of his own kind.

They sow the seeds of their own destruction, yes. But they destroy others, too. Because Hulten, that poor distorted Peter Pan, would not grow up beyond his crime novelettes, the Man With The Cleft Chin was foully murdered.

Who is to blame? God knows: He sees everything; and it may be that, on a certain Day when all the people of the earth are gathered for judgement, an awful finger will beckon a certain bespectacled story-writer or some plump, respectable film producer, while a dreadful Voice says: 'You, who made dirt desirable and murder romantic, come into Our Presence and answer for the slaughter of Hulten, Jones and the Man They Slew!'[21]

Kersh expanded upon his ideas about the retarded adolescence of criminals in *Prelude*. The murderer relives the thrill of killing the little girl, and now knows what Friedrich Nietzsche's Zarathustra meant when he spoke of the murderer who 'thirsted for the pleasure of the knife'.[22] He plans to carry out many more murders, with different instruments, to keep the thrill fresh. And, as for the police: 'The danger that followed the kill was, so to speak, the savoury that rounded off the roast.'[23] Just as Karl Hulten had Elizabeth Jones, the murderer has a girlfriend, Catchy, and blames the murder on her, for she gave him the confidence to make his desires a reality. He dreams he is a conqueror full of purity and strength.

**

At Asta Thundersley's party, just as the murderer is hidden among dozens of suspects, so Kersh's central premise is hidden within the chatter of their conversations.

Hemmeridge, a writer of mystery novels, says 'one murder makes many'.[24] When we go to a wedding or see a baby, it puts an idea into our head. Likewise with murder – if the murderer gets away with it, it will encourage others to come out of the woodwork and murder. Hemmeridge continues, saying that most of us do our killing vicariously, through books: 'One of those Americanish tough-guy books in which the hero is a bit of a murderer thinly disguised as a private detective and goes about slapping glamorous female prisoners in the face or tearing their clothes off or something.'[25] Monty Bar-Koch Ba asks why they are so concerned about one child when Hitler has been in power for two years, over which time he has raped and murdered thousands and thousands of Jewish girls, yet Hitler is received by politicians and there is no uproar. Mr Pink points out that when a murder becomes safe, that is when a lynch mob gathers or is made legal, then everybody agrees to and accepts the murder because 'in every man there lurks a hungry beast'.[26]

And so Kersh's design becomes clear. He has placed his story in bohemian London and dressed it in the mystery genre, but his real concern is that society, any society, can incubate murderers and allow them to kill without repercussions. It is his way of trying to understand how a society can create a man like Adolf Hitler and, over a decade, helps him perpetrate genocide on a global scale.

**

Kersh wrote *Prelude To A Certain Midnight* in London and Perce, Quebec, finishing it in early 1947. The novel was published in America by Doubleday on May 15, 1947, and well reviewed by some. HW Hart, *Library Journal*, May 15, 1947:

Kersh's portraits of the eccentrics and minor artists who inhabit the bohemian world have the vitality of first-rate satire; his novel is also a parable on evil and its indulgences, eloquent with indignation and disgust.

Stephen Stepanchev, *New York Herald Tribune*, May 25, 1947:

The novel is wholly successful in its integration of meaning, story and character. The Kersh cosmos and the people who inhabit it carry his insights easily, without forcing. There is a curious relevance even in the mingling of bohemian and criminal elements, for in Kersh's view both are Nietzschean rebels, obsessed by a wish for freedom and power.

It achieved sales of 7,000 copies. The British release by William Heinemann on September 7, 1947, was met with review fatigue by the majority of the press, who had read and featured fourteen Kersh books over the previous six years. However, both *The Times Literary Supplement* and Richard Church in *John O'London's* recognised the essential truth behind Kersh's storytelling devices and wordplay.

Prelude To A Certain Midnight is a novel of outrage. Kersh is outraged by murderers and also points the finger of guilt at the enablers, the people who encourage and give confidence to killers, as well as to those who stand by and allow atrocities to occur.

Prelude To A Certain Midnight is Gerald Kersh's proof that the abominations of places like Belsen were, so to speak, not local phenomena.

Paul Duncan

Notes and Sources

1. Brophy, John, 'The War Has Found Us A Great Novelist', *Sunday Graphic*, February 21, 1943
2. Kersh, Gerald, *Clean, Bright And Slightly Oiled*, London: Heinemann, 1946
3. ibid.
4. Kersh, Gerald, 'Sitting Alone By The Ashes', *The People*, September 10, 1944
5. ibid.
6. ibid.
7. England, Piers (Gerald Kersh), 'Piety And Charity', *The People*, January 7, 1945
8. Personal correspondence
9. Kersh, Gerald, 'Ashes Of The Bonfire', *The People*, May 13, 1945
10. ibid.
11. Kersh, Gerald, 'Victory Through A Mist', *The People*, May 27, 1945
12. ibid.
13. Kersh, Gerald: 'Things We Must Never Forget', *The People*, June 17, 1945
14. ibid.
15. ibid.
16. Kersh, Gerald, *Prelude To A Certain Midnight*, New York, NY: Doubleday, 1947
17. ibid.
    ibid.
18. ibid.
19. ibid.
20. ibid.
21. England, Piers (Gerald Kersh), 'Pity These Modern Peter Pans,' *The People*, January 28, 1945
22. Kersh, *Prelude To A Certain Midnight*
23. ibid.
24. ibid.
25. ibid.
26. ibid.

Prelude To A Certain Midnight – Reviews

Richard Church, *John O'London's*, September 19, 1945

Gerald Kersh, for all his American terseness and violence of image, writes with a sense of rhetoric, and that is what makes his books so vivid and exciting. Kersh's themes are now notorious; as hard as jazz; as wild as swing. He uses sawn-off sentences and knuckle-duster epithets. But I perceive behind all this a sensibility to truth, as keen (I might say almost as touchy) as that revealed by Kipling.

Lionel Hale, *Observer*, September 21, 1947

Mr Gerald Kersh has a kind of feverish invention which well suits the Bar Bacchus, the rendezvous for his curious London characters in *Prelude To A Certain Midnight*. The clientele of the bar includes drunkards, perverts, authors, and at any rate one child-murderer – a very pretty kettle of queer fish.

Times Literary Supplement, October 4, 1947

Mr Kersh's most original quality as a novelist is a violent disregard of the conventions of what may be acceptable as 'true' in fiction. His best work has the strangeness and improbability of truth.

NE, *Liverpool Post & Mercury*, September 12, 1947

It is, in fact, a remarkable essay in the sordid things in life, with a most ingeniously devised chain of events depending on the search for the person responsible for the grim sex-murder of a ten-year-old girl. With few exceptions, the characters are queer eccentrics, like Asta Thundersley, a female dragon of masculine appearance who 'for a kicked puppy would drag the Home Secretary out of his bath', and who in fact takes it on herself to lead the search for the murderer. There is a nightmare quality about this strange book and a curious unreality about many of its characters.

Harrison Smith, *Saturday Review Of Literature*, May 31, 1947

This novel is worthwhile for the not unpleasant tingling it will produce along the reader's backbone, though it will not be conducive to pleasant walks in a city park at night.

BOOK ONE

I

Hardly any of the old crowd go to the Bar Bacchus now, yet for twenty-five years it was one of the three most popular meeting places in London. Suddenly nobody wanted to go there any more. The old customers developed a distaste for the bar at which they had for so many years intoxicated themselves with mixtures of alcohol and intimate conversation, where they had cashed cheques, borrowed money, made eyes at one another's husbands and wives and uttered strong words about deep matters.

People said that the 'atmosphere' of the Bar Bacchus had changed. But they could never tell you how it had changed or what had changed it. It is difficult – I believe that it is impossible – to explain a change of atmosphere. The atmosphere of a place is the soul of that place, and when it departs the place dies. One may make equations: A New Manager, *plus* the New Manager's Friends, *minus* certain Old Familiar Faces, *plus* a Strange Barman, *plus* the Tension that goes with Unfamiliar Voices, *minus* Intimacy, *equals* a Change of Atmosphere. But this is not satisfactory. One might as well describe an oppressive quiet in terms of decibels, or explain a grief in cubic centimetres of salt tears. One might as well expect an oceanographer to draw up the loneliness and the darkness of the Mindanao Deep on a plumb-line.

The Bar Bacchus died. The virtue went out of it. Its soul drifted away, so that now, although nothing about the place has visibly changed, it is nothing but a shell that once enclosed a character and an individual heartbeat.

Of all the old habitués, only Amy Dory goes there regularly, generally in the evening. She is better known by her nickname Catchy. More years ago than she cares to remember, when she was only twenty-eight years old and still beautiful, a certain novelist who never got around to writing his novel and whose very appearance no one remembers was sitting at the bar ten minutes after opening time. His name is Ember, and he is one of the few men that ever burned with unrequited passion for Amy Dory. After the manner of such men, he had to talk about it. Since none of his friends would arrive for at least five minutes, he talked to the barman, Gonger.

He said: 'She gets hold of you, that woman. Do you understand what I mean? She gets hold of you. I mean, she goes with everybody. Let's face it, she's as common as a drain, Gonger. But I mean, common – common, like one of those catchy bits of sentimental music that everybody gets hold of. In everybody's mouth. You find yourself singing "*Amy Dory, Amy Dory, Amy Dory*" until she sort of interferes with your sleep. I mean, you can't get her out of your head. A catchy tune. She has to have her run. There's nothing you can do about her, do you see what I mean? She's *catchy*.'

Gonger, the barman, gave him a warning look as the door opened and Amy Dory came in. Ember turned, changing colour, but said in a hearty voice: 'Hallo, Catchy!'

One of his friends who was coming behind her asked: 'Why Catchy?'

'Because she's catchy,' said Ember.

From that day her name was Catchy. After many years it still sticks. It is a fact that she was extremely attractive in those days, although her beauty was of the commonplace sort. She had regular features, an excellent figure – she called it '*a good bod*' – and a fine head of hair, remarkable in its luxuriance and colour. It was gleaming red-brown. Her eyes were of the same colour; they were large and clear, candid yet submissive – motherly yet doglike when she looked at men. Catchy's face had something of the shape, the warm colour and the texture of an apricot. She used to be much beloved. There was no doubt that her heart was big and warm – she couldn't bear to see anyone suffering. And she was good company: she made you feel powerful. 'Whatever you say,' was her slogan. The weaker you were, the more submissive she became. The more foolish and indecisive you were, the more she looked up to you.

She was by instinct neat, orderly and tasteful in her dressing. Yet, if by virtue of your helplessness you won her heart, she never made you feel that your unwashed teeth, dirty socks, filthy linen or stained bed were in any way offensive to her. She wanted, as she said, to be 'good for you'. There isn't the slightest doubt that Catchy had a kind heart, the sweetest of natures. There was (as someone said to her at that time) something of the saint about her; she gave everything, took nothing and forgave those who ill-treated her – or rather, she convinced those who ill-treated her, when they begged pardon, that there was nothing to forgive. Thus Catchy made many men happy; generally neurotic, misunderstood men who needed her most. The majority of her friends were writers, actors – artists of one sort or another who loved to tell her all about themselves and explain their disabilities to her. She learned a great deal about people and came to be regarded as a Mother Confessor to all the world.

Not only did she absolve, she excused. Having excused, she justified. She knew how to make people happy when she was beautiful, and when the Bar Bacchus was a place with an atmosphere.

2

But the Bar Bacchus lost its soul and Catchy lost her body. If you had known her then and could see her now you would see what I mean when I say that she has gone through the years like a woman dragged backwards through a thickset hedge. Time has made a sad mess of her – time and trouble. She has had trouble, she will tell you a few minutes after meeting you. Those bright brown eyes that used to be so steady and candid against the baby-blue whites may now be likened to a couple of cockroaches desperately swimming in two saucers of boiled rhubarb. Her magnificent hair has acquired a coarse texture. There is something bohemian about it: it will not lie down; it resists the comb; it is hair in revolt. She is too tired, now, to fight against it.

A few months ago she made her last effort and went blonde. This merely made matters worse. The mixture of hydrogen peroxide and ammonia with which she bleached it made it even coarser than it had been when, with angry determination, she first stirred up the chemicals with a toothbrush. When the mixture was dry she washed her hair in the handbasin, looked at herself in the grimy, freckled mirror and wept. The same evening she attempted to commit suicide.

She tied her head up in a kind of turban, went to the Bar Bacchus and told a friend whom she happened to meet that at last she proposed to end it all. After she had spent all her money, she went home and swallowed twenty aspirin tablets. Nothing happened. Catchy is still alive. Everyone knows that Catchy has gone through the motions of suicide at least half a dozen times. She has scraped at the tendons of her wrists with a blunt razor-blade, drunk hair lotion, swallowed a sixpenny bottle of iodine, taken aspirins and turned on the gas fire without lighting it. But it has always happened that somebody has been near her to rescue her in case she needed saving.

Catchy, I repeat, is the last of the old school at the Bar Bacchus, and she is far from being the woman she used to be. Her cheeks are at once puffy and shrivelled, and her skin is of the colour and texture of dusty curds. She still takes a certain pride in her appearance: her nails are meticulously varnished dark red, but she seldom remembers to wash her hands. The fact that she cannot bring herself to wash off the remains of yesterday's powder, cream and rouge is neither here nor there – she remakes her face scrupulously every morning, laying a fresh coat of paint upon the cracked, stratified remains of the old. Catchy's teeth too are in a precarious condition. After the birth of her child – she was married once – two or three of her side teeth fell out and were replaced with a bridge. Years later the bridge fell out. By then she had lost the will to do anything about anything, and so she put the fallen bridge into a cold-cream pot. For the past five years she has been intending to go to a dentist. But she never has time. Meanwhile some of her real teeth have gone and others are going, so that she has acquired a tight-lipped, enigmatic smile, like the Empress Josephine.

As for Catchy's fine physique, it is a thing of the past. Her torso is blown up round and taut. Yet her arms and legs remain elegant in shape, and her hands would still be beautiful if only she could find time to wash them. Still she retains her old taste in dress. She used to be a well-dressed woman with a flair for style and colour. Now, shuddering away from the clutching hand of Time, she dresses as if the years had not passed, in short skirts and low waists. In general, however, her manner has not changed. She is still kind, sympathetic, anxious to talk things over and listen to your troubles, willing to have something to forgive you for, eager to be good for you, ready to combine the functions of a mistress and a mother. But this is out of the question. People do not like to be seen talking to her in the street. It is not that she is uglier, older or wilder-looking than other women of the bohemian half-world; there is about her an indescribable air of neglect and decay that causes passers-by to turn and look at her. Catchy rushes past in the manner of a demented woman who is looking for something very important and cannot remember what. She is conspicuous for her expression of crazy tragedy, especially when she has been crying. Then her face swells until it resembles a painted toy balloon, the colours of which have run in the rain. She cries at least once every day. She drinks as much as she can because there is something she wants to forget.

The first few drinks really do cheer Catchy up, and then she can be a lively companion, well worth listening to; humorous in her turn of phrase, vivid in her narratives and anecdotes of people she has known. For she has a keen eye, a good ear and an excellent memory – all too excellent. Usually when she is at her most hilarious and scandalous, she will encounter a little stale crumb of something that brings back that which she has been working so hard to forget. It chokes her. She falls silent; gulps, coughs, sobs, and at last weeps in a hoarse, loud, howling voice. At this point she ceases to become good company and becomes very bad company indeed. Catchy throws out her hands like grappling hooks, holds you fast, and tries to tell you something which does not make sense, something hopelessly incoherent. It is distressing to hear her uncontrolled sobbing and moaning. There is something weighing upon this unfortunate woman's heart, but no one has any idea of the nature of it. When she stops talking suddenly and you hear in her throat a noise like a tight corset bursting all its hooks, you excuse yourself, if you are wise – you duck away as you used to do when you heard a V-1 bomb cut off overhead. You know what is coming and hope that it will miss you. They all have their sorrows, their incommunicable sorrows, these broken people who belong to the Mad Twenties and seem to nourish themselves mainly on other people's liquor and wash themselves only in their own maudlin tears – these pumping-stations on the shores of a Dead Sea. Best not to listen to them: it will probably end by your having to see them home in a taxi. More likely than not they will fall down and cut their heads or be sick on your feet. It is best not to involve yourself in the unprecedented sorrows of Mercedes – who once loved a man who didn't love her. Wisest to keep beyond the range of the flamethrower that is the anguish of Fifi, who was divorced by the husband she loved because he could not see eye-to-enlightened-eye with her passion for a female book reviewer. The voice of Catchy when she starts on the story of her great sorrow is not unlike the voice of a cat in the night – that cry that drags you back from the frontiers of sleep because your foggy consciousness tells you that something human is emptying its heart of sorrow too deep for words, trying to tell you something. You sit up and there is only the howl of a beast in the dark. So you fall asleep again.

And so when Catchy begins to cry out, you start for an instant into an anxious alertness, if you do not know her. But you do know her. Nothing she says can possibly mean anything to you: 'Oh, why, why, why? Tell me, darling – darling, dear darling; for God's sake don't desert me, but tell me why! You understand, you do understand – don't you? Yes, you do! Then tell me, for God's sake tell me, what did I ever do? Oh dear God, if you knew – if you knew how unhappy I am, how miserable! Do something for me! I haven't the courage. Kill me! Do this for me, kill me, kill me, and I won't cry out. Darling; I am brave, so much braver than you think! Kill me! What right have I got to live? *Do* something to me! Do something *horrible* to me! Burn me with a red-hot iron... You think I'm afraid, ha ha ha! Me, afraid?'

At this point, she stubs out a lighted cigarette in the palm of her hand and leans forward flickering her wild brown eyes at you.

'I'm not afraid. Do you see, do you see that? And *that*? Afraid! You're afraid, not me! You're a coward, a dirty cheap coward! I'm not afraid. So what have *you* got to be afraid of? I'm only a woman. Well then, kill me! Just kill me. Darling! Put your hands around my throat and strangle me. Or strangle me with a stocking. Yes? Will you –'

She starts to take off one of her stockings. You say: 'No, no!'

She says, with something between a smile and a whimper: 'Oh, I see, you're afraid. You're a coward. You're a dirty, cheap, common, rotten, lousy, stinking, bloody coward – that's what you are. Oh, darling, darling, darling, I could so admire and adore you if you weren't a coward. I'd do anything for you. I'd lie down and let you walk on me. I'd be your slave. I'd look up to you like a king on a throne. I'd wash your feet and drink the water. Don't you see, I want to worship you! You're so strong, so ruthless, so powerful! You're so real, so hard... but no, I was mistaken. You're all alike, you – liars, cowards! And I *did* so look *up* to you! I thought you were God, God Almighty. I said my prayers to you. I wanted you to strike me dead. And now I don't believe in you any more... Oh, please, please, my God, my beautiful God, don't take away my faith! Strike me dead! Dead at your feet, your beautiful, beautiful feet! You must! I want to confess, confess, confess, and confess and confess, to you – to you, my king, my God!'

If you're still there thirty seconds later, you'll hear her say: 'I didn't want to do it, I wouldn't do anything! But punish me, kill me – strike me down dead. Strike me dead! Strike me...'

But if you are a sensible man, you're on your way elsewhere. Christopher, the doorman of the Bar Bacchus, will see her to the street. Then Catchy will make a recovery. She will draw herself up, take a firm grip on her handbag – her poor old greasy alligator-skin handbag which looks as if it contained fifteen pounds of walnuts, into which no one has ever dared to peep – and lurch off home.

3

She can always rely upon her feet to take her home. She has been living in the same place for many years. It is a little flat on the top floor of a second-hand clothes shop. The lettering on the fascia reads:

S. SABBATANI

MISFITS
WARDROBES

The shop has an air of dilapidation. As you walk by, you wonder how the devil anyone can possibly make a living out of it. It was last painted ten years ago, and then with a cheap brown-red paint. The shop window is of a sort of plate-glass that is no longer made nowadays. Slightly corrugated and flawed with bubbles, it is strangely framed in four pieces of wood like Greek columns.

Here you may see displayed a bundle of garments like Eton jackets made of coarse white cotton; a green-and-blue-striped suit labelled 'Savile Row'; some bundles of gloves marked '*Assorted sizes. West-End make*'; two or three pairs of second-hand or third-hand shoes carefully polished and mounted on trees; and an assortment of dusty dress shirts. There is also a bundle of whangee, rattan and malacca walking-sticks such as no man has carried since 1903; and an overcoat or two ticketed '*West-End make. Property of a Lord*'. In addition to these things, there are sidelines: boot polish, collars, saddle soap and one or two massive old battered dressing-cases fitted with strange bottles and seven-day sets of cut-throat razors with the initials of unknown bankrupts stamped all over them in blackened gold.

Catchy lives on the top floor. She goes in by the poor old blistered side door, climbs resolutely, keeping in touch with the handrail of the banisters, which are painted the same colour as the outside of the shop. She tries to walk quietly because she is afraid of her landlady, Mrs Sabbatani. On the top landing she pauses for breath, by the little gas stove outside her door, fumbles for her key – still snivelling a little – and finds it. She works it into the keyhole like a soldier threading a darning needle, gets inside, switches on the light and throws herself into a shiny grey-black rickety old easy-chair by the gas fire, looking around the room, as if she expected to find someone waiting for her. She sees most of what she put into the room a dozen years ago; and a dozen years of wear and tear, neglect and decay. The furniture is her own. It cost something once upon a time; but now, even as prices are at present, she would have to pay a man to take it away. From where she sits she can see springs coming out of the bottom of the divan like the entrails of a disembowelled horse. The bedclothes are neither here nor there; you might imagine that the patchwork quilt has gone mad and engaged a gay plaid travelling-rug and a filthy Witney blanket in mortal combat – from which the sheets have recoiled in terror to the foot of the bed, where they are trying to dig themselves in. The pillow is grey with eye-black, tears and dirt. The electric light has a beaded shade; the upper edges of the walls are in a striated half-shadow. She can see, if she strains her eyes, the oblong of pink wallpaper in its frame of dust where her picture, in the nude, by Schuster, used to hang until she sold it for the wherewithal to drown her sorrows eighteen months ago. There is another picture, too: a concatenation of triangles. She wept when she took it to the dealer and offered it for sale, because it was painted by Toon, whom she loved. She wept when the dealer said he would not have it as a gift. Now, whenever she sees it she wants to weep again.

Where, she asks herself, is Toon? *Where* are they all? And where is she, Catchy, who was so much beloved? A tear rolls down and makes a black star upon the ashy surface of the Kilim rug which Toto gave her, saying that it was a bridal rug. She would light the fire, only she has forgotten to get any matches. Tentatively she stirs the debris on her dressing table. She could have sworn that she had matches. Her hands move jerkily: a couple of books, an ashtray belonging to the Café Royal, a small piece of mildewed cheese, a dirty towel, an empty aspirin bottle and a hair comb fall to the floor with a clatter. Catchy pauses, horrified, slightly unsteady on her feet. She does not want to disturb Mrs Sabbatani. That poor woman Mrs Sabbatani loves her so much, relies upon her so much, and is so sweet, so kind, so delicate when she touches at the matter of arrears of rent. Thank God, thinks Catchy, thank God she has a little lavatory and handbasin of her own so that she need not disturb Mrs Sabbatani... After three provocative blows she hits the switch. The washbasin looks like a dried-up riverbed. But she has her own WC – spattered, derelict, deplorable. Yet it is her own, and nobody else's...

At the back of Catchy's throat something sounds like that tight corset bursting all its hooks. She begins to cry again.

'Help me! Help me! Do something – anything!' she cries, turning her bloodshot eyes upwards. The lavatory ceiling, marked with a brown stain that looks like the map of South America, gives no answer.

4

At last she goes to bed as quietly as she can. But the ruined divan twangs like a zither struck by a bored and vicious child. Downstairs Mrs Sabbatani hears it and sighs. Her sister-in-law, an elderly spinster, nods angrily and says for the thousandth time: 'So she's here again, the drunkard. What for are you keeping her here, what for? Why don't you throw her out, why don't you? Drunkards she wants, they should burn the house down yet!'

The widow Sabbatani – sad, pale and exhausted – screws up her eyes as if in anticipation of a blow and says: 'It's not so easy to get an old tenant out of an unfurnished room.'

'If they don't pay their rent? No?'

'Enough already, Sarah! What are you breaking *your* head for? So if Mrs Dory owes a week's rent, she'll pay.'

'Pay! Pay!' says Sarah with bitter mockery. 'How will she pay? When will she pay, why should she pay? Pay!'

'She gets an allowance from her husband,' says Mrs Sabbatani. 'She gives me what she can.'

At the sound of the word 'husband' Sarah throws down her needlework, lets out a hollow laugh and says: 'Husband! Allowance! She's a prostitute. A prostitute to have in the house! I've got no patience with you.'

'She's here again with her prostitutes,' says Mrs Sabbatani, with some irritation. 'You've got prostitutes on the brain. She's a married woman, a separated married woman. She mixes up with educated people.'

'So how much does she owe rent, with her educated people?' asks Sarah.

Mrs Sabbatani does not want to admit that Catchy has paid no rent for nearly five months.

'A few weeks,' she replies.

'A few weeks? She should live so sure! A few months!' Sarah says.

Harassed almost to tears, Mrs Sabbatani cries out in Yiddish: 'Sarah, what do you want of my life? What do you want of my years, Sarah?'

'She should be thrown out into the street, into the street,' says Sarah. 'My only wish is, Sam should be alive –'

'Sam *should* be alive,' says Mrs Sabbatani, glancing up with wet eyes towards a large framed photograph of a man in a bowler hat, which hangs over the fireplace. At this, her sister-in-law pauses for a few seconds. But then Catchy rolls over in bed and there is the plaintive whine of strained wire.

Sarah says: 'Sam would have thrown her out into the street. Into the street, Sam would have thrown her out.'

'Sam had nothing against the poor woman,' says Mrs Sabbatani, 'and my Sonia thought the world of her.'

'What was, was. What is, is,' says Sarah.

'Drop it already!' says Mrs Sabbatani. 'I should throw out a poor woman into the streets? Will she make me rich with her few shillings? It's a *mitzvah* to let her alone.'

'Fine friends they make,' says Sarah with a sour smile. 'Drunkards they want in the house. Prostitutes they want in the house. I'm in her way. Better she should have prostitutes; drunkards better, she should have! She's so rich, already, she can give the house away to such a class of people.'

'And supposing?' cries Mrs Sabbatani, with as much asperity as she is capable of – which is not much. 'Do *you* keep me? Do I owe *you* anything?'

Now Sarah begins to weep, beating herself in the face with an agonised hand and rocking forward and backward in her chair: 'The bit of bread I eat in the house she throws up in my face! I'm in her way, she wants I should go away to a home! *Weh ist mir! Weh ist mir!* Sam should be here to see it.'

Now Mrs Sabbatani soothes her, saying: 'Sha, sha! May I never move from this chair, Sam never had anything against Mrs Dory. And she thought the world of my Sonia. Whenever she sees a picture of my Sonia, she cries like her heart would break. I'll make a nice cup of tea.'

This has been going on, night after night, since Sam Sabbatani died and Sarah came to live with his widow and cheer her up. Having lost her daughter and her husband in one year, Mrs Sabbatani was so broken by grief that it was thought she might go out of her mind. So Sarah came to comfort her. Now, every night, as the divan springs twang out their weary discords under the weight of Catchy's body, Sarah raises her voice in protest, and the end is always the same. Mrs Sabbatani is soft, slow and sweet as honey; and as obstinate to cling. She always has the last word: Sam had nothing against Mrs Dory, and the child Sonia thought the world of her.

5

More than ten years have passed since the death of Sonia Sabbatani made its little sensation in that part of London. In those days Catchy was still clear-eyed and desirable; she paid her rent regularly and kept her little flat clean. Sabbatani's shop was prosperous. The paintwork was fresh and glossy; the lettering of the fascia was bold and legible; the window was filled with a tasteful display of gents' second-hand suits, most of which were practically all that the price tickets proclaimed them to be. There was a ticket which announced that gents' evening dress and morning dress was available for hire. Sam Sabbatani had a good reputation as an honest and obliging tradesman, and a dexterous man who could alter anything to fit anybody. He had an eye for commodities and for faces, but you could see by the composition of his fat, grave face that he would never make his fortune – he was like a rich province in a state of civil war. His heart had a fifth column behind the fortified walls of his hard head. He was conscious of this and sometimes tried to silence the sly, insidious voices that, at the crises of certain transactions, whispered: 'The client needs money. He's not a businessman. There's no business in him. What difference does a pound make? He asks three-pounds-ten. You could get that suit of clothes for fifty shillings, because he wants the money. But will a pound note break you? Don't be silly! Look at the boy's face: would he sell his best suit for three-pounds-ten if he didn't need three-pounds-ten? Perhaps there's a wife and child ill in bed. Say, God forbid, it was you with your Gertie or your Sonia. There could be rent to pay, there could be groceries. Give him what he asks. What is a pound note? You'll get it back. Put an extra ten shillings on the price when you sell the suit: put an extra ten shillings on the blue serge you bought yesterday...'

Then Sam Sabbatani, with a melancholy look at the garment he was buying, would turn to the customer with his Asiatic bulldog face and say: 'All right, three-pounds-ten,' and push the money across the counter.

As often as not, the customer went away thinking that he'd been a fool not to ask for five pounds.

When, however, someone came to try on the blue serge suit, the price of which Sabbatani had raised ten shillings, there would be another skirmish in the mysterious region between his solar plexus and his cerebellum... 'Look, a respectable boy wants to get a job. Have a look at what he's got on. A dark-grey hopsack, made by a city tailor. Cost six pounds new; made to measure, one fitting. Look – a tie for eighteen pence, a shirt for five shillings, shoes for seventeen-and-six, all nice and clean. Times are bad. Look at his face. He's making a frown, and a mouth. He's trying to show you he doesn't care. Poor boy, does he think he's a businessman? By him a pound is already important. Give him the blue serge for a pound less! What's a pound note? Will a pound break you? A good suit of clothes makes a man feel better. It makes him confident. Better still – let him think he's got a bargain out of you – much better still – he'll go away, get his job, get married, make a nice family, be a Somebody. It can make all this difference. All for the sake of a pound note. Give him the suit. Put another thirty shillings on the crocodile-skin dressing-case with crystal fittings. Anybody that'll pay ten pounds for a dressing-case will pay eleven-pounds-ten.'

Thus twisting his face into an expression of melancholy anger, Sam Sabbatani would say: 'All right, take it.'

When it came to alterations if the suit did not fit, Reason spoke: 'Make the alterations free of charge. That way you get yourself a loyal customer.'

By this time, Reason had been undermined by the fifth column. The heart of Sabbatani chuckled in quiet triumph. His head growled impotently. His face scowled.

If anybody asked for the crocodile-skin dressing-case with crystal fittings, it invariably happened that he was a struggling actor invited to an important house party, and Sam Sabbatani, with a face of doom, knocked off thirty shillings.

He even trusted people. When Catchy's friend, the one she called Osbert, asked for the loan of a decent suit to wear at lunch with a publisher, Sabbatani, with a glare and a growl, let him have it.

6

Sabbatani was a burly, stooping man of middle height, who liked to wear his hat indoors and could not touch a thing without working out an estimate of its market price. While embracing a long-lost brother, he would instinctively have pinched up a handful of the back of his coat and judged the cost per yard of the cloth from which it had been cut. And yet there must have been something all-too-human in the man. When his daughter Sonia died, Sam Sabbatani threw away the will to live; and after his death it was demonstrated that he had more debtors than creditors.

He owed money to a clothes manufacturer in East London, who said: 'Write it off. Poor Sam!' The amount of the bill was thirty or forty pounds. A dozen men in his own neighbourhood owed him about sixty pounds between them. Five of these men sighed with relief; three laughed out loud; two of them simply paid their debts; one claimed that Sam Sabbatani owed him a suit which had been sent for alteration; and the twelfth called with a bunch of flowers and said: 'I believe Sam kept his books in his head, Mrs Sabbatani. I want to tell you how sorry I am. You remember my name, perhaps? Osbert – Tobit Osbert. I owe you fourteen shillings for the hire of a suit. Sam trusted me. You haven't got the record of what I owe, I dare say. Two days at five shillings a day, and four shillings for repairs. May I pay you now? And I'm sorry these aren't nicer flowers, Mrs Sabbatani…'

Sam Sabbatani's widow wept. 'You're the third what comes to pay a bill like this,' she said, looking at the flowers. 'People are good.'

'You are good to have such faith in people,' said Tobit Osbert, a tall, quiet man with a dreamy face and a gentle voice. '*You* are good, Mrs Sabbatani.'

'God is good,' said Mrs Sabbatani. 'The kettle's boiling. A cup of tea?'

'You're too kind,' said Tobit Osbert, sighing.

Then Mrs Sabbatani remembered her husband's sigh before he went away with the strangers. She had been sitting in the shop parlour. As the doorbell tinkled, Sam leaped up and went out, leaving a cup of tea which he had not yet touched. After a minute or two, something in the tone of a stranger's voice made her sit up and listen.

Then: 'I don't believe it,' said Sam Sabbatani.

'It may be a mistake, but you must come and identify –' said a stiff-backed man, in a clipped monotone. 'Pull yourself together.'

Sabbatani said: '*Why* should anybody? How *could* anybody? It's a mistake. No offence – anybody can make a mistake... I don't *believe* it.'

She saw her husband turn towards someone she knew – a flat-footed old police constable who tramped a local beat. The policeman looked wretched and nodded. Then Sam sighed: he seemed to suck into his lungs all the air in the shop, leaving everyone else gasping for breath. That was a terrible sigh.

'Sam!' cried Mrs Sabbatani.

'Wait,' said her husband.

'Keep calm, ma'am – back in a minute or two,' said the man with the stiff back. His voice was as gentle as he could make it. His hard mouth was chopping off chunks of reluctant sweetness, like a toffee-cutter.

'Wait, Gertie, for God's sake,' said Sam.

Half an hour later they returned in a taxi.

'Where is she?' asked Mrs Sabbatani.

Sam Sabbatani caught the point of his right-hand lapel in a clenched fist and tore his coat. Then he burst into tears.

The man with the stiff back said: 'Mr Sabbatani, I sympathise. But you've got to pull yourself together. We've got to have a talk, now. Now. D'you hear? Now. Hold yourself in, Sabbatani. Sit down. Get some strong sweet tea, George...'

Later, Mrs Sabbatani asked: 'But what for? Why? Why should anybody do it to her? A child! Sonia! Why? What for?'

Sam Sabbatani looked at his wife and then at the detective, who said: 'Just for nothing, ma'am. For nothing at all, Mrs Sabbatani. A madman. Could happen to you or me.'

'If I could find who it was!' cried Sam Sabbatani.

'All right, Mr Sabbatani: that's what we're here for...'

'Sammele, Sammele!' said Mrs Sabbatani, weeping. 'Why should it be?'

Her husband could not speak of the abomination; yet it had to come out. The evening papers were already printing the story.

Sonia Sabbatani, who would have been eleven years old next birthday, had been gagged and bound, raped and strangled, and thrown into the cellar of an empty house. She had told one of her classmates that a friend of her daddy was going to meet her and tell her a great secret.

But she named nobody, and Sabbatani had a thousand friends.

7

Six months later Sam Sabbatani went to bed with a stomach ulcer. In normal circumstances he would have laughed it off. After the operation he contracted pneumonia: there is more than one way of dying of a broken heart. A man who really does not want to go on living will find deep water or a gas oven in which to drown or suffocate; inside himself, if need be. 'Murderer! Murderer!' cried Sam Sabbatani, in his last delirium. 'Where is he, the murderer? Murderer! Murderer! *Murderer*!...' Then he thought that he was back in Bessarabia in the days of the pogroms. 'Hide the children!' he shouted in a voice that echoed through the long cold corridors of the hospital. 'Hide the children! In the cellars! The Cossacks are coming! They cut Reb Shmuel's heart out – they cut the Rebbitzin's breasts off – they tore little Esther Krejmer to pieces! Hide the children! Where are the men? Quick! Out! Give me the cutting shears! Dovidel – take the fur knife! Mottke, take an iron bar! Hold them back a minute, the murderers, while the women hide the children! Where are the men?... Men!... Men! Women, women! – hide the children! The murderers are coming!...'

But at last he lay back rattling in his throat under the oxygen apparatus. He was buried in the Jewish Cemetery at North Ham, where the remains of Sonia had been lowered into the ground a few months before. There is a little place reserved for Mrs Sabbatani next to Sam's grave, over which stands a tall, ornate gravestone of pale marble.

This stone cost more than she could afford: members of her family remonstrated with her. 'It's for all three of us,' said Mrs Sabbatani.

But her time has not come yet. She must wait and live, and in order to live she must carry on the business. And what is the business worth? There is nothing worth honest buying, and next to nothing fit to sell. Clothes are like blood. Nobody sells them, and you need coupons to buy them. It is necessary to play strange games – leer here, nudge there, fiddle on the black market. Sam (she thinks) would have seen them all in hell first.

Meanwhile, Mrs Amy Dory, whom everyone calls 'Catchy', cannot pay her rent. And if Catchy could pay her rent, what good would it do? Ten shillings a week can make no difference now: times have changed: nothing will ever be the same again...

So thinks Mrs Sabbatani in her loneliness and her unhappiness. Her heart goes out to Catchy, who also has a sorrow. When Sarah is out of the house, and Catchy is at home, Mrs Sabbatani asks her to come down and have a cup of tea. The cup of tea carries a supplement of fried fish, stuffed fish or something of the sort; bread and butter, cheesecake, apple strudel – anything there happens to be in the house.

Mrs Sabbatani's heart goes out to this wretched Catchy, who drinks too much and does not eat enough. It is a bad thing for a woman to drink. Still, there must be a reason. Catchy has troubles. Therefore it is a *mitzvah* – a charitable act – to be kind to her. What Catchy's troubles are is neither here nor there. One fact remains forever: when Sam died, Catchy wept; and she thought the world of Sonia. When Mrs Sabbatani and her family were sitting on sawn-off chairs in deep Hebrew mourning, Catchy and her friend Osbert came to offer condolences.

Catchy was inconsolable, because other people were wretched. Catchy felt only for others, through others.

Now, therefore, Mrs Sabbatani feeds her secretly, when Sarah is not looking. Your own flesh and blood mourns your bereavement: that is normal. But when strangers weep, it is beautiful. Every tear shed by an outsider is a confirmation of the magnitude of your loss. Whenever Catchy thinks of Sonia and Sam, she cries bitterly.

Yet what is it to Catchy?

8

Mrs Sabbatani knows, or should know, that Catchy is ready to weep at any hour of the day or night on the slightest provocation. How many times has she seen her coming home with her mouth twisted into a quivering oblong; bubbling at the nose and dripping at the eyes, sobbing heartbrokenly because she has seen an organ grinder with one leg, or a dog with a bandaged paw? Yet this good widow cannot bring herself to believe that Catchy hasn't a special personal feeling for her and her troubles. In any case, Catchy weeps: that in itself is enough. God knows through what steamy, stinking jungles and scummy backwaters a psychiatrist would have to paddle before he found the source of her tears! Mrs Sabbatani is of the opinion that her unprofitable tenant is a victim of misplaced devotion. She is well aware of the meaning of love, yet she cannot pronounce the word except with a certain ironic emphasis and a half-smile; for in her world no one ever talks of love. You and your husband get over the nonsense of sighing and pouting and billing and cooing early in your married life, and settle down. Love is more than an 'affair': it is the bedrock and the prop of life at home. As such it is taken for granted but never discussed. The word *Love* pertains to romantic stories, dramas or picture shows. She has read stories and seen films about great tragic loves, and she thinks that she knows what they mean; although they have little enough to do with her. She agreed with Sam when, after having seen Greta Garbo in *Wild Orchids*, he grunted: 'Love! Schmove! They should have a few children to bring up; they should have the cooking to do, and a house to keep clean, and look after the shop. *Love*!'

(Yet Sabbatani died of grief.) Still, Mrs Sabbatani cannot get it out of her head that Catchy is devoured by a romantic yearning for someone – she suspects Osbert. She always liked that kind, quiet, considerate gentleman. But years have passed since she saw him last. He has grown prosperous and has a wife and a smart flat in Kensington now. No one sees him any more.

Once in a while she asks Catchy for something on account of arrears of rent. On such occasions – she always waits until Sarah has gone to the pictures – she approaches the subject in a round-about way.

'A nice cup of tea? And look, I made a nice cheesecake. Look, it's still warm; I made it this afternoon. Just a little bit. I made it with pure butter. Come on, you don't look after yourself enough.'

Then Catchy crumples and twists herself and drips grey tears like a wrung dishcloth and wails: 'Oh, you're so sweet, so sweet, so sweet! You're always looking after me. And I don't deserve it, Mrs Sabbatani! Oh, darling, darling, I owe you so much, so much!'

'Well, if you *could* let me have a *little* on *account...*'

'Oh, Mrs Sabbatani, Mrs Sabbatani! Why don't you throw me out? Dear, darling Mrs Sabbatani, why don't you throw me out into the street? It would be good for me. It would make me pull myself together. It would serve me right. I'm bad, bad – I'm no good! Don't you see, I'm no good?'

'Sha! Sha!' says Mrs Sabbatani. 'You're a nice girl. Sha, sha, then.'

Still weeping, Catchy begins to laugh. 'A nice girl! You don't know what Asta Thundersley said about me.'

'Go and have a nice lay down, and I'll bring you up a cup of tea,' says Mrs Sabbatani, who is afraid that Sarah may come back at any moment and catch her fraternising with this wet-faced, wild, disreputable woman who smells of gin and stale cigarette smoke. She follows Catchy upstairs with a cup of tea and something to eat on a plate. When she sees the bedroom, her heart contracts with pity and her nostrils with disgust. 'A minute,' she says going out; and comes running back with cleaning materials. She brushes up ashes, shakes sheets and blankets into position – although she can hardly bring herself to touch them – wipes up dust, scrubs the dry grey incrustations off the bathtub, and does all that a human being can do in two minutes to mitigate the offence of the water closet.

Meanwhile Catchy whimpers: 'Don't do it! Don't do it! I'm no good. I'm no good. Ask Asta, she'll tell you. Asta Thundersley will tell you all about me. I'm a bitch, I'm everything – everything that's wicked. Ask Asta. Throw me out, throw me out – please, please throw me out!'

Mrs Sabbatani, embarrassed, looks at the filthy mantelpiece, and says: 'Asta? What do I know about Asta? Why should I ask Asta? What for Asta?'

'That lesbian,' says Catchy.

'Lesbian? What is it in English, Mrs Dory? I'm not an educated woman,' says Mrs Sabbatani, apologetically. 'String beans, broad beans, human beens, butter beans, has-beens, less-beens. I get mixed up.'

Catchy comes up bubbling and spluttering out of a great laugh.

'Darling, you're priceless! Has-beens, less-beens, human beens – may I have that? May I use it?'

But the waiting ear of Mrs Sabbatani catches the click of the closing street door. Sarah is back from the shadowy embraces of Tyrone Power. 'Drink up the nice tea, eat up the nice cake. Excuse me,' she says, and runs downstairs.

'*What is it in English?*' says Catchy, laughing in the act of swallowing a mouthful of cheesecake and spattering particles like a charge from a sawn-off shotgun.

9

Asta Thundersley is perhaps the only living creature for whom Catchy professes hate. At the same time, she fears her with a great, paralysing fear so that she would not say what she thinks about her except to people Asta Thundersley is not likely to meet.

Asta is a dangerous woman to cross. Most people are afraid of her. She has a knack of hammering you into abject submission. Physically she resembles a man, a man to be reckoned with. Imagine a retired middleweight boxer, turned gentleman farmer, impersonating his aunt; dressed in a coat and skirt. She must be fifty now, but she looked exactly the same fifteen years ago. Once in a while, when she feels that much may depend upon her personal appearance, she has her grizzled brown hair marcelled into tight waves and crams her torso into one of those silk dresses that change colour according to the angle of the light. On such occasions she puts on a hat like a pot of geraniums and a pair of high-heeled shoes. She is a fusspot, a busybody, with a finger in every charitable pie; a maiden lady of diabolical energy. An ill-used child sends her out like a roaring lion. For a pregnant housemaid she will tear down half the town. Secretaries Of State hide when they hear that Asta Thundersley is on the warpath, for she has a tongue like a cavalry sabre and knows neither shame nor fear; she hacks and slashes her way, without regard for rules or common decency. Asta is one of those strange creatures that recognise no neutral state between right and wrong. To her, black is black and white is white; she hates the one, loves the other, and never listens to reason. For the sake of a boy birched by a petulant Justice Of The Peace she will start a crusade, dragging in everyone upon whom she can lay her great red hands. If she happens to say: 'Mr So-And-So, are you my friend?' Mr So-And-So knows that she is about to ask him, in the name of friendship, to do something for a baby, a convict, an evicted tenant, an old-age pensioner, an expectant mother or a litter of kittens; and if he hesitates, he loses her friendship. If he loses Asta's friendship, he becomes her enemy, in which case his life will be made a burden to him. She is a woman of independent fortune, most of which she squanders on leaflets, pamphlets for the prevention of this, that and the other and lost causes in general. Asta has no sex. This shiny, red, social reformer is nothing but a pip, a seed of social conscience enclosed in a fleshy envelope; a sort of berry.

Once she slapped Catchy's face. If Asta had been a man, Catchy would not have resented the blow; on the contrary, she would have become warmly submissive, saying: 'Yes, yes, dominate me – dominate me!'

She would have derived a certain pleasure from the blow, even from a woman, if it had not been delivered in indignation and accompanied by certain words which it was impossible for her to forget.

It was what Asta Thundersley said that really hurt: the words that preceded the blow she will never be able to forget or forgive.

Catchy maintains that Asta, more than anyone else, has been the ruin of the Bar Bacchus.

Asta used to live in an elegant little house in the neighbourhood, and took to dropping in between 11.30 and noon for a couple of cocktails, and in the Bar Bacchus, as elsewhere, she made her powerful presence felt. She made no secret of her likes and dislikes and behaved like an autocrat of the old school: 'Hey, you, boy! Get a bit of rag and wipe this confounded bar! Somebody's been slopping beer or something all over it. Shaky hand, I suppose, confounded drunkard! Hey, *you* – switch the electric fan on. The place stinks of stale smoke. Why don't you get yourselves a proper ventilating system? It's enough to turn one's stomach. But I suppose the crowd you get in here would die if they saw a bit of daylight or got a breath of fresh air – like clothes moths. No wonder everything's going to the dogs. God, what a generation!'

She looked pointedly at a slender young man who wore a brightly coloured scarf instead of a tie and whose manicured hands were adorned with two or three intaglio rings.

He, goaded by irritation into a state of mad courage, said, in a shaky voice: 'If you don't like the place, what do you keep coming here for?'

Asta looked him up and down. Her astonished glance travelled from his suede shoes up along his loose corduroy trousers, and from button to button of his white tweed jacket, abruptly stopping at his big brown eyes. 'I beg your pardon?' she said. 'Were you speaking to me, young man? You couldn't have been speaking to me, surely? You wouldn't have dared to address me in that tone of voice, I believe?'

The young man put down his glass and went to the door. Before he went out, he turned and said to Gonger: 'If you allow your oldest customers to be annoyed like this, I, for one, am not coming back again. Goodbye.'

Asta began to chuckle. 'Don't you worry,' she said to Gonger, 'he'll be back.'

'Why don't you let people alone?' asked Gonger. 'They don't interfere with you. What do you want to interfere with them for?'

'I don't like pansies.'

'I mean to say,' said Gonger, that intrepid man, 'you don't own the place, *do* you now?'

'No, thank God. If I owned your stinking place I'd have to be nice to every Tom, Dick and Harry. But since I don't own the place, I can say what I damn well like – and so I shall, young fellow, and if you don't believe me, just try and stop me, that's all. Just you try.'

'I wouldn't dream of trying, miss,' said Gonger.

'I should think not. It would take a better man than you or a dozen like you. Give me another drink. And when I ask for a Tom Collins, I don't ask for a Tom Collins so that you can get away with a short measure of gin. I ask for a Tom Collins because I want a Tom Collins, and that means to say that it's got to have the right amount of gin in it. Is that clear?'

'You don't think', said Gonger, 'that I'd be crazy enough to try and get away with giving you short measure, do you?'

'And don't think that I am the sort of fool who falls for that line of talk, young fellow. Before I fall for that stuff, I'll fall for the three-card trick. Hurry up, I haven't got all day.'

Then Gonger would mix her a Tom Collins, brazenly giving her short measure again. And she would drink it, saying: 'That's better.'

There was something sympathetic about the Battleaxe, as she was called. Many people liked her in spite of her savage tongue and belligerent manner. Like the carcass of Samson's lion, this muscular busybody was capable of giving out sweetness. Furthermore, she was what is known as a Character, and all the world loves a Character. It was difficult to be dull in her company. She kept you on your toes: she was almost certain to say or do something unpredictable. There was a time when, to the ill-concealed, ineffable joy of Gonger, Asta Thundersley was pursued by an enigmatic young man, whose sole topic of conversation was the fact that he had never had a Mother, not a real Mother, not a proper Mother – not a Mother who was a comrade, not a Mother who was a Mother, not a Mother who guided him; just an ordinary Mother like everybody else's Mother – not a Mother he could look up to. The ideal Mother, he maintained, was Miss Thundersley – a Mother who drank Tom Collins, smoked all day long, and could tell a good smutty story.

Asta listened to all this for several days, with a hideous contortion of the face which was her idea of a motherly smile. At last, on a Saturday morning when the bar was crowded, she produced from her handbag a small towel which she folded into a triangle like a baby's diaper and approached the young man waving this object in one hand and a safety-pin in the other, shouting: 'You want me to be a mother to you, you silly little man? Right! Let's start, from the beginning! I'm going to change your nappy!'

No one doubted for a moment that if the young man had stayed, something scandalous would have happened; but he fled, and never set foot in the bar again.

In this manner she antagonised certain people. It was quite clear that she was a little crazy; one of those strong-minded lunatics dangerously compounded of love and anger; contemptuous of the opinions of mankind.

10

She liked to startle people. If she had been born poor, she would no doubt have tried to have her way with the world by walking up and down Whitehall between sandwich boards or chalking on walls. But she was rich and a member of an influential family. She had access to great people who could not refuse to see her: they had known her mother, her father or one of her uncles.

Some women might have been held back by reticence. Not

Asta Thundersley, that uproarious extrovert. For herself she would ask nothing. But for a kicked pup she would drag the Home Secretary himself out of his bath. She overdid things; never knew when to stop. Once, for instance, she interested herself in the case of a woman who, having old-fashioned ideas of child management, beat and starved her stepdaughter. The child, who was six years old, ruined the experiment by dying of ill-treatment: she had always been a difficult child. The stepmother was sentenced to six months in prison. Asta was outraged at the lightness of this sentence, and for five years, no matter what anyone said, she managed to introduce 'six months for torturing a child to death' into every conversation. If, say, you were talking about the parcel post, she got away from parcels to the subject of string; from string to rope; from rope to murder; and so to a peroration: 'Kill your wife's lover as a gentleman should, and you'll swing for it. Torture babies to death, and you only get six months in quod!' With her, every issue became a monomania, something fiercely personal.

Even in the old days, when Catchy had such a shape that she could earn her living as an artist's model, Asta Thundersley was regarded as a species of maniac – an over-energetic woman who ought to have been born a man; in which case she might have become a cabinet minister, and then she would have gagged herself with party politics and the consciousness of her own importance.

She picked up cronies and made friends in the unlikeliest corners, for she had a childlike craving for the indigestible sharp pickles and belly-aching green apples of society. There was, for example, an old ruined heavyweight boxer, who called himself The Tiger Fitzpatrick, whom she found one evening when she was rescuing fallen women (or something of the sort) near the East India Dock Road. The Tiger Fitzpatrick, drunk but still thirsty, came out of a dark turning, grabbed her wrist and said: 'Listen, you!'

Without changing her expression, Asta Thundersley kicked him scientifically on the shin. Her legs might have belonged to a billiard table, and her kick was something to be remembered. As The Tiger let go and hopped back with a yelp of pain and incredulity, she beat him over the head with a massive umbrella and said: 'Take your hands off me, you dirty bully, you beery ape! Now, what is it?'

The Tiger Fitzpatrick, somewhat sobered, muttered: 'I'm broke to the wide.'

'Serve you right! You smell as if you deserve to be, you drunken sot. How dare you lay your hands on me? I've half a mind to give you the hiding of your life.'

The Tiger cringed and said: 'I couldn't fight a lady, lady.'

'Oh no, not you! I know you. Don't tell me. You couldn't fight a lady, oh dear no! But you can try your hulking great brute strength on a lady, can't you? You can bully a lady, can't you? – or you think you can, don't you? What do you want money for? Beer? Eh?'

'Yes, lady,' said The Tiger Fitzpatrick with humility.

She looked at this shattered Hercules as he stood, hanging his head in the feeble light of a bracketed streetlamp in the rain, and observed that this head was like a head of moist clay half hammered back to utter blankness – all but the ears, which resembled old boxing gloves. Yet there was something pathetic in the twitching and flickering of it. She thought of God's breath breathed into the wet red earth in Eden. 'Why don't you get yourself a job?' she asked.

He answered: 'They won't give me no job.'

'Because you don't deserve one, I suppose? Because they know you'll get drunk and make a beast of yourself, like you are now – is *that* it?'

'Lady,' he said with dignity, 'don't you know who I am? I'm The Tiger Fitzpatrick.' He paused, waiting for an exclamation.

'Who's he?'

'I was nearly in the running for a fight with Johnny MacTurk. Lady, where have you been all your life? Didn't anybody ever tell you anything? Didn't you ever hear about how I went seventeen rounds with Tully Burnett? And there you are, talking like an educated lady! Four more fights and I'd of had a chance at Bob Fitzsimmons. But I was robbed of the verdict when I fought Ernie Tombs. God Almighty,' said The Tiger with pain in his voice, 'you must have heard what Tombs *did* to me? I'd got him going in the sixth. I could have knocked him out stone cold in the eighth, and he knew it – I knew it. I said I'd let him go up to the tenth, but in the seventh – see? – I'm jabbing to the body with my left hand – and he knows, *he* knows, *he knows* what's coming! And the next time I let him have it with the left, Tombs sees it coming and jumps clear off the canvas and takes the punch right in the groin. Honest to God, it wouldn't have hurt a new-born baby, but Tombs rolls on the canvas, rolls and rolls and grabs himself down here and shouts – 'foul, foul, foul,' like a dying man... and there it is. See? Some feller wrote a bit about it in the *Liverpool Echo*... Look, I got it here.'

He fumbled in a pocket, got out two pieces of strawboard fastened with elastic bands, separated them and, like a librarian handling an ancient and priceless document, lifted into the light six column-inches of newsprint transparent with wear and tear.

Asta said: 'I see what you mean. You're a boxer, I take it.'

'All I want is a chance at this so-called Braddock,' said The Tiger Fitzpatrick, trembling with cold, drink and advancing age under the rain.

'Where do you live?'

He shrugged an embarrassed shoulder.

'Where are you sleeping tonight?'

'Well, lady, I haven't made up my mind yet, if you see what I mean, lady.'

Asta gave him three half-crowns and her card and said: 'Look here, you, whatever you call yourself – take this and go and get yourself something to eat and a bed. You know where to get a bed?'

'Yes, lady.'

'Get a good night's sleep, do you hear? Have a good breakfast. Get a shave. Is that clear? Wash your filthy hands. Do you understand? Then come along to this address, and I'll give you a job – 9.30 tomorrow morning. I know you, you drunkards; the moment I turn my back, you'll rush into the White Horse and drink yourself silly.'

'Oh no, I won't, lady.'

'I know you, you sots, better than you know yourselves. Go away!'

She left The Tiger in the dim lamplight, looking from the three half-crowns to the card she had given him.

Next morning at 9.15 he knocked at her door. Even Asta realised that she could not reasonably ask any of her friends to give such a man a job. Besides, he needed a strong influence. At any moment he might run off the rails, get drunk, go crazy, try and rob people in the streets. Having thought the matter over for thirty or forty seconds, she took him into her own service.

The Tiger Fitzpatrick became her butler.

He fraternised with her housekeeper, Mrs Kipling, who had, in her day, danced suggestive dances and sung lewd songs in East End music halls but who now (as visitors said) was like something out of the Book Of Revelation. She had been plump; now she was thin, but her flesh had shrunk faster than her skin, which hung in peculiar folds. Her hair had been red, but it had gone white and she had made it red again – fantastically red – carmine tinged with blue. Her health had gone with her youth: her stomach made noises. Every morning Mrs Kipling rouged herself, blowing out her lank cheeks and drawing under each cheekbone a cyclamen-coloured disc. She lived, now, in invisible limelight. Everything that she did, said and wore was intended to strike a target twenty feet away, and the perfume she used clung in the air for a long time. She was careless about the house, concealed dust under rugs, scratched what she was employed to polish, stole what she was expected to protect and burned everything she was asked to cook. From time to time she had what she called 'attacks', and then she would go weeping and groaning into her room – which was hung from ceiling to floor with theatrical photographs – and came out an hour later singing 'Ta-ra-ra BOOM-de-ay' under her breath, which smelled strongly of whisky. Mrs Kipling got on well with The Tiger Fitzpatrick. She spoke of her triumphs, and he spoke of his. The Tiger had, at least, got his name into the papers: she knew his press cutting by heart. There was, indeed, something compelling about the wide-eyed gesticulatory enthusiasm of The

Tiger Fitzpatrick when he spoke of boxing and devoted himself to prophesying the results of the big fights.

It is a fact that in fifteen years he has never managed to forecast a winner. Yet he still has half-pitying, half-mocking friends in the profession who give him tickets. Shortly after he put on a black coat and a striped waistcoat in the service of Asta Thundersley, he was presented with two ringside seats for the Leppard-Coffin bout and asked his employer if she would like to come. He was anxious, he said, to do her a good turn. No man in his right senses could possibly doubt that Coffin would win in four rounds – probably in the third. He, The Tiger, owed Asta much – would she give him a chance to repay her by putting her shirt on Coffin? She put ten pounds on Coffin and went with The Tiger Fitzpatrick to the Albert Hall, where she shouted down several thousand people, brandishing her big red fists in the air and stamping her feet until Coffin, having run away for two rounds, was knocked unconscious in the third and booed out of the ring. The Tiger explained, with violent blows at the ambient air, that Coffin had been robbed. Asta lost her ten pounds but developed a taste for the ring.

Since then she has been conspicuous in the crowd at every notable prizefight. Sometimes The Tiger Fitzpatrick accompanies her, whispering dark secrets in a voice that can be heard four rows away. If she had laid her bets in direct opposition to his forecasts, she would never have lost. But she has faith in her butler. He has not been drunk more than thirty times in fifteen years – that is to say, not so drunk as to be incapable of walking. She feels that he is a demonstration of the power of militant humanitarianism and would not lose him for all the money in the world. For his part, The Tiger glumly worships the ground upon which Asta treads. Once, in the Black Swan, the body servant of a gentleman who lived two doors away made Miss Thundersley the subject of a ribald remark, whereupon The Tiger, looming over him, said: 'Put your hands up, you bastard, and fight like a man!' – meanwhile throwing across what he believed to be a punch like a thunderbolt. The punch landed with deadly accuracy exactly where the other man's chin would have been if he had still been there, but he had finished his drink and left a quarter of a minute ago. The Tiger Fitzpatrick no longer needs to hit anyone: a look at his face is enough. This perhaps is just as well.

Once in a while, he helps Asta in her garden. With a spade The Tiger is more trouble than he is worth; the essential pressure of the foot reminds him how Kornblum trod on his instep, once upon a time, in Birmingham, and this makes him so angry that he cuts everything to pieces. If he is given a hedge to trim, he does very well indeed for the first twenty minutes; but soon the snapping of the shears reminds him of the quick left-right with which Roland Gogarty knocked him cold in Sheffield. And so he fights the battle over again to the detriment of the defenceless hedge. It is dangerous to let him weed. As the hoe comes down there comes back into his memory a vivid recollection of how Pancho Quixote held him for one operative moment with a chin hooked over his shoulder while he butted with his head and hammered his kidneys with his right hand; then God help the geraniums!

Asta Thundersley, however, who is violent as a cow buffalo, has a light hand with growing things. She loves children and vegetables. Holding out a handful of seeds like little knots of coarse brown string, she will say to The Tiger Fitzpatrick: 'Look! Onions. Each of these is an onion, millions of onions. And what a nice thing an onion is! Layer on layer, what a miraculous thing an onion is!'

The Tiger usually replies: 'With sausages.'

Once, picking up a windfall apple under one of the two soot-intoxicated trees in her garden, Asta tore the fruit apart and said: 'Six, seven, eight pips... Isn't it odd, Tiger? You can count the pips inside an apple but not the apples inside a pip?'

'Just spit them out,' said The Tiger Fitzpatrick. 'You get appendicitis through swallowing pips.'

Asta Thundersley called him a punch-drunk idiot and hurled the jagged halves of the apple at his head. Later, he picked them up, cut away the bruised parts and ate them.

Next day, Mrs Kipling cooked him an apple pie. She was jealous, she loved him, but The Tiger was not interested in her or any other woman as a woman. He had got out of the habit of that sort of thing many years before, although he was – and still is – something of a ladies' man; a Casanova, all talk and reminiscence.

If anything was needed to make The Tiger's aspect thoroughly nightmarish, that thing was a bowler hat. He has taken to wearing a bowler hat. A woman, of course, was responsible for this – some painted scarecrow or expiring balloon who told him that in 1912 she knew a gentleman who worked in an office, and this gentleman wore a bowler hat day and night and was a nice gentleman.

Mrs Kipling has made no secret of her intention to tear this woman's eyes out.

'Take it easy,' says The Tiger Fitzpatrick, who has got very heavy in the past few years. 'Take it easy...'

II

Another of Asta's unpredictable friends was a demented theologian who was working on a crack-brained scheme: he proposed to modernise and dramatise the whole of the Bible and so bring the modern world to God. You may still see Mr Pink, as he is called, in the bohemian pubs. He sees no harm in a glass of beer and cracks little jokes of a slightly clerical flavour. 'Our Lord turned the water into wine, Mr Landlord; you appear to have worked the miracle in reverse' – that sort of thing. He is a quaint, not unattractive figure, in spite of a badly scarred chin. While elucidating a point of doctrine one evening, gesticulating with a cigarette, he set his celluloid collar alight and burned off his little silky beard, of which he used to be inordinately proud. He has always taken a finical pride in his appearance and gets himself up like a parson on holiday at the seaside, in a prim but natty grey alpaca coat, black trousers, a high stiff collar and a narrow tie. In all weathers he wears a straw boater, much too small for him, into which he screws his big round head. He laughingly refers to this hat as his 'little crown of thorns'; it leaves a vivid red ring around his bald scalp. Mr Pink is never to be seen without an old-fashioned umbrella with a silver handle and an armful of papers. There never was such a man for carrying papers. All day long, he sheds sheets of notes as a dying chrysanthemum sheds its petals. If you are in a hurry, you will be well advised not to help him pick up his dropped papers, for if you do he will engage you in conversation, and it is impossible to resist his shy, childish eagerness and the trusting look of his clear blue eyes. In no time at all, he will tell you all about himself – that is to say, the work to which he has devoted himself:

'...the modern trend, my dear sir, is to the staccato, the crisp, biting, slangy phrase. I have not the slightest doubt that Our Lord in his lifetime talked so as to appeal to the great mass of the people – simply, dramatically, colloquially. Twenty years ago, struck with this idea, I determined to translate the gospels into the sort of language the younger generation prefer to read and talk in this day and age – to retell it all as if it were a story. Perhaps I don't make myself clear, sir? –'

Out comes a quire of paper closely covered with illegible scribbling. He flips over the sheets, muttering to himself: 'Judas, Judas, Judas... Judas and the Priests... that awful scene of the betrayal of Jesus... Judas, Judas, Judas, where's Judas? Aha! Here he is. Allow me to read it. Or no, perhaps it is a little long. I see you're in a hurry. Here, sir, is a shorter passage, the tremendous drama of Peter when the cock crows. I have put it into modern dialogue. I should greatly prize your opinion...'

In an incongruous, high-pitched, academic voice Mr Pink reads:

– *Say, aren't you one of Jesus' mob?*

– *Who, me?*

– *Yeah, you!*

– *You're nuts, I never saw de guy in my life.*

(A cock crows. Enter servant girl.)

– *Listen, boss!*

– *What is it, honey?*

– *This bastard with the beard was with that God-damn radical agitator.*

– *Who, me? Honest to God, de dame's screwy! I was not!*

– Why, you lying son of a bitch, you were so!

– Who, me? One of that mob, well whadda-ya know about that? Ha, ha, ha! I wouldn't touch dat guy Jesus with a disinfected bargepole.

– Guess you made a mistake, honey.

– Well, maybe I did at that, Moe.

– What do you say we go nibble a drink?

– Okay by me.

(Exeunt. A cock crows again.)

– Holy Jesus, holy Jesus! What a rat I turned out to be!

'...Do you see? Does it strike you as clear? Does it hammer home the lesson? If you had time I should have liked to read you some of my notes on the modernisation of The Lamentations – quite forceful. Or perhaps Joseph in Egypt and Potiphar's wife:

– Joe, I feel terrible. I got a terrible pain, Joe.

– I am sorry to hear that, madam.

– I got a lump coming up here – just here – I think I got a cancer, Joe.

– Let us hope not, madam.

– Put your hand here, Joe; no, not there – here. Yes, right here. A bit lower. I guess I got cancer of the womb or something. Oh Joe, Joe, Joe!

– But, madam, please!

– God, Joe, you don't know what it is to be starved for affection. Potiphar doesn't understand me.'

At this point, perceiving that Mr Pink is likely to go on all day, you excuse yourself and make a getaway. But Asta Thundersley can listen to him for hours. His life work should be finished in another nine years. According to his schedule he has only the Books of Hosea, Joel, Amos, Obadiah, Micah, Nahum, Habakkuk, Zephaniah, Haggai, Zechariah and Malachi left to dramatise. Among other things he is a Christian socialist, and every May Day, without fail, he puts on a tired old red tie which looks like a boiled geranium. He is punctilious in acknowledging his debts and has given Asta his IOU for £392 . 7s . 2½d. The tuppence-halfpenny represents a stamp he borrowed.

There is something saintly about Mr Pink. He never disliked

anyone in his life, except a girl nicknamed 'Peewee'. This is short for Pauline. When she was a baby she could not say *Pauline* and had to pronounce her name as best she could. Now she is a raw-boned woman of forty with dark-grey eyes as cold and unsteady as windblown puddles, whose face is always fixed in a maddening expression compounded of hate and resignation. Peewee was supposed to be a medium. She professed to have a Control named Tiny Wing, the spirit of a Red Indian. Peewee could fall into a trance at a moment's notice and then, in the accent of a cockney imitating Maurice Chevalier, she would speak with the tongue of Paul The Apostle. On one occasion she had a seance at Asta's house. Mr Pink quivering with rage at question time asked Paul The Apostle to translate the cry of Jesus at the Ninth Hour – '*Eli, Eli, lama sabachthani?*' – whereupon Peewee came out of her trance with a hollow groan and said that she could not go on because there was a Doubter present. Asta lost faith in her at the time of the murder of the second-hand clothes dealer's little girl, Sonia Sabbatani. Peewee said that she knew who had committed this crime. She saw, she said, a dark thickset man with a heavy lower lip and a blue jaw – a man who had the habit of glancing from left to right out of the corners of his eyes, and dressed in clothes that might have been either blue, brown or grey.

Asta was sure that this was not the case, because, as it happened, she was convinced that she knew who had raped and murdered the child.

Asta made no secret of her conviction in this matter. But she discredited herself by her own fierce impetuosity. She saw criminality in the most unlikely people, just as she saw virtue in outcasts. It was not in her nature to gather evidence and present it: she had to rush out of her corner with her head down and her fists flailing, looking for a face to punch. When Peewee, in a trance, started to tell her patroness what she saw, Asta leaped out of her chair with a bellow, shook her and said: 'Now, you bitch, I know you're lying! And *you* know you're lying! I *know* you know it! Don't tell me!'

Peewee pretended to have a nervous crisis; Asta poured a jug of ice-water over her and kicked her out of the house, to the

inexpressible delight of Mr Pink and The Tiger Fitzpatrick. Mrs
Kipling wept because she had had faith in Peewee – she who had
wasted whatever change was left on the morning after the night
before in the booths of soothsayers and fortune-tellers. Mr Pink
made reference to the Witch of Endor, with a sort of Talmudic
chuckle. But at that point he looked up, saw Asta scowling at him,
coughed, gurgled and became silent suddenly, as if a knife had
been drawn across his throat.

Still another of Asta's friends was an artist who painted large
canvases, one Johnny Nation, who had been trained to be a doctor
like his father before him. He drew nothing but dried-up livers,
kidneys preserved in formaldehyde, tangles of tortured nerves and
guts.

Nation drew with remarkable skill and accuracy. Asta hoped
to wean him from his bad habits. Meanwhile, to give the young
man a chance to live, she bought his pictures. Now her house was
full of them: panels of bowels and bladders and dropsies, tumours
wearing spectacles, wombs in aspic, ulcers in floral hats and
corneous moles like human faces. She hung them up between
Indian watercolours, caricatures by Sem and bits of framed
embroidery of the time of Queen Anne. Her house, in fact, was
like a madhouse. Asta kept a cook and cooked for herself, employed
a butler and presented her own guests to herself. She had a secretary
who could not efficiently read or write, Mrs Fowl, a reduced
gentlewoman, who sometimes helped with the sewing. What with
her household and her charitable works, Asta Thundersley found
little time to eat or sleep. And still she got fat!

12

Her increasing weight used to worry her. What was the use of a
crusade against hunger and oppression, led by a woman who
looked as if she had been stuffed with chickens, peaches and cream?
She tried – not wholeheartedly – to get thin, but God had seen
fit to enclose her hungry soul in a hundred and seventy pounds

of meat: there was nothing Asta could do about it. So she became more vehement in her outcries, and by this very vehemence she discredited herself. Asta might be in the right seven times out of ten, but she had a way of hanging the cap-and-bells on Reason and lending the aspect of lunacy to a trivial error.

Nobody who was present is ever likely to forget the Bishop of Suchester's tea party, to which Asta Thundersley brought another of her friends, Tom Beano, the leader of a group of militant freethinkers.

'So,' said Beano, feeling the bishop's stomach, 'this is how you sell all you have and give to the poor, is it, you swollen prelate?' Then he made a speech, denying God: there was a scene.

Beano loved scenes: he was responsible for the Buttick Street Riot. On that occasion Beano tried to overthrow the Salvation Army in one desperate *coup d'état*. After the band had played, a melancholy, blue-lipped man in uniform told the audience that he had once been a drunkard, a liar, a fornicator, a thief, a profane swearer, a coppers' nark, a teller of filthy stories and in general a dirty dog – but now, now (*Hallelujah!*) he was saved, saved, saved – now, now, now he was washed in the Blood of the Lamb (*Praise the Lord! Oh praise, praise, praise the Lord!*).

Beano had arranged that his supporters should be ready for a certain signal. Everything had been rehearsed. As the saved Salvationist made a dramatic pause, Beano roared:

'Sister Hannah! YOU shall carry the banner!'

In a squeaky falsetto chorus his supporters responded:

'But I carried it last time!'

'You'll carry it this time and like it!'

'But I'm in the family way!'

'You're in everybody's bloody way! January, FEBRUARY, MA-A-A-ARCH... Left-right, left-right, left, left, left, left...'

Then the fight started, and that is how Beano lost his front teeth and the job he used to have in a shipping office. Beano and Mr Pink used to have some interesting discussions concerning the existence of the Deity. Mr Pink always ended by saying, with maddening calm: 'I have faith, my friend.'

'So have I, my friend,' said Tom Beano, unshakable.

'Faith in what? Faith in God, Mr Beano?'

'Faith in the non-existence of God, Mr Pink.'

'Then you're a blind fool, Mr Beano, if you don't mind my saying so.'

'And you are a blithering idiot, Mr Pink.'

'Thank you, Mr Beano,' said Pink, with irony.

'Thank *you*, Mr Pink,' said Beano through curled lips

Asta picks such people up as the whim moves her and seldom drops them. She always feels personally responsible for the welfare of her wistful, watchful hangers-on, who sit hungrily about her big red presence like stray dogs about a butcher's shop. Yet she has made several true friends who love and understand her. Curiously enough, most of her real friendships developed out of enmity: Asta's best friends are people whom she originally attacked.

Once you persuaded her that she had done you an injustice, Asta would take off her skin to make a waistcoat for you: she was yours for life. Now, for example, Chief Inspector Turpin might be her brother: he is one of the few men she really admires. Yet at the time of the murder of Sonia Sabbatani, when Turpin was only a detective inspector, she was ready to tear him to pieces.

Turpin was a big man with a tucked-in chin and a spirally wrinkled neck that resembled a gigantic screw by means of which his small head was fixed to his thick shoulders. His fists were freckled, and his face was pale. When Turpin talked he barked, kept his white-grey eyes on you as if he was waiting for a sudden, belligerent move.

Now his hair is white: his scalp resembles one of those wire brushes with which suede shoes are cleaned. When the Sabbatani case was in the newspapers, Turpin's hair was almost red; he is thinner now, so that his face hangs in folds. The watery sepia ghosts of freckles still speckle the backs of his hands, but he is not the lean, tense man he used to be, although his eyes are more arrogant and his voice more brusque.

13

Asta met him first in the Bar Bacchus: he was pointed out to her
by Gonger. 'Detective Inspector Turpin of the Yard,' he said in a
graveyard whisper.

'Ho!' cried Asta Thundersley, loosening her shoulders with
a series of angry shrugs, like a boxer before a fight. 'Ho!... Hi,
you!'

'Mom?' said Turpin.

'Where's the beast that murdered Sonia Sabbatani?'

'Couldn't say, mom, I'm afraid.'

'He couldn't say!' said Asta. 'He couldn't *say*! *Why* can't you
say? A friend, a customer of her own father, did it. Rottenest, dirtiest
case in the world, and he can't say! What do I pay taxes for?'

'Ha!' said Turpin, finishing his lager beer.

'You're a detective inspector, aren't you?'

'Yes'm.'

'Aren't you a public servant, then?'

'Yes'm.'

'Find the beast that murdered Sonia Sabbatani, and I'll give
you a hundred pounds. There!'

'Much obliged to you,' said Detective Inspector Turpin dryly.
'See what I can do.'

'See what you can do? Bah! Catch the beast, lock him up and
hang him – d'you hear?'

'Yes'm,' said Turpin, rising and brushing ashes off his blue
trousers and moving towards the door.

'No you don't,' said Asta. She interposed her powerful body
between the detective inspector and the way out of the Bar Bacchus
and continued: 'Look here, you, whatever you call yourself. Find
who killed Sonia Sabbatani, and I'll give you a hundred pounds
for yourself. In notes. Do you hear?'

'Couldn't accept it, 'm. Find the man if we can in any case.'

'Look here!' Asta bellowed, holding the detective inspector
back as he tried to go out. 'A little girl is murdered. Have *you* got
any daughters?'

'Two.'

'If one of your daughters was Sonia Sabbatani, what'd *you* do?'

'What I'm doing now,' said Turpin. 'That's what I'm here for.'

'Here,' said Asta, 'here a child is murdered –'

'Listen, madam,' said Detective Inspector Turpin, 'do listen. This murder was, as they call it, a Sex Murder. That is to say, a sort of a murder without obvious motive –'

'The motive *is* obvious!' said Asta Thundersley, getting hold of the detective inspector's lapels. 'Sex is the motive, rape is the motive, beastliness is the motive!'

'Quite so. You know how these things are, don't you? Some of the nicest people go in for that kind of thing – there's no way of identifying them. Is there, now?'

'Bah!'

'Ask yourself, Miss Thundersley,' said Turpin, 'if it's as easy for us as you seem to think. As you say, sex is the motive – beastliness as you said just now, and quite right too. Well now, you see, almost anybody might commit a crime like that. Respectable fathers of families have been known to, er, commit certain offences against children. People you'd never suspect are always strangling ladies of easy virtue with silk stockings, for instance. This sort of murderer is the hardest sort of murderer to lay your hands on, because he's not a habitual criminal. He is not known to the police. A burglar, or a forger, or a confidence trickster – he leaves, as you might say, his autograph on his work. A certain kind of thief might be specially expert at opening, say, Yale locks with a bit of celluloid. Or another might, as a skilled craftsman, have his own particular way of cracking a safe. They can no more change their style than you or I can change our handwriting or our fingerprints. They give us something to work on, and sooner or later we make an arrest. And besides, in the criminal world there *is* always somebody or other who will give information to the police; or at least somebody we can get information from in one way or another. But the sort of men that do jobs like this Sabbatani job, they're lone wolves. Ordinary, clean-cut crooks hate and despise them. They're always the last sort of people you could possibly suspect. For all we know the man who killed that poor kid is having a quiet drink in this bar at this very moment. Or perhaps he's too respectable to hang about in bars: perhaps he believes it's wicked to drink. Or perhaps he's hard at work earning money to keep his mother, wife and children. Or he might be a doctor, at a lying-in. Or a tramp on the roads. There *is* no earthly way of saying, is there? That's where our headache comes in, don't you see? But don't you worry, we'll get him in the end.'

'Oh, yes! Of course you will get him in the end! Bah! Don't talk to me! I know you. I know the police. They couldn't even catch a cold. I know them. Oh, they're remarkably efficient when it comes to picking up some old hag, paralytic-drunk on Red Biddy; or running in somebody without visible means of support, or lying in wait for tarts in Gerrard Street. But when it comes to a murder –'

With some amusement Turpin asked: 'As a matter of curiosity, 'm, I wonder what you'd do in a case like this if you were the superintendent. God forbid. Here are your facts. Little girl goes to school. In the afternoon thick fog comes down, real London pea-souper – can't see a hand in front of you. Four o'clock comes, the little girl doesn't get home. Mother, worried, goes to the school to meet her with a torch. School is in Ingersoll Road, half a mile away through half a dozen dark, dirty streets. Mother gets to the school at five. Asks for Sonia and is told that the child has been kept in for being a bit too high-spirited but has been released with a caution at ten past four because of the fog. Mother walks streets –'

'– She *felt* something terrible had happened,' said Asta, with tears in her bloodshot bull-eyes. 'She felt it in her heart.'

'Quite so, quite so. Everybody always does, or at least they say they do after the fact. Mother walks streets shouting *Sonia, Sonia, Sonia* and gets home three-quarters of an hour later. Still no Sonia. Waits till six. Very properly rings local police station. No news. At half past seven she rings again. Enquiries have been made at local hospitals. Still no news of Sonia. At last body of little girl is found in the coal-cellar of empty house (condemned property) in John

Cornelius Street. An Offence had been committed and the child strangled. Medical evidence says death occurred sometime during that foggy afternoon. Nobody saw anybody or anything. No witnesses could possibly be reliable in any case, because the whole town was stone blind… Well?'

Asta Thundersley gritted her big teeth and, after a long pause during which she pinched her cheeks, twisted her ears and stood on one leg like a dropsical stork, while Detective Inspector Turpin watched her out of the corners of his eyes with a little expectant smile, she said: 'Arrest every known pervert in London.'

'You'd have your work cut out,' said Turpin.

'What the hell are you paid for? To hang around grinning like a Cheshire cat and wasting the public money in saloon bars?'

'All right, Miss Thundersley, I beg your pardon. You're the boss now. You're going to arrest every known pervert. What do you mean by *pervert*?'

'People who go in for that sort of thing, of course,' said Asta, angry because she felt that she was not on solid ground.

'You mean,' said Turpin, with an irritating smile, 'arrest everyone whom you know to be a child-murderer, is that it?'

'I mean everyone who *might* be a child-murderer,' said Asta Thundersley, breathing hard.

'On what charge would you arrest them, miss?'

'For questioning.'

'Ah, Miss Thundersley, I see you're one of these Hitlerites.'

'Do you want me to knock your silly head off?' asked Asta Thundersley in such a tone that the detective inspector realised that she might at any moment try to do so.

He said, hastily: 'You can't just arrest people because they *might* have done this or that. You ask them to call and see you, or ask permission to call on them and have a few words with them… But all right. Have it your way. You're the boss now, remember.'

'Well,' said Asta, a little out of countenance, 'interview (if you like that word better) people who have tendencies that way.'

'You wouldn't find enough policemen in the world to do it, would you?' asked Turpin.

'What do you mean by that, Turpentine, or whatever you call yourself?'

'Well, Miss Thundersley, I come back to what I said before. Anyone, absolutely anyone, could be the culprit. Take these queer people whose idea of fun is to give their girlfriends a good hiding. Where are they?'

Asta Thundersley said: 'All over the place, I believe.'

'Well, I put it to you, since you're the boss now, anyone who has fun that way might be the man we're looking for. But how are you to find out? I'm going to be crude. Sometimes this sort of nonsense with dog whips, or whatever it might be, is something between husband and wife, as it might be. Your queer fellow has his fun, if you can call it fun, with the connivance and the assistance of what a normal person would call the "victim". The willing victim.'

'Well, Turpentine?'

'Turpin. The name is Turpin. You can put it this way. Say, for the sake of example, I am a timid sort of man. I am as quiet as a mouse. This has nothing to do with present company, but – just for the sake of example – I am as quiet as a mouse and you (you realise, of course, that I am only talking for the sake of talking), you are one of those soft little women, one of those little fluffy ducks who wants to do nothing but please someone.

'I am timid. Why am I timid? I'm timid because I shrink away from people. I'm timid, in short, because I am afraid. What I really want to do is show myself to the world as a great big savage hairy creature with a pair of fists on me like hammers and the courage of the devil; I want to use those fists that I haven't got. I'd be a real thug, a tough guy, if I could. But I can't. I'm always, if the truth must be told, one of those shrinkers-back – full of all sorts of hate. You see, I'm dead yellow. And what happens is, I cover it all up by pretending to be sweet and soft and gentle. But underneath I'm waiting for just one chance to get at someone. If, say, you give me a good smack in the face, I won't do anything about it except store it up in my mind. And then at last, one of these days, the thing I've been storing up breaks out. But I don't get my revenge on you, you see. I get my own back on something weak. See?

'How does it break out? You can mark my words, hardly ever of its own accord. Somebody's got to help it. Who? I'll tell you who.

'The person that helps a softie to get his revenge is always the willing victim I think I mentioned a little while ago. You know what I mean; somebody who gets a thrill out of suffering: it might be a woman; it might be a man. Up comes the willing victim; which is all that this shy torturer, as you might call him, this murderer who's afraid to commit his murder – this willing victim is all that he needs to make him feel powerful. He never felt powerful before.

'But you (I am not speaking personally), you are much stronger, better looking and socially more important, perhaps, than he is – and you somehow enjoy submitting to him. I'm being direct and brutal, 'm, since you asked for it. You make this man feel stronger; you give him a feeling of self-confidence – which is half his battle – because you lie down and let yourself be ill-treated by him.

'And so there comes a certain night – or it might be a foggy afternoon – when somebody falls into his hands. More often than not it's a child. The weakest man is stronger than the average child, isn't he? So what happens? All of a sudden he feels that he's something like a man of power, and he rapes that child. After he has raped that child he knows that if she lives she'll recognise him; and her identification together with the medical evidence will make things hard for him. See? And generally he's a respectable man. So what does he do? Tries to wash out the evidence. How? With a child it's easy. Get hold of her throat and hold on tight.

'Then he goes back to whatever job he does for a respectable living. I can tell you, anyone might have murdered Sonia Sabbatani... But you're the boss, miss, and you're telling me what you would do if you were superintendent,' said Turpin.

Asta Thundersley said: 'I am to take it, I believe, that everyone who enjoys being hurt adds to the cruelty of the world. Is that it?'

'I suppose you could put it that way, 'm.'

'You could put it this way: that anyone who enjoys being hurt is bound to find someone who enjoys hurting him, or more probably her.'

'Yes'm.'

'What you indicate is this: that any woman who gets a thrill out of suffering and submission will, as it were, stimulate some man, in play, to feel he's compelling her to suffer and submit. Am I right?'

'You're not far wrong, 'm, I should say.'

'The idea is, Turpentine, that if he learns self-confidence in being violent with her, he will be violent with somebody else without invitation. Is that it?'

'Yes, in a way, that *is* it.'

'Then she's the mother of a murderer, isn't she?'

'If you put it that way – yes, that's it.'

'I take it that it depends entirely upon the individuals concerned. They have no right to encourage that sort of thing, is that right?'

'Never more right in your life, Miss Thundersley.'

'But what about the beast that killed Sonia Sabbatani?'

'Circumstances being favourable, any man can get hold of any child and do whatever he likes and go home and have a cup of tea and get away with it.'

'Then why aren't you looking for the murderer?'

Turpin waved goodbye.

14

The job of work upon which Detective Inspector Turpin was employed concerned a man called Jack Emerald. One of Jack Emerald's nicknames was 'Chicken Eyes': he was one of the most resourceful burglars in the business. He had been sent to Dartmoor after his third conviction on a formidable charge concerned with five-thousand-pounds'-worth of jewels belonging to a countess but had escaped, slipping a handcuff, knocking a six-foot policeman unconscious, vaulting a six-foot wall and taking a running dive into the countryside. This was in the early autumn of the year, and Chicken Eyes Jack Emerald, having been at large for ten weeks, had been the subject of leading articles in several newspapers.

Rumour, reinforced by whispered information, said that he had dressed himself up as an artist.

This was regarded as unlikely but not impossible. Turpin was well aware that all sorts of strange organisms lurk in the guts of the fine arts. The edges of the two underworlds overlap. The fringes of art tangle with the fringes of crime. Artists *ratés* frequently become crooks; similarly, professional criminals almost invariably regard themselves as artists – and sometimes they are artists, in their way, like Chicken Eyes Jack Emerald. In any case, the bohemian is second cousin to the spiv: he has a similar lighthearted amorality, a similar slack-mouthed here-today-and-gone-tomorrow easy-goingness, a similar tendency to hide himself under a certain kind of clothing and barbering, or lack of barbering; a similar light-fingeredness with his neighbour's property; a similar delight in strange slangs and jargon; a similar urge to be conspicuous coupled with the same secretiveness; a similar fatal weakness in self-revelation and a similar intemperateness; a similar blind detes-tation of law and order and established things. They are fellow rebels.

Turpin knew all this, and he knew something else more important: that Chicken Eyes had a weakness for a young lady called Cigarette, who wrote poems and short stories and had, shortly after the beginning of her association with Chicken Eyes, taken to talking authoritatively about the Underworld. Cigarette was a rebel. Against what was she in rebellion? Everything. She was an unhappy woman, and for her unhappiness she blamed her mother, whom she described as 'an unmitigated bitch'. The mother of Cigarette had compelled her daughters to wash their hands and faces and brush their teeth every morning, to pull the plug when they used the lavatory, to say please and thank you and to come home before midnight. Cigarette's sisters, girls of no spirit, submitted like tame mice to this brutal ill-treatment; not Cigarette. She, as she put it, got the bloody hell out of it as quickly as she could. She came of a good family – solid landowners in the Midlands. But she seemed to be eaten up by a homesickness for the gutter. 'I am a Rebel,' she used to say. By this she meant that if everybody else thought it right and proper to clean their nails, change their underclothes, blow their noses into handkerchiefs, stand up when the band played 'God Save The King', stub out a cigarette end in an ashtray or return a borrowed book or umbrella or coat, she was determined to do the opposite.

Ideologically she was a feminist. Cigarette was constantly conscious of the degradation of her sex. It irritated her, for example, that men proposed to women. How dare the sons-of-bitches stand around smirking and looking upon women as mere creatures to be proposed to? Cigarette invariably proposed, frankly and directly: 'Look here, don't you think it would be a good idea if you and I went to bed?' Only she employed a four-letter word. Of course she was talked about, but her principle was to give any gossipmonger who opened his lips something really worth talking about. Thus she would go out of her way to make scandal, and practically burst her lungs diving down to the muddiest depths of degradation, just to outdo gossip and exceed saloon-bar report.

At the time of the flight of Chicken Eyes she was about twenty-nine years old – a big redhead with a sneering mouth. She had, by that time, given up being filthy and dressed in a somewhat masculine style but with a certain elegance, ordering her clothes from Waldemar's and telling them to send the bill to her mother, whose banker sent Cigarette thirty-two pounds on the first of every month. She said that it suited her convenience at the present moment to be well-dressed: Chicky liked her that way. Chicky, it is scarcely necessary to say, was Chicken Eyes Jack Emerald. She had found him in a public house near Charlotte Street. He had been pointed out to her two days after his acquittal in the Goldclang jewel robbery case. Everyone knew that Chicken Eyes had done the job, but the police were unable to prove it. He got away with it, and, going out to refresh himself, was pointed out to the young lady. At that period of her life – two years before – she was in the habit of lounging about the town in an outrageous state of dishevelment. She sauntered up to him and said: 'Are you Jack Emerald?'

'Well?'

'They call me Cigarette. Does that convey anything to you?'

'No.'

'What do you think of me?' she asked, pressing herself against him.

Chicken Eyes replied: 'I think you could do with a good wash.'

'Don't you like me?'

'No.'

'Don't you think it would be a good idea if you and I –'

In spite of her dirt and the fact that (it being a warm May day) Cigarette was wearing nothing but a stained black silk dress, there was unmistakably an air of breeding about her. There was authority in her tone and in the glance of her haughty eyes. She said: 'Do you come home to my flat, or do I go home to yours?'

Chicken Eyes looked at her, felt a surge of wrath, but wavered and at last said: 'You can come back to my place if you like.'

He lived in a large Edwardian block of flats built of red brick – Something-Or-Other Mansions – near the Gray's Inn Road. In the taxi on the way home he said not a word. As soon as they arrived and Chicken Eyes' door clicked shut behind them and the yellow electric light went on, he took her by the scruff of the neck, thrust her into the bathroom and washed her from head to foot with a nailbrush. Thereafter she adored him. She became elegant. She lived only for him. But her family got wind of the affair: her mother cut her allowance. So Cigarette had to work from time to time. Chicken Eyes did not like that, but there was nothing he could do about it. Burglary is an underpaid profession, or art, whichever you choose to call it. Cigarette had a knack of writing spicy little stories and naughty little paragraphs. She had begun to contemplate a novel. The two lived together in one of those strange states of armed truce in which so many couples seem to pass their lives. They quarrelled every other day, and when they quarrelled the air was thick with pots and pans. They lived in perpetually recurrent estrangement and reconciliation. An outsider might have said, observing them, that Chicken Eyes and Cigarette were implacable enemies. Yet the fact of the matter was that in their way they loved each other: only they could not live with each other. Yet they could not live without each other.

Turpin knew that, whatever happened, the escaped burglar would inevitably come back to the girl called Cigarette.

It was pretended that no one knew of the existence of this strange relationship.

One morning, not long after his conversation with Asta Thundersley, Detective Inspector Turpin called on Cigarette at about a quarter to ten, humbly begged her pardon for having disturbed her – which she said he had not – and begged the favour of a few words with her. She was wearing a brick-red dressing gown over an almost transparent nightdress of a lighter colour. Turpin observed that the make-up of her mouth was smeared, her hair disordered and that she gave out a strong odour of perfume. Cigarette had not slept alone. Over a cup of tea he said: 'Speak to me as it might be man to man. You know we're going to get Chicken Eyes in the end. Where is he? He was here last night, you know. He was, wasn't he?'

'I don't know your friend Chicken Eyes, and I don't want to know him,' said Cigarette. 'Do please ask me exactly what you want to know. If I can tell you anything I will. Can I say fairer than that?'

'Where is Jack Emerald?' asked the detective inspector abruptly, watching her eyes. He saw Cigarette's eyes flicker; looked in the direction of the second glance and observed that it indicated the kitchen door. Meanwhile, Cigarette was saying: 'I haven't the faintest idea what you mean; I assure you, not the faintest idea.'

Having looked closely at the outside of the building before he entered it, Detective Inspector Turpin knew that the back door of the kitchen opened on to a fire escape and that this fire escape went down into the back doubles of West Central London. It was safe therefore to assume that Chicken Eyes was not in the flat.

'This, 'm, is nothing but a routine investigation, you understand. We are looking for a man called Emerald, and we were told he might be here.'

'Emerald? You can't possibly mean that burglar, or whatever he is, who keeps running away?'

'Well, as a matter of fact, yes – that is who we do mean. This is a nice flat you have here.'

'A dump, nothing but a dump.'

'How many rooms?'

'Three rooms, bathroom and kitchen. Why?'

'I just wondered, 'm; I'm looking for a place myself. I hope you don't mind my calling on you like this. It's a routine business, you understand. I've no right to –'

'Oh, I quite understand, Mr –'

'– Detective Inspector Turpin, 'm.'

'Turpin!' Cigarette began to giggle. 'No relation to the famous Dick, I suppose?'

'Well, I don't know, 'm. Nobody ever told me anything about it. Well, I'm glad this business is all over. I hate disturbing ladies.'

'Have a drink, Turpin?'

'It's a little early, 'm, but I wouldn't say no. I've been up since four o'clock this morning.'

'Whisky, gin or sherry, Dick Turpin?'

'Well, what are you having, 'm?'

'Whisky, if you will, Turpin.'

About three-quarters of an hour later the detective inspector said: 'The caretaker tells me there is a flat going. I wonder if you'd mind very much if I just sort of took a kind of look, sort of.'

Cigarette said: 'The house is yours, Dick Turpin. The house is yours, Dickie-boy. Come and look... here you are in the lounge. Well, there is a bit of a dining-room and quite a nice bedroom. Most important part of the house, don't you always think? Here, see?'

Turpin saw the disordered bed. On the floor, on the left-hand side, lay the lower half of a pair of small-sized pyjamas. 'How are the bathrooms?' he asked.

'As you see,' said Cigarette, pushing open the door; and there was a battered tube of shaving cream and a razor.

At about half past eleven Turpin said, casually: 'He won't be back in a hurry, though.'

'Who d'you mean?' asked Cigarette, snarling.

'You know who I mean. I mean Chicken Eyes,' said Turpin, suave as death. 'I wouldn't mind betting you a ten-pound note the Chicken won't be back this side of lunchtime. I happen to know that he won't.'

'And how do you happen to know that he won't?'

'That who won't? Who won't what?'

'This Chicken, or whatever you call him.'

'Ask Millie Cloud,' said Turpin, chuckling.

'And who the devil may she be?'

'Ask Chicken,' said Turpin, breaking into a hearty laugh and filling the glasses.

Twenty minutes later she said: 'You're a liar, a liar, a liar! A dirty, dirty, dirty, dirty liar! There isn't, there isn't – ISN'T any Millie Cloud! I can prove it, prove it, PROVE it!'

'All right then, I'll bet you twenty-five pounds.'

'There isn't any other woman, d'you hear? There isn't, isn't, isn't any other woman! Wait and see.'

'All right, I'll wait and see,' said Turpin, refilling her glass. 'Do you mind if I use your telephone?'

'Use whatever you bloody well like.'

Turpin dialled. Cigarette remembers that she heard him say: '…Oh yes, OK… right you are, George… yes, stand by, George. Yes, George… no, George… yes, George… goodbye, George.'

Two and a half hours after that Chicken Eyes Jack Emerald escaped for the last time. He was a sure-footed man and confident of himself on a parapet. But he had had an almost sleepless night and made one false step. That was enough: he fell six storeys, landed flat on his back on the pavement, bounced, and that was the end of him.

The papers called it a 'death-leap'. It was nothing of the sort. Emerald had told Cigarette one night that a fortune-teller had predicted that he would die through being struck by a ball. (He had been something of an athlete once.) Cigarette wrote the story in the *Sunday Special*. The fortune-teller's prophecy had come true: after all, the earth is a ball. She got £20 for the story and spent the money in the Bar Bacchus, maudlin and mocking in turn. Two days later her mother started to pay Cigarette's allowance again.

The Chicken Eyes Emerald affair took up most of the national front pages, squeezing the mystery of Sonia Sabbatani into the corners of the newspapers.

The police were not sorry for this: they did not know where to look for the murderer.

But Asta Thundersley raged like a raving lunatic.

BOOK TWO

15

She wanted to do something to somebody. She felt a need for a hushed Old Bailey, a Black Cap, a Sentence, a rope snapping taut and a gratified crowd outside grey walls half cheering while a man in uniform pinned up a bit of paper. She was out for blood. First of all she tried to get hold of the superintendent at Scotland Yard; but he had had about enough of Asta Thundersley and was not available when she called, nor did he reply to a six-page letter which she sent him. She made several attempts to get hold of Detective Inspector Turpin: he, aware that he had managed, with all the goodwill in the world, to put a new bee into Asta's bonnet – which was already droning like a kicked hive – thanked God for an assignment that sent him to the north.

For the first time of her life, Asta was conscious of a sense of frustration. She realised that the police had their difficulties but felt that if she were the police she would manage to do something drastic and sensational. In any case, she was determined to make trouble for someone, somewhere, somehow. The home secretary was out of town. The secretary for Scotland was the only other cabinet minister whom she knew, and he was, or pretended to be, ill. London, which she had hitherto seen as a concentration camp for persecuted dogs and starved children, now became, in her eyes, something like a criminal sanctuary full of ravening child-murderers. She could not live in peace while the killer of Sonia Sabbatani was at large. So at last she decided to do something about it on her own.

She began by calling on the Sabbatanis. She knew them. Sam Sabbatani used to send to her house every week or so for clothes to be sponged and pressed. Now, when she saw him, she was shocked. His child had been dead for seven days, and the Sabbatanis were observing the prescribed eight days of mourning. He had not shaved for a week, and his cheeks, which were sunken and flabby – for he had been unable to eat since his daughter disappeared – were covered with a black-grey mat of sprouting beard. Mrs Sabbatani, in the first burst of her grief, had torn out some of her hair: there was a little raw patch on her forehead. The room was full of people; at least ten men and a dozen women. Asta arrived in the evening after they had finished the mourner's prayer: she heard the last mutter of it and the concluding *Amen* as she came up the stairs; then, as she entered the room, the prayer having finished, conversation broke out. She darted forward, got Mrs Sabbatani in her wrestler's grip, shed a few genuine tears and said: 'Oh, my dear, my dear! Oh, my poor dear! What can I say? What can I do?' In that moment she ceased to be a crusader and wanted only to be able to work a miracle – to produce Sonia Sabbatani alive and give her back to her mother.

'So nice of you to come.'

'I don't suppose there's anything I can do, Mrs Sabbatani, is there? If there is, say so.'

'Do? Do? What is there to do? It is nice of you to come. It is nice of you to think of it. What more is there to do?'

Sam Sabbatani, who had been listening, seemed suddenly to go out of his mind. He burst into tears and began to shout in a language which Asta Thundersley could not understand: a thunderous, reverberating language made terrifying by the intensity of his emotion. He shook his fists at the ceiling and shouted. Sam Sabbatani was calling upon the head of the murderer the curse that is written in the book of Deuteronomy: 'Cursed shalt thou be in the city, and cursed shalt thou be in the field! Cursed shall be thy basket and thy store. Cursed shall be the fruit of thy body, and the fruit of thy land, the increase of thy kine and the flocks of thy sheep! Cursed shalt thou be when thou comest in and cursed shalt thou be when thou goest out! The Lord shall send upon thee cursing, vexations and rebuke in all that thou settest thy hand unto for to do, until thou be destroyed and until thou perish quickly; because of the wickedness of thy doings whereby thou hast forsaken me! The Lord shall make the pestilence cleave unto thee until He hath consumed thee from off the land whither thou goest to possess it! The Lord shall smite thee with a consumption and with a fever, and with an inflammation and with an extreme burning, and with the sword and with blasting, and with mildew – and they shall pursue thee until thou perish...'

It went on. Even Asta Thundersley was shocked to silence by the frightful vehemence of the man: '...And thy life shall hang in doubt before thee; and thou shalt fear day and night and shalt have no assurance of thy life! In the morning thou shalt say, would God it were even! And at even thou shalt say, would God it were morning! For the fear of thine heart wherewith thou shalt fear, and for the sight of thine eyes which thou shalt see...'

The old man in the round hat, and another old man with a rabbinical grey beard and a skullcap, forced Sabbatani back into his chair, while a woman thrust into his trembling hand a glass of tea with a slice of lemon floating in it, and an aged man with a clipped silver beard told him: 'It is a sin to curse like that. You don't repeat that curse. *Sha*, then!'

Asta was glad that none of her friends or enemies were present, because the time had come when she, of all God's creatures, was struck dumb. She had understood the intonation and the gestures but not the words; Sabbatani had been speaking Hebrew with a Rumanian accent, the old man in the round hat had been speaking Yiddish with a Polish accent and the old man with the bristly beard had been speaking something that sounded like a mixture of Aramaic and Lithuanian – which everybody else appeared to understand, since, when he had finished speaking, there had been some nodding of heads and clicking of tongues. Asta withdrew to the back of the room, edging towards the door, and there she almost collided with Catchy, with whom she had exchanged a few civil words from time to time in the Bar Bacchus. Catchy's eyes were shiny and purple with weeping; they opened and closed slowly like squeezed antirrhinums.

'Have you ever heard anything more terrible in your life? No, but have you? That poor child! These poor people! And someone did it who *knew* them! Oh, darling, what is one to do? Look at him! Look at poor Sam! He used to be fat, fat as a pig – and shaved,

shaved like a billiard ball. And now look. Oh God, dear God, is it possible to imagine? And look at Mrs Sabbatani. Those eyes! That hair! When she heard the news she tore a handful out – but by the roots, the roots – and her poor dear blood ran down! Oh, Miss Thundersley, Miss Thundersley, what *can* one do, what *can* one do?'

This question recalled Asta Thundersley to herself. She said: 'Do, Catchy? Do? I don't know what I'm going to do, but you mark my words – something is going to be done. Something or other, as I'm a living sinner! You wait and see!'

A belated condoler, saying as he came in: 'I wish you long life,' trod on her foot, for the room was crowded.

She brushed him aside; looked towards Mrs Sabbatani and saw a densely packed mass of muttering people; postponed her intention of rushing over and going into details; turned and rattled away down the stairs on her hard flat heels. Asta went out purposefully, as she had come in. But in the wet, dreary street a puff of wind, like a derisive sudden laugh, sprayed her with ice-cold rain. She turned up her collar. A hundred yards away a policeman in a blue greatcoat stamped through a puddle of rain in a disc of lamplight. The wind whistled, and the rain came down, striking the shop window and making a noise that sounded like a sort of signal: *What to do? What to do, what to do, what to do? To do what? To do what, to do what?*

Full of impotent anger, Asta Thundersley went home.

16

But it was not in her nature to do nothing. Next day she was up at six o'clock; fed, bathed, dressed and out of her house within the hour and on her way to the scene of the crime.

What did she propose to do, having got there? She had no idea. She knew only that she had to do *something*, anything, with all the vigour God had given her. She went, first of all, to the shop of Sam Sabbatani and there asked a policeman the way to the Ingersoll

Road School. He said: 'Ingersoll Road School. Take the first on your right, go straight on, bear left, take the first on your right and the second on your left and then you'll find it, just round the first corner at your left, mum.'

Asta said: 'Is that the best way to get to it?'

'You know, mum, there is no use going there before nine o'clock, don't you?'

'Why don't you mind your own confounded business? What do you take me for? A schoolteacher looking for a job? A new girl, or something? I am asking you a civil question. Give me a civil answer. Is there any other quicker way? God Almighty, man, give me a straight yes or a straight no, can't you?'

The policeman looked her up and down; but having let his glance travel from Asta's knees to her face he bit off and swallowed a little retort that he had been rolling on his tongue and said: 'Well, no, mum. The way I told you is, actually, the best way to get to the Ingersoll Road School. I mean to say, the best way for the present. Leadbetter Street is still up. I dare say Leadbetter Street will be up for about another four or five days. When Leadbetter Street's open again, then the quickest way is to take the first on your right, second on your right, bear right and there it is on your left.'

'Then why don't you keep a civil tongue in your head?'

'I try to, mum, but why don't you try walking up and down all night on a night like last night?'

'Officer, I sympathise with you. I'm not a schoolteacher, you know.'

'Aren't you, mum? You know what? There was something about you that made me think perhaps you might have been.'

'Exactly what?'

'I can't say exactly, but just for the moment I thought you might be a new schoolteacher. Not long ago some girl came down from the north to take a job in a school around here, and she looked –'

'– She looked what?'

'Nothing. I forget. No,' said the policeman, 'that is your best way to the Ingersoll Road School, but it won't be open until nine.'

'And how long did you say this other road of yours had been closed?'

The policeman said: 'I didn't say, mum. But if you want to know, Casement Street, the first on the right, has been closed halfway along ever since the gas mains blew up three weeks ago. Why do you ask?'

'I ask, policeman, simply because I want to know. Is that clear? All right, then. Good morning to you.'

Asta Thundersley walked away. She took the first turning on the right and went straight ahead into a street of soot-soaked brick, bypassed a great hole in the road and found herself in an alley, the left-hand side of which was the frontage of a brand-new slum, the windows of which looked out upon an ancient red wall. After that she had to make her way around the periphery of half of a crescent; could not decide whether at this point she ought to turn left or right or walk straight on and was lost. She had an idea at the back of her head that she had been told to turn left; she turned left and found herself by the railings of a square full of rotting grass and dogs' dung, surrounded by houses that looked all alike and overshadowed by a church spire like an ice-cream cone. The streets were empty. It seemed reasonable to Asta Thundersley that by this time someone, anyone, should be approaching the doors of the church. She waited. Nobody came. As she calculated it, the nearest main road was to be found by turning to the right, the left and the right again. She walked, turned right, and left, and right, and found herself in a street that seemed to have no beginning, no middle and no end. So she walked. After fifteen minutes she arrived at a turning, turned and found another street. This street appeared to go on without perspective to the end of the world. Asta walked on. She turned left, she turned right; she turned right, and then she turned right again and walked straight on.

Soon people appeared in the streets: girls on their way to work, pale with a bluish pallor under their face powder, and men whose pockets bulged with packets of sandwiches, filling the first pipe or lighting the first cigarette of the day. Asta asked first one and then another the way to Ingersoll Road School; nobody knew. One man said: 'First right, second left', but said it as if he was, so to speak, picking it out with a pin. Another said: 'Are you sure you don't mean the Pross Crescent Kindergarten?' The third, with the quiet smile of the man who knows that he is irrevocably in the right, said: 'Ingersoll Road School, mum? Easy. First right, second right, bear left, straight on as far as you can go, turn right at the traffic lights, straight on till you come to a red-brick building, and there you are… Not at all, it's a pleasure. Good morning to you. Not at all, glad to have been of some assistance.'

In the end she found herself near the river, where she saw a policeman admiring the sunrise. In a thoroughly bad temper, Asta approached him and shouted: 'I suppose if I was some poor down-and-out without a roof to my head you'd be on my tail already. But if I was a murderer trying to give himself up, I'd have to fill in a form or something before you put in an appearance. Don't talk to me, I'm fed up with you, fed up with the whole lot of you!'

'What's all this about, mum?'

'I'm looking for Ingersoll Road School. Be so good as to direct me to it, will you? I warn you, I'm a friend of the superintendent.'

The policeman put his finger in his mouth and sucked it, took it out and looked at it; inserted the fourth finger of his left hand into his right ear, blushed, said: 'Just a minute', unbuttoned a pocket and pulled out a reference book and said: 'Ingersoll Road School, let me see.'

At that moment a taxi passed, and Asta Thundersley cried *Hey!* in a tone that stopped it like an invisible brick wall. As she ran towards the taxi she shouted over her shoulder: 'And a fat lot of use you are, you parasite! You drain on the public money! You bloated creature! You wait! I'll show you! Don't talk to me!' When she told the taxi driver to go to Ingersoll Road School he said that it was a matter of a few yards up the road.

'I wasn't asking you what it was a matter of. I told you to take me there, didn't I?'

'OK.'

He drove her two hundred yards and stopped in front of a building that stood in the middle of a black rectangle of asphalt surrounded by a red-brick wall, and said: 'See?'

Asta gave him half a crown and went in at the entrance under the sign that said *GIRLS*.

She was aware, first of all, of a smell of chalk. One of the teachers had arrived – a light-haired woman who looked older than her years and had no eyebrows. Asta Thundersley got hold of her and said: 'Are you the headmistress?'

'I am Miss Leaf. Is there anything I can do for you?'

'Give me the headmistress.'

Miss Leaf said: 'I don't think she'll be in for a few minutes. But if there is anything I can do for you –'

'My name is Asta Thundersley.'

'Oh, yes?'

'I want to speak to the headmistress. Who is the headmistress?'

'Miss Handle. If there's anything I can do... what did you want to speak to her about, if I may ask? I only want to help, you understand...'

Asta Thundersley had followed her into the classroom, hung with maps, educational pictures and pinned-up pastel drawings of leaves, horse chestnuts and bananas. There was desk space for thirty-odd children. At the back of the room there was a big glass-fronted cabinet which contained a peculiar octagonal wheel used for unwinding the cocoons of silkworms, several birds' eggs, a walrus's tusk, some specimens of raw cotton, several lumps of mineral ore, a stuffed sparrow and a celluloid doll confiscated from a naughty girl who had been caught in the act of nursing it in the course of long division.

Asta looked about her. The blackboard was going grey. On the window-ledges there stood pots that sprouted leaves which, to Asta Thundersley, were completely uninteresting. There was also a little tank full of newts and a number of jam jars containing tadpoles. She had been educated at a private school, a special sort of school, to which parents used to send their more ferocious and unmanageable children. She had never been to a school like this.

The first thing she looked for was a safety exit, because her most recent mania had been concerned with exits in case of fire.

'Say the place catches fire? What happens?' asked Asta. 'What's the first thing you do?'

Miss Leaf said: 'Save the register.'

'Save the register! I've never heard of such a thing in all my life. What about the children?'

'Oh, they have fire drill.'

'What I wanted to ask you was this: what about Sonia Sabbatani?'

'She was in my class. The poor little girl!'

'Was she a good girl?'

'Oh yes, a very good girl. A little high-spirited. Something of the tomboy. But a good girl, quite definitely a good girl.'

A door slammed. 'That'll be Miss Handle,' said Miss Leaf in a hushed voice. Heavy heels thudded in the passage. Miss Handle came in. Looking at her, Asta observed that after all these years she had come face to face with her match.

'Yes, madam?'

'I am making certain enquiries relative to the death of Sonia Sabbatani,' said Asta. 'My name is Thundersley.'

'Well, Miss Thundersley?'

'Well,' said Asta, 'I'll tell you. I am determined, madam, to get to the bottom of it.'

'I think the police are best qualified to do that. I realise that individual effort can occasionally attain its ends, but I really do believe that this sort of thing is best approached through the proper channels. I am a very busy woman, Miss Thundersley,' said Miss Handle, who had seen, in Asta, an adversary of her own calibre.

Asta mentioned the names of three or four well-endowed and influential charitable societies for the prevention of things, of which she was a representative, and said: 'I'm determined to help dig out the man who killed Sonia Sabbatani. I know that the police are doing whatever police can do, God help 'em. But you don't understand how I feel about this.'

'I think I understand only too well,' said Miss Handle. 'But what can you possibly do about it? Have you asked yourself that?'

'I don't know,' said Asta. 'There's always a chance in a million that I might just happen to pick up something everyone else has overlooked. It's been known to happen. Is there nothing you have in mind – you know, something so trivial that it didn't seem worth mentioning – anything at all about the child or anyone connected with her? The police', Asta added grimly, 'have to go to work according to their proper procedure, or whatever they call it; but *I* haven't got any proper procedure, I can assure you! I've only got improper procedure. So –'

'Miss Thundersley, I believe it to be a fact that outside interference hinders rather than helps the police in such cases.'

'How could I hinder the police? There's nothing to hinder them about. They're up a blind alley – a blind alley in a thick fog at that. There's nothing to work on.'

'Miss Thundersley, I fancy that the detectives at Scotland Yard are not in the habit of making public every shred of evidence upon which they happen to be working.'

This was unarguable. The headmistress continued: 'And I have already answered more questions than I believed possible. A charming man, the chief inspector, although not quite like the detective of fiction.'

'What questions did they ask you?'

'That is not a proper question to ask, and I don't think it would be proper to reply to it, Miss Thundersley.'

'Did they talk to the little girl, Sonia's friend, who was told by poor Sonia that a friend of her father's was going to…' the words stuck in Asta's throat, '…going to *show her a secret*?'

'Yes, they did talk to Violet Almack. I was there at the time. The Chief Inspector was most tactful and charming – he put the child quite at her ease at once. She could only repeat what Sonia had said to her: that a friend of her daddy… etcetera, etcetera. Nothing more. And in case you propose to ask Violet about it, I want to say in advance that I strongly disapprove.'

'No, I don't propose anything of the sort. Poor little things! Let them have a little bit of innocence while the going's good! No, no – not for the world! But tell me one thing, Miss Handle. Which way would Sonia have gone home so as to pass by the place where that coal-cellar is?'

'Well, Miss Thundersley, she might have gone by any of four or five different ways. She might have started in a wrong direction in order to make a game of skill of getting home. You know what high-spirited girls are, I dare say?'

'I was one myself. But tell me – which way would Sonia have gone if she had been going directly home?'

'In that case she would have sidetracked the excavated street and gone the longer way – as it is until they get the road mended. Especially in that fog.'

'Thank you, Miss Handle. You may, and will, call me the damnedest old fool in the world. But I tell you, I'll hang someone for this if it's the last thing I do.'

Miss Handle said, with an intonation of sarcasm: 'I wish you luck, I am sure.'

'Thank you for your good wishes. I am much obliged to you. And I can assure you that I generally achieve what I set out to do.'

'I haven't the slightest doubt of it, Miss Thundersley.'

'Thank you, Miss Handle.'

'Good morning, Miss Thundersley.'

17

Asta went out, cutting little crescents into the floorboards with her angry, stamping heels. The fact was that she had not the beginning of an idea of what she proposed to do. First of all, she decided, it was necessary to look at the scene of the crime. She had no difficulty in finding the place: as soon as she asked the way a dozen men, women and children seemed to spring out of the earth. They all shouted directions. One girl asked her if she was on a newspaper. Asta said no. The girl did not believe her and followed her, walking about eighteen inches behind her and keeping up a running commentary full of geographical information: 'This is the street. All these houses are going to be pulled down. They're condemned. Unfit frooman 'abitation. That's Mrs Switch's house they've begun to pull down there. It was full of bugs. My mum says they pigged it, they didn't live in it, they just pigged it. You wouldn't keep a self-respecting pig in such a house. They used to let rooms. They made ever such a lot of money. My mum says anybody can make money that way. My mum says they lived twelve in one bedroom so as to let rooms. See where that grease mark is on the wall? They had a gas stove in the bedroom. You ask my mum.'

'Why aren't you at school?' asked Asta.

'I've got ringworm.'

At the far end of the street a policeman stood, contemplating a pillar-box. In the remote distance someone was playing a barrel-organ. Asta, looking at the front of the house, was overwhelmed by a sort of sickness of heart. It was not merely that the house was derelict, not that it was unoccupied, unused, unusable, and forever abandoned, it was that she could somehow perceive in the aspect of the place exactly what they meant when they said that it was Condemned. It was finished. It was better torn down and wiped off the face of the earth. She could see how, for the past fifteen years or so, no tenant of the house had been able to bring himself to spend as much as it cost to paint the railings or the window-frames. The place was condemned property: nothing was worthwhile. The house which, as the little girl had said, had been full of bugs and was now half torn down, gaped at the rainy sky. Asta could see the greasy pink paper of the bedroom. It had been worth nobody's while to hang paper there. There must indeed have been a gas stove in that bedroom: she could see the greasy black outline of it. Above this outline there was nailed an oblong of painted green tin, curling away from the wall at one corner. The demolition men had not yet started to break up the house in which Sonia Sabbatani had been murdered. It was exactly like every other house in that street: four storeys high, built of a muddy-mustard-coloured brick and sinking, as it seemed, into a squalid basement bristling with spearheaded rusting railings.

Little boys had smashed the windows with stones. Every frame enclosed a shivered frieze of dust-encrusted grey glass. Through a splintery star of dark space in the ground-floor window she could see an empty, desolate room and, on the only visible wall, an oblong of patterned paper, lighter than the rest, where a framed picture must have hung. The brass-headed nail was still protruding from the wall above it. Asta would have sworn that the picture which had hung framed in this space was of a little girl and a mastiff, with the caption: *Love Me, Love My Dog.*

Now, standing in front of this empty house, Asta was almost afraid. She wanted to go home. She remembered certain bad dreams of ruins in wildernesses. So she became angry; stamped up the three dirty steps to the front door and wrenched at the doorknob. She had expected to feel the resistance of a turned lock – indeed, she hoped to find the door immovably shut.

But it opened.

She found herself standing in a short, narrow passage leading to a steep, narrow staircase. There was a smell of dereliction, of damp and, as it were, of darkness. On the left, beyond the door, she could see a heart-shaped mark where an umbrella stand had stood. Beyond it a gas bracket protruded. She went in. Her footsteps reverberated. This house enclosed something of the misery, the loneliness and the hollow silence of the outer dark. The street door slammed behind her with the noise of a gunshot. A foul wind was blowing through the passage. The house was evil. It was rotten; full of a dirty twilight and the stale stinks of a hundred and fifty dreary years. A flake of wet plaster came fluttering down past Asta's face, startling her so that for the first time in thirty-odd years she uttered a cry of terror. Then, ashamed of herself and (because she was still afraid) even angrier than she had been before, she went forward.

18

She had a shadowy, wrong-headed idea that she would find a clue, some shred of evidence – button, hair or rag – which the police might have overlooked.

First she went upstairs. In the attic there was nothing but mildew. The second floor back contained only some decomposing shreds of torn ticking stuck to bits of broken wood; this had been a mattress which someone had gutted for the sake of its horsehair, for which he might have got threepence or fourpence a pound. The next room must have been a bedroom also. There was a gaping cupboard containing a broken clothes-hanger and, in a vile newspaper parcel, unspeakable evidence that the last occupant of that sordid room had been a woman, not too particular in her personal habits. 'Slut!' said Asta; and the sodden, echoing house called her a slut in her turn. *Slut* said the passage; *slut* said the staircase; *slut* muttered the cupboard. On the next landing there was a bathroom. Asta shuddered at the rusty iron bathtub on high, ornate, cast-iron legs, and the water closet which, it seemed, was worked by means of a handle, like those electrical generators used for firing off charges of high explosive. It was stuffed with used newsprint like the head of a plagiarist. Asta went down to the first floor. She walked warily because wet rot, dry rot, the wear and tear of countless feet and sheer weary decrepitude had made the stairs dangerous. A picture, about as big as this open book, hung on the wall: she noticed it as she passed. It had not been worth taking away – it was a vulgar little print cut out of a cheap magazine. Somebody had loved this picture well enough to put it in a sixpenny frame and nail it up. It depicted a scarecrow of a woman with a black bonnet all askew, horribly drunk between two sturdy policemen, shrieking at the top of her voice. The caption read: *Hark, Hark The Lark At Heaven's Gate Sings*. The front room on the first floor must have been the most important bedroom of the house. There Asta saw a broken glass vase and a wonderfully designed red, blue, purple and gold-lustre chamber-pot of remarkable capacity, minus the handle, which lay, badly broken, inside it. Asta could see as clearly as if she had been present at the time how the lady of the house, in the excitement of packing, had broken this thing, which was part of a wedding present: she had picked up the fragments of the handle, fitted them together, wondered tearfully whether they might be seccotined or riveted together, but had given it up, putting the fragments neatly all in one place in case some poor devil might find a use for them. The floor was littered with bits of paper and studded with tin tacks that had held down linoleum. In one place the floor had given way, and a hole patched with the lid of a biscuit tin, hammered flat and fastened with nails. Stamped on the surface of this piece of corroded metal, still perfectly legible, was the name *PEEK FREAN*. There was also a common kitchen chair, broken and glued, broken and screwed, broken and nailed and finally irreparably broken and abandoned. As Asta touched it with her foot two or three fat slate-grey insects with more legs than she cared to think of darted out at dazzling speed and ran into a crack. She lit a cigarette, beginning to wish that she had not been such a fool as to stick her nose into this putrescent corpse of a house.

A man must have occupied the bedroom next door: the black marks of a brilliantined head were clearly visible on the top stratum of the wallpaper, which, peeling in the damp, seemed to be opening like the pages of a fantastic picture-book illustrative of sixty years of popular taste. The linoleum in this room had not been worth taking up: it was falling to pieces. Originally it must have been blue with a red lozenge pattern; Asta could see traces of this pattern upon a background of something that resembled sackcloth. Four indentations marked the place where the bed had stood, and upon the adjacent wall there was a rash of reddish-brown blotches where bugs had been thumbed to death.

The ground-floor front was, of course, the sitting-room. There was a ruined cushion: it had been stuffed with chicken feathers but had burst. These feathers lay, now, in the form of a straggling letter 'S', on the floor, so wet and dirty that they looked heavier than lead. The grate was red with rust. Scattered about the hearth lay a broken poker, part of an old brass fender, green with age, and a tennis boot covered with fungus. There was also a handsome ashtray, badly cracked, with the inscription *Galeries Lafayette*. And the whole place seemed to be full of broken, knotted and rebroken string and spoiled brown paper.

Asta went downstairs again. This journey to the basement of

the house was a dangerous one. As she went deeper the stairs grew more and more treacherous. At the bottom something gave way under her heel, quietly and as it were deliberately, like a soft-shelled crab upon which one accidentally treads, and Asta had to disengage her heel from a bit of rotten wood. The scullery was a desolation. Someone had stolen the scullery sink – there were hideous scars upon the wall. Perhaps that same marauder had got away with the old-fashioned lead pipes, for where the pipes had been there were surfaces, rough and sore-looking, like picked scabs. Here again lay ten thousand odds and ends of brown paper, white wrapping paper, silver paper, newspaper and looped and knotted lengths of all kinds of string – all wet, sodden, mildewed, untouchable.

To this part of the house a little light penetrated between the area railings. Asta Thundersley's heart felt like something she had eaten that had disagreed with her.

Near the kitchen there was an ancient wash-house with a copper boiler built in a round cylinder of half-rotten brick that had once been whitewashed and a window as big as a pocket handkerchief that was not designed to open. The smell of five generations of filthy linen hung in the thick grey air of the wash-house. As Asta hurried out of it she saw an archway. It was the opening of a malodorous little vault, the roof of which was the pavement of the street. Looking up, she saw the rusty undersurface of the lid of the coal hole. There was coal dust under her feet; and now her feet were as sensitive as teeth – she walked on her toes. In the coal-cellar there was a crushed tea chest of peeling plywood, a few shovelfuls of wet coal dust and a demolished leather sofa.

This was the love nest of the undiscovered murderer. Here the beautiful child Sonia Sabbatani had been ravished and found dead, with her head in a puddle, some lengths of knotted string about her wrists, gagged with abominable rags.

As the police surgeon lifted Sonia, one of the fat grey insects had run out of her ear.

19

Asta wanted to be sick. She had never before been so afflicted with loathing. She had never experienced such a sense of disgust. For the first time in her life she found herself disturbed by two equally powerful impulses: she wanted to run away, hide her head, forget all about this thing; and at the same time she wanted to rush forward with her head down and find out all about it. She turned to go home. Then something happened that made her heart stagger between two beats. A heavy, solemn footstep sounded in the passage just over her head.

It is unlikely that Asta Thundersley actually became pale, but she felt herself going pale; she felt that a great cold funnel had been thrust into her bosom and that all her vital parts, reduced to pulp, had been squirted down into her lower gut. She felt cold, she felt damp and her belly rumbled so that the arch of the squalid coal-cellar picked up the echo and threw it back. Asta's first impulse was to look for a place to hide. But then she became angry again, gathered herself, tensed her muscles, set her teeth, rushed upstairs and found herself face to face with a policeman who, in his turn, became greenish-white and recoiled.

He said: 'What are you doing here?'

'What are *you* doing here?'

'I was informed that someone had been nosing around here.'

'Oh, you were, were you? I wouldn't mind betting that you were informed by a little girl with ringworm. Is that so?'

'Well, it was a little girl who told me. She said somebody was nosing around.'

'Oh, she said somebody was nosing around? Well I can tell you for a fact that somebody *is* nosing around. *I* am nosing around. On whose behalf? On my own behalf. Anybody's death diminishes me because I am involved in mankind. Is that quite clear? I am involved in mankind. Get that into your thick head, you and your ridiculous helmet. I'm looking. Is there any law against looking?'

'That front door ought to be locked, ma'am.'

'Don't ma'am me. My name is Thundersley, Miss Asta Thundersley.'

'I didn't mean to bother you, ma'am, but that front door ought to have been locked.'

'By the by, officer, do you happen to know whether the police force is looking for traces of coal dust?'

'I must get back on the beat, mum.'

'Get back wherever the hell you like, you bloodhound without a nose!'

The policeman went out. Asta Thundersley went away to where she thought she might find a taxi.

20

At the cab rank she met a man she knew. His name was Schiff. He was a kind of scientist, a German who called himself an Austrian and got himself up to look like an Englishman in ginger tweeds, big brown boots and a fair moustache. No one knew exactly what his background was, but everyone knew that he had something to do with medicine. Now he is working for a firm that manufactures nose syringes and fountain pens. Then he was looking for a patron and had his eye on Asta Thundersley. She told him what was on her mind.

He quoted Groddeck: 'Why are you concerned so much about sadist-masochism? What says Groddeck? "What you have read and learned about sadism and masochism is… untrue. To brand as perversions these two inescapable human desires which are implanted in every human being without exception, and which belong to his nature just as much as his skin and hair, was the colossal stupidity of a learned man… Everyone is a sadist; everyone is a masochist; everyone by reason of his nature must wish to give and to suffer pain; to that he is compelled by Eros." So said Groddeck.'

'I don't give a damn what Groddeck said,' said Asta Thundersley. 'If I had your friend Groddeck here I'd give him a piece of my mind. Didn't Groddeck ever come across –'

'"Humanity created for itself a god who suffered, because it felt that pain was a way to heaven, because sorrow and bloody torment is esteemed divine.'"

'Bah! To hell with your filth! Does it make murder good, you fool?'

'"Was your skin never reddened by the sucking of the mouth? Did you never bite into an encircling arm and did it not seem good to you to be bruised… Why, most dear lady, even the child wants to be punished – he yearns for it, he pants for a beating as my father used to say. And he uses a thousand tricks to attract punishment. The mother soothes the child on her arm with gentle pats and the child smiles; she washes it and kisses it on its rosy little bottom, which only just now was so full of dirt, and as the last and greatest treat she gives the dancing baby a slap which sets it crowing for joy." So said Groddeck. Of Groddeck, the Master, Freud said: "We shall gain a great deal by following the suggestion of Dr Groddeck… and we need feel no hesitation in finding a place for Dr Groddeck's discovery in the fabric of science." Pay no attention, dear lady. All this is not your world.'

'It *is* my world, and if, Dr Schiff, you have nothing more to contribute, you can go and –'

Schiff said: 'Dear lady. Dear, good, kind lady. I beg you. Do not look at it like this. Everything is not so easy. There is a good reason for everything. Let us have no sweeping generalisations. Nothing occurs without a good reason.'

'To hell with your good reasons,' said Asta, with the memory of the derelict house still in her mind. 'There isn't any good reason for anyone to do what that man did. I'm going to find who did it, and, so help me God in heaven, I'm going to hang him. I don't want him on earth.'

She started to walk away, but Schiff followed her. Asta habitually walked fast, and he was a short-legged, short-winded little man. Still, he kept up with her and trotted beside her talking in gasps: 'Consider, consider. There is much you want to do. Socially, socially, I grant you very properly. You are a lady with money.'

'None to give to you, I assure you.'

'Not so fast, not so fast. Give? Who said give? It is I who want to give. I want to give advice, advice worth money.'

'I suppose you want me to invest in some wildcat scheme of yours, is that it?'

'Listen,' said Schiff, as Asta slowed down. 'I knew Georg Groddeck. I have studied psychology in Vienna. I know what I'm talking about. There is something you want to achieve. As a millionairess or a multi-millionairess you will achieve what you hope to achieve five times more quickly.'

'I'm not a millionairess or half a quarter of a millionairess. And if I didn't know where my next bit of bread was coming from I'd still achieve what I wanted to achieve, as you put it; so stick that in your pipe and smoke it, Mr Schiff.'

Schiff said: 'I wasn't suggesting that you were a millionairess, or a half, or a quarter, or an eighth of a millionairess. I was only going to tell you how to become – not a millionairess but something like a tenth part of a millionairess. I wanted only to tell you how to make a hundred thousand pounds. I am a psychologist. Also, I am a chemist. I am a psychological cosmeticist. I was with Groddeck, and I knew Coty. Listen. This is the era of the new self-consciousness. This is the period of the self-inflicted psychic wound; the age of masochism. Now, you do not win a lady's heart by saying: "Dear lady, you are so sweet." You say, as brutally as possible: "Holy God in heaven, woman, you stink like a dead pig – for Jesus Christ's sake wash yourself." You say: "Look at yourself! You are as shaggy as an ungroomed horse, you untidy bitch – do something about it, or you will never get married." Now I, Miss Thundersley, have evolved a deodorant. Because I know you, and trust you, and like you, I will give you the formula. It is as follows: *glyceryl monostearate, triethanolomine stearate, glycerine, hexamethylenetetramine, a dash of perfume and water*. It is a very good deodorant. It holds back the sweat. It takes away the stink. What more do you want? It is a genuine article. I have a good name for it: *POO*. But, psychologically speaking, the formidable aspect of the advertising campaign is that the copy contains the following statement: *Contains hexamethylenetetramine*. Naturally, it must. It could not exist without *hexamethylenetetramine*. But consider, psychologically, the impact of that word – *hexamethylenetetramine* – slap bang in the public eye! And consider also that long word in relation to the brand name of the product – *POO*. And consider again, psychologically, the value of the brand name, *POO*. A ridiculous name? I grant you that. Completely ridiculous, and even, in a way, slightly improper, since it suggests someone holding the nostrils. Poo! Poo! What happens? The name *POO* in itself breeds publicity. It makes its own publicity. People say: "Get yourself some *POO*." They say things like that. It passes into the language. In the end, a critic says of a play: "It needs *POO*." It may be argued that the purchaser may not like to ask for a product named *POO*. I have a way around that. Actually we call it PO^2. In other words, pee double O, which spells $POO – PO^2$. I am absolutely convinced that given a little support it would make a fortune. Or then again, an astringent lotion. And what does it take? A little alum, zinc sulphate; menthol for an illusion of coolness, witch-hazel, alcohol, diethylene glycol and, of course, water. The operative thing is this: one says, *This astringent contains diethylene glycol*: psychologically it's irresistible. I have also a toothpowder –'

Asta Thundersley managed, by some unprecedented effort of will, to hold back an avalanche of icy, crushing words. It occurred to her that this learned man Schiff might be of service to her. She said: 'I never looked at these things that way before. I should be very glad indeed to help – I mean to say that I have been wondering for a long time what to do with a few hundred pounds that I have lying loose. But before I can really give my mind to these things – before I can rest content – I must see that the man who killed Sonia Sabbatani goes where he belongs. I wonder if you can help me?'

Schiff's round face became alternately red and white with hope and fear while she was speaking. He thought deeply, biting his nails, and at last said: 'Do you suspect anybody?'

'I suspect everybody.'

'If I were you, Miss Thundersley, do you know what I'd do? I'd have a party. Invite everybody, everyone you know. Let everyone come who might possibly have anything to do with this affair. Let one or two of your most trusted friends listen. I'm a psychologist. I'll help to guide the conversation into certain channels. I tell you that one must wash and dredge the conversation of one's friends as one of these prospectors for gold dredges the mud of a dirty, shallow river. Through listening to my friends, I have found out many interesting things about them. And sometimes I've been of service to many friends by listening to what their friends said. The thing to do is to get them, dear lady, to relax. At a social gathering there is nothing like alcohol to make people relax, reveal themselves, as it might be described, a catalyst – which hastens the human-chemical reaction. I have a recipe for a drink which I believe I am not far wrong in describing as, psychologically speaking, a catalyst. I evolved it myself. It comes out of much trial and error, dear lady. It does not taste strong, and yet it is strong. In point of fact, the power of this drink lies in the fact that the most potent combination of ingredients are made to seem innocuous. As a matter of fact, I had half hoped to put it on the market. I couldn't think of a good name for it. You will see for yourself. Besides, it might be a little difficult to market this product on account of the high cost of essential ingredients. For you, I will write down the recipe. The point is this. Ladies and gentlemen, who like to drink, have a tendency after a glass or two, to talk. Then something starts. People reveal themselves. Give a party, dear lady, give a party to all whom you suspect – keep your eyes open and your ears open, and let me keep my ears and eyes also open for you, eh?'

Asta scratched her head and said: 'Schiff, I haven't got any faith at all in your psychological revelations. But I begin to feel that a little party would do me no harm at all.'

'And you will invite everybody?'

'Look here, I must go home now and make a list. So give me a ring tomorrow.'

'One little thing. My formula, the one for the fruit cup, as it is so called, was the result of research. Of this I want to make you a present. But a certain something I was expecting has not arrived. Will you lend me fifteen pounds?'

'I can let you have ten.'

The psychological Schiff was right again. If he had asked for twenty pounds, Asta would have said that this was out of the question; if he had asked for ten pounds, he might have got five. But asking for fifteen pounds, he got ten. He went his way north-westwards, and she went hers to the mellow and elegant little red-brick house in Frame Place by the river.

21

On her threshold Asta was shocked at the sight of a heap of massive leather luggage, stamped with the initials *TOT*. There were portmanteaux, hat-boxes in which one might have grown rhododendron bushes, dressing-cases, portable writing-desks, shoe cases, cabin trunks and old-fashioned tropical zinc-lined trunks – all made of massive cow hide and constructed to last for a hundred years. This luggage, and the initials, belonged to her elder sister, Thea Olivia Thundersley, another old maid, who had spent the past thirty years of her life wandering over the face of the earth, visiting members of her family. She had devoted the last half-century to the manufacture of a patchwork quilt. Thea Olivia's ambition was to herringbone-stitch into this quilt a little bit of everything. It already contained relics of precious old brocade, tapestry and paduasoy of forgotten pattern and texture; a fragment of an engineer's dungarees; a portion of a silk shirt; clippings of rich cravats and neck-ties; a corner of one of old Sir Hanover Thundersley's fancy waistcoats; polygons of magnificent satin, snippets of ribbon, pieces of the robes of mandarins looted at the time of the Boxer Rebellion, triangles hacked out of gorgeous Paisley shawls and oddments of rare cashmere. She carried her Work, as she called it, in a receptacle like a dispatch case made of red leather and stamped with initials in gold. This contained as much of the quilt as she had finished. In another article of luggage – this was not unlike an octagonal hat-box, but at the pressure of four little springs, it shot out four legs to stand on so that it became a sewing basket – she kept, in their proper compartments, gold-eyed needles, multicoloured silks, scissors, piercers and other pearl-handled tools, all highly polished. Most of the space inside this extraordinary receptacle was filled with countless bits of material which she had accumulated for her patchwork. When she was tired of sewing, she sorted, categorised and made little bundles of duplicate patterns in the manner of a stamp collector.

In a separate silk compartment she kept snipped-off geometrical clippings of soldiers' uniforms; a neat oblong of scarlet from the tunic of one of her uncles who had been in the Guards; a segment of green khaki from the breeches of her brother who had gone down in South Africa; and half a trouser leg of dark blue from the mess uniform of a cousin who, Asta suspected, had been her sweetheart.

Asta's first recollection of Thea Olivia was of a downward-looking, soft-spoken girl of twelve – drooping, almost voiceless, sweet-natured, dreamy-eyed – and damnably obstinate.

Thinking of her, Asta never failed to remember a curious exhibition she had seen in a booth when she was a girl. A tiny-boned Japanese ju-jitsu man, with a fixed sweet smile on his face, was demonstrating his skill against all comers. An enormous, oafish navvy, with muscles as hard and fists as terrible as the sledgehammer he was accustomed to wield, came forward and got hold of him in what seemed an unbreakable grip. Still sweetly smiling, the Japanese submitted. With a scornful laugh the labourer threw his arms about him and dashed him to the ground and then was lying on his stomach five yards away, yelping with pain while the little smiling Japanese was kneeling upon him in a businesslike way, with one hand in the small of his immense back and the other clamped about the toe of the big-booted right foot. Thea Olivia reminded her sister of that little Japanese wrestler.

Asta gave all the orders and did most of the talking and was feared in the family. The Thundersleys protested, argued, slammed doors, recriminated but obeyed her. Thea Olivia never argued with her, never protested, never recriminated, never could stand the sound of slamming doors, yet never in any circumstances obeyed anyone, unless obedience exactly suited her convenience. Asta, therefore, felt her heart sink as she looked upon the half-ton of cowhide luggage which The Tiger Fitzpatrick was dragging, hundredweight by hundredweight, into the house.

'Why, Tot!' she cried, with uneasy heartiness.

'Asta!'

The sisters embraced.

22

'You might have let me know you were coming, Tot.'

'Oh, but I did, Asta dear.'

'I don't remember getting a letter or a telegram, Tot darling.'

'But, Asta dear, I said in July that I'd come and see you in the winter.'

'Oh well, oh well, you're welcome, you're welcome. How's the quilt going?' asked Asta with a snorting laugh.

'Coming along very nicely, Asta dear, thank you. How is the Cruelty To Animals?'

Asta detected an undertone of mockery in her sister's voice and said shortly: 'It still goes on.'

'I told you it would,' said Thea Olivia, with her shy, pale smile. 'Oh dear, look at you Asta! How in the name of goodness did you manage to get yourself so dirty? What on earth is that on your shoes? Soot?'

'Coal dust,' said Asta and told her sister how she had got it.

Drinking tea and smiling, Thea Olivia said: 'Dear Asta – dear, darling Asta!'

'What the devil's the matter with you?'

'We do, all of us, love you so very much – you are so kind. Dear Asta.'

'What are you driving at now? Spit it out, woman, and don't beat about the bush.'

'I met Cousin Shepperton at Lausanne.'

'What is there particularly funny about that, Tot darling?'

'Don't lose your temper or I shan't tell you, Asta dear. Sheppy said: "If I remember rightly, Asta has been putting the world right for the past twenty years, and it's a hundred times worse than it ever was."'

'Shepperton is a blithering dolt, and you, Tot, are a nitwit.'

'Oh, I know I'm silly, Asta my love, but do tell me. I'm only asking to be informed. What are you going to do that Scotland Yard can't do?'

This question threw Asta into a state of blind exasperation, because she had not the faintest idea what she could do. She would have overwhelmed anyone else with frantic abuse. But she always felt the need to explain herself to Thea Olivia, who reminded her of their father – a quiet, prying, gentle, perfumed, poisonous little old man.

'Someone I know did it,' she said.

'No, really?' asked Thea Olivia, putting down her cup and sitting upright. 'Do I know him? But how do you know, Asta dear? Do be careful, won't you? Remember what an awful silly you made of yourself when you accused that poor lady of giving her baby gin out of a bottle, and it turned out to be pure milk in a green gin bottle? Don't be too impulsive. How do you know? Who is he? Do tell me.'

'That's exactly what I am going to find out.'

'Dear, good, kind Asta! Kind, sweet Asta! You always were the same. Wild, impulsive, angry for everyone else but yourself. *Nice* Asta!'

'Oh, for God's sake, Tot, go and patch your quilt.'

'Of course I will, if you want me to, Asta dear.'

Asta crossed the room in two great strides, embraced Thea Olivia and said: 'No, no. Please don't. You mustn't. You know me. I'm an absolute beast. I'm sorry I'm so bad-tempered. But all this has got on my nerves. Imagine how I feel. That poor child! And nothing done. Something the detective inspector – a nice man, if I was a man I'd like to be a detective – something he said gave me a kind of crazy idea that someone around here killed that poor little girl. I haven't got any evidence, but it rang, so to speak, a bell in my mind. Have some more tea. Eat a bun. Have some brandy. I don't mean to hurt your feelings. I'm all wound up and don't know what I'm saying.'

'Something about bells ringing in your head?'

'Somehow I'm sure in my mind that somebody around here did it. And I know everybody, and they all know me. It's the sort of murder that one of those plausible, educated types of man goes in for. Don't start laughing at me, Tot, because I'm not happy about this, not a bit happy, Tot. You mustn't laugh if I tell you that what I'm going to do is invite pretty nearly everyone I know to the house to a party and somehow try to get...'

As she paused, angry with herself at her own embarrassment, Thea Olivia suggested: 'Clues?'

'There's no need to say *clues* in that tone of voice!'

'Well, if you want my advice – drop it, Asta. You can't do any good, and you're almost certain to make a silly of yourself again – the same as you did that time when you got mixed up about that business of cruelty to a horse; when you had the terrible quarrel with Aunt Elizabeth because she said we ought to get two doctors to have you certified. No, please, please Asta darling, don't fly into one of your rages – they terrify me out of my wits. Who are you going to invite to your party?'

'I'll tell you later.'

That evening, after Thea Olivia had bathed and rested and bathed again and eaten – with the ethereal look of someone whom two spoonfuls of soup will choke – as much solid food as would satisfy a hungry farmer's boy, she sipped a cup of coffee and a glass of anisette while Asta, consulting a foolscap sheet blackened with wild scrawls and agonised doodles, told her whom she proposed to invite to her party.

23

'Tot, if I didn't know that you were as secretive as the grave, I shouldn't have breathed a word about all this,' said Asta. 'But I know you. You're sweet and kind and co-operative, and you won't breathe a word to a soul.'

'I won't, Asta dear, if only because I'm awfully afraid you're going to make a silly of yourself again over this.'

'Whatever else you were, you never were a sneak, Tot; that much I will say for you. A sly little – however, you could always be trusted with a secret; I can say that, at least. You *like* keeping secrets!' cried Asta, in a rage. 'God knows what secrets you keep!'

'I won't if you don't want me to.'

'Look here, Tot, are you going to start all that over again? Are you looking for a quarrel?'

'Dear Asta! Do go on.'

Asta composed herself and continued: 'Well, all right. Party. You know Mr Pink, you know Tom Beano, you know Peewee. You've met Doctor Schiff.'

'I've *met* him, yes.'

'And what's the matter with him?'

'Nothing, nothing, Asta darling; nothing.'

'For God's sake, Tot, control your vicious tongue! You know Mrs Dory, Catchy Dory? Girl with beautiful figure? No? You'll like her... Sir Storrington Thirst?'

'No, I don't know him.'

Asta would have said to anyone else that Sir Storrington was a wide, flat man shaped like a bed-bug, who crept into the cracks of conversation and crawled out between rounds of drinks. She said, simply: 'A baronet. You've heard of Cigarette?'

'The woman who was mixed up with that burglar?'

'Was it her fault, poor girl? She isn't the first girl to be misled by a crook, and, mark my words, she won't be the last. She's coming, anyway. Have you met Tobit Osbert?'

'Not that I remember, Asta.'

'A critic.'

'Dramatic?'

'I forget. It doesn't matter. A critic. He's coming. Detective Inspector Turpin, of course, you haven't met. A charming man – I wish I was a man: I'd be a detective. Oh, and you won't know the fellow they call "Shocket The Bloodsucker".'

'*They*, Asta?'

'Boxers. Shocket's a fight promoter.'

'I don't think I quite understand, Asta darling.'

'He promotes boxing matches. Don't you understand? He'll come. But I'll have to invite Titch Whitbread – Shocket The Bloodsucker won't move an inch without Titch just now. And Titch wouldn't come unless I invited Cigarette, because he's keen on her. Then there's Sean Mac Gabhann.'

'Pardon, dear?'

'Sean Mac Gabhann – an Irishman. Sean Mac Gabhann is Irish for John Smith. He comes from Cumberland.'

'What does he *do*?'

'He's an Irishman. Then there's Ovid Moffitt, the poet, and Dawn Knight, the actress. Inga Balzac, George Cheese and Beeps Wilking –'

'Pardon, dear? Beeps, did you say? Male or female?'

'Male,' said Asta, impatiently.

'But why "Beeps"?'

How could Asta explain that Wilking, when drunk, liked to sound the hooters of parked cars, crying '*beep-beep-beep*'? She brushed the question aside.

'Who else, Asta sweetheart?'

'I have Monty Bar-Koch Ba –'

'A Spaniard?'

'A Zionist. He doesn't believe in the Arab Problem.'

'A Jew?'

'I don't know: he eats ham. And there's Ayesha Babbington – the sculptress – and her boyfriend, Bubbsie Dark. They have all the vices. There's Johnnie Corduroy, in films, and Hemmeridge –'

'What does he do, for goodness' sake?'

'He... he isn't absolutely normal, Tot, my dear. In point of actual fact, he's a... Never mind. Then there will be Soskin – a dentist, a refugee, you never met him – and Goggs, a pork butcher.'

'Goggs, a pork butcher. Yes?'

'What are you looking at me like that for?'

'I think you've gone out of your mind, Asta. Who else?'

'Tony Mungo,' said Asta, with a defiant growl, 'a bookseller, etcetera.'

'What kind of *etcetera?*'

'He sells other things *you* wouldn't understand. Never mind. And there's Mr Roget, James Geezle and Alan Shakespeare.'

'They do what?'

'Geezle is a tattooist. Roget takes care of his mother and Alan Shakespeare has money of his own. If I think of anybody else I'll let you know. You don't have to come down unless you want to, Tot, my love.'

'But Asta, my dear heart, I do want to.'

'Behave yourself, then.'

'If you think I don't know how to conduct myself in order not to disgrace you in the presence of your friends –'

Asta Thundersley suddenly felt tired and discouraged. Between a yawn and a sigh she said: 'I'd be grateful for any help you could give me, Tot, my sweet. I know I seem crazy. I don't care about that. The only thing is that I feel helpless.'

Asta's angry, glaring eyes flickered and became wet.

'There, my dear – there, there, there,' said Thea Olivia, stroking the back of her sister's head. 'You mustn't wear yourself out.'

'Yes, I must,' said Asta, shaking herself like a wet spaniel and gritting her teeth. But then she started to weep, somewhat in the manner of a boy whose feelings have been hurt – sniffing, swallowing, holding back, bursting out and pausing to blow her nose while Thea Olivia tried to comfort her.

'Oh, go to the devil!' said Asta at last, throwing a salty wet handkerchief into the fireplace and striding out of the room.

'I will, if you want me to.'

'No, darling – please – good-night.'

'God bless you, my sweet.'

'God bless, Tot.'

24

Asta went to her room in one of her highly infrequent moods of black depression and rare doubt, feeling – for the third time in her life – feeble and lost, defenceless and lonely.

The first time she had felt like this had been at the turn of the century: as an ugly, noisy, boisterous, irrepressible girl in her ninth year she had fallen in love with a handsome cavalry officer twenty years older – a straight-backed, dignified man with a great moustache. This love was more than she could contain. She had to tell someone about it and chose for her confidante her young and pretty Aunt Clara, who listened to her with all the gravity in the world, uttering occasional sympathetic interjections as one woman to another – and when the whole story had come out threw her head back in an uncontrollable gust of laughter. This cruel yet melodious mockery came back into Asta's memory as she stood in the elegant old bedroom and watched the firelight winking on the polished walnut posts of the bed upon which she had been born. She told herself that it was stupid to remember such foolish things. Yet how could she help remembering? It was soon after this humiliation that she had decided to be a missionary – strong yet gentle, fearless yet kind, bold as a dashing cavalry officer, yet full of understanding – plunging through stinking, steamy jungles, laughing at nothing but danger, bringing the Peace of God into the hearts of fierce, cruel black people. But all this was so long ago, so terribly long ago! She had wanted desperately to give herself to all the defenceless and lonely people of this sad and bewildering world in which so many cry in vain for comfort, and where tender hearts like peaches carelessly thrown into a basket get bruised and go bad. She wanted to interpose herself between the cruelty and the vulnerability of mankind. But she realised, even at that tender age, that Good must be militant; that it is not for nothing that Evil is symbolised by the subtle snake that twists and turns and fascinates and must be struck quick and hard and can never really be charmed into harmlessness. She was by nature an extrovert; she became thunderous, unmanageable, had to throw her weight about, make her presence felt.

The second occasion of Asta Thundersley's descent into the shadows occurred – what nonsense one thinks of alone at night! – twenty years later. She had owned a white terrier bitch, which, in some inexplicable way, had grown to resemble her. The bitch, Jinny, had the same sort of tenacious goodwill under the same kind of forbidding exterior, and a half-fierce, half-humorous expression that had caused her to be called 'Asta Thundersley's Twin Sister'. Between Asta and this animal there was an affection, a tacit understanding. One day Jinny was run over by a taxi. Her hindquarters were smashed. The vet told Asta that there was nothing to be done: Jinny had to die, and it would be better if she died immediately. Asta loved Jinny better than any other individual in the world.

That was an atrocious hour.

'What will you do?' asked Asta, shedding tears for the first time in twenty years – not counting the times she had wept alone.

'My method is to give them a strong sleeping tablet in a spoonful of milk and, when they're asleep, put them into the lethal chamber. She won't feel a thing. She won't know. You can stay with her and stroke her if you like, until she's quiet. Upon my word of honour, it's the only kind thing to do.'

Asta looked into the vet's eyes for several seconds and then, standing like a condemned man when the safety catches of the firing squad click open, said: '*Do it.*'

And Jinny was only a dog.

Now this was Asta's third descent into hell.

She could not drive from her mind the appallingly vivid recollection of the grief, the hopeless grief, of the Sabbatanis. She could see them, as the firelight flickered, rocking to and fro as on a seesaw of which the point of balance was the limit of endurance – in and out, in and out, in and out of the frontier of utter despair.

She remembered the coal dust on her shoes, the squalor, the melancholy and the rottenness of that vile empty house, that abandoned evil place with its deep wet cellar. She could see it all. She could see the red-brick school in the yellow fog.

The child comes out. Somewhere, not far from the gate under

the sign that says *GIRLS*, someone is waiting. Who? As yet nobody knows. There is the fog, and a Figure with blurred outlines. No doubt his coat collar is turned up. He is quiet, persuasive, soft-spoken. The odds are that the child knows him. He says: *'Do let me see you safely home in all this nasty fog: your father sent me to see you safely home…'* And then leads her, chatting very pleasantly, perhaps telling her an amusing story, down the dark, dirty street to that condemned house; and there he tells her that he has got something there for her. A live teddy bear, it may be, or – most likely – nothing at all, just a mystery. *'I bet you a penny I can show you something you've never seen before.'*

He makes a mystery, a secret; and they go down, down that dreadful passage, down those rotten stairs, past that dark wash-house, into that grave – that stinking grave – that vault, that coal-cellar –

– And then, when the little girl says: 'Well?'

(Asta Thundersley could not bear to think of what happened then.)

Again she trembled with desire to do something about it and cursed herself for her incapacity to do anything at all. Almost deliriously she wished that Evil were, in fact, a great serpent and that she was a horned antelope: she would cast herself into the jaws of the serpent and perish – and in swallowing her the serpent would swallow that which must destroy him. Suffocating in his coiled maw, hers would be the last laugh, because with her last breath she could gasp: *'My horns will pierce you – I have let in the daylight – writhe and die!'*

Having draped her ungainly body in a linen nightdress and put herself to bed, Asta forced herself to be calm.

Out of the emotional chaos of the past twenty minutes there came an idea – one of the ideas for which she could give no reason and for which, nevertheless, she was prepared to fight to the death.

It was somebody who knew the Sabbatanis that raped and murdered the little girl.

After that, sleep was impossible. She was thinking, in her disorganised way, of the people she proposed to invite to her party.

Could it have been Dr Schiff? No, because whatever Schiff might have in mind, above everything he had in mind the safety of his person. Schiff (thought Asta) could even run away to save himself. As she saw things with her peculiarly focused eyes, this was unthinkable. It was permissible to beg, borrow or steal for another but not for oneself. One might sacrifice one's self-respect by running away for the sake of some other living creature. But no proper person ever ran away to save his own skin. She discounted Schiff. Yet anything was possible.

But what of Sir Storrington Thirst? He was a man of good family. Yet there must be, surely, something extraordinary in Sir Storrington. How could a man who called himself a man – not that she liked men – be so shameless? If he wanted a drink he would steal the price of it out of a blind beggar's tin cup or sponge on a woman. He would dash his title into your face, slap his pockets, put on an expression of astonishment that would not deceive a little girl of nine years old… and forget his wallet three days running. For the sake of a free drink Sir Storrington would invent slanders against his own mother. He kept his address secret – came and went, here today and gone tomorrow. Yet, as she knew – he had made a funny story about it – he had been one of Sam Sabbatani's customers. He had borrowed a dinner suit from a younger brother, sewn into it a label off one of his old suits and sold it (with *Sir Storrington Thirst, Savile Row* clearly marked upon it) for two or three pounds more than it was worth. He had a habit of laying his hands upon you.

Surely, such a man might be capable of anything?

It was so hard to decide. What of Tobit Osbert? Asta knew nothing to his detriment, yet the man was, so to speak, a little too mealy-mouthed to be a proper man. You could see, simply by looking at him, that Osbert was keeping secrets. But then again, what if he were? Thea Olivia was keeping secrets – secrets with which she had been entrusted – so that you never knew which way to take her. What to make of Osbert, and how to define what lay at the back of his soul?

As for the girl, Cigarette, she couldn't possibly have done

anything in this connection. But she associated with the sort of set that might easily give birth to the murderer of Sonia Sabbatani. Certainly not that poor burglar, Chicken Eyes Emerald – he was nothing but an honest burglar, a reclaimable man, Asta decided. Shocket The Bloodsucker? No. It was impossible to doubt that he was bloodsucker by name and bloodsucker by nature, because of the formidable percentages he extracted from the unhappy boxers for whom he arranged matches. He was a bloodsucker but not a sucker of blood.

Titch Whitbread? No. Whitbread was, as the posters persistently insisted, a killer. But he was a killer only in the way of sport. She had talked to Titch Whitbread and remembered the conversation: 'I saw you fight and congratulate you. It was a good clean fight, and you deserved to win. But that poor boy – what's his name? Kid Carpet – how is he?'

'I saw him while we was dressing, lady, and he didn't look too bad. I mean to say he didn't look much cut about.'

'I'm glad to hear it. Did he have anything to say?'

'Well, he sort of said, kind of, that he was saved by the bell in the seventh round – if you get what I mean, kind of style.'

'And what did *you* say?'

'Well, I said to him, I said: "I dare say you're right, kid." He said: "But if you hadn't slipped sort of on to my right, kind of style, I don't know how it might have finished up." And I said: "It was a nice fight." And then he said: "Thanks very much. I never had a nicer set-to in all my life." And so we shook hands once again, and that was that.'

'There was no ill feeling?'

'Ill feeling? Why should there be ill feeling?'

Yet who knew? Boxers are beaten about the head. The Tiger Fitzpatrick, for example, was not what you might describe as sane. People like Ovid Moffitt, George Cheese, Beeps Wilking or Bubbsie Dark might do anything; let alone the man that was not quite a man – the one called Hemmeridge. God only knew.

Consider Soskin, the dentist. What kind of a man became a dentist? Dentists worked backwards, in reverse. Dentists approached things in a mirror – like actors. Of all the men that held absolute power for their brief moment, dentists were supreme. Asta remembered one afternoon when, while Soskin was drilling a hole in one of her teeth, she rolled up her eyes and saw him looking down at her with what seemed to be an abominable smile. It was true, she realised, that she had been looking at his face upside down. Still, how was one to know? How was it possible for a man deliberately to choose to be a dentist?

And Tony Mungo? There again was a man who, if one watched him carefully, might be suspected of any secret excess. He liked to play tricks with people. She detested Tony Mungo. He knew a great deal about natural history, and on Saturday afternoons loitered about the museum in South Kensington. Sooner or later someone would try to tell him something, then Mungo would seem ignorant, wait until the other man had finished and then let loose such a flood of factual information as swept the informant away in shameful disorder.

Geezle, again, was a tattooist. What kind of a man was this that could live by pricking out patterns upon the bodies of his fellow men? Concerning Roget, who took care of his mother – he was waiting for her to die and dared not to get himself a wife for fear of offending her. In such a man, surely, a thousand things were bottled up – bad things, dirty things.

Again, there was Alan Shakespeare, with money of his own; completely idle, useless; a bored man. Could there be anything like boredom for breeding viciousness?

Take the case of Goggs, the pork butcher, the charcutier, or sausage-maker. There, potentially, was something evil. Why should he choose the business of killing pigs and grinding them up into mincemeat and stuffing their muscles into their own entrails? Why should he do it? And why should this squat, thick-set man with hacked hands put on a gentleman's clothes before and after work and hang about the Bar Bacchus?

Also, there was something sinister about Irish John Smith, the one that called himself Sean Mac Gabhann. What was he after? Why was he hiding himself? Why the pseudonym? Surely he was a man who pretended – and all the world knew that he was a liar – to have killed his man in the Troubles. Such a man was playing a deep and violent game. If he wanted to *seem* violent, he wanted to *be* violent. If he wanted to be violent, why wasn't he? Because he didn't dare to be. *Such a man surely might pick on a child in a fog?*

Any man might pick on a child in a fog…

25

Here they were – the secretive Baronet Thirst; the literary slasher Osbert; Shocket the general of face-punchers; Titch Whitbread the defeater and at the same time the defeated. There was the persecuted-by-vocation Monty Bar-Koch Ba; the hater and the hated.

The man Soskin chose to pull out teeth for a living. Goggs pretended to be proud of being a professional butcher, yet tried to look like something else when he wasn't slitting pigs' throats. Mungo? When all is said and done, a man who finds pleasure in other people's discomfiture is a cruel man, a man animated by a mean little lust for power at the expense of another.

There was Geezle getting his living out of degenerates – for apart from old soldiers and sailors, no one but a degenerate goes and gets his skin pricked out with dragons and snakes and butterflies.

Roget? Anyone who is waiting eagerly for another person to die is murdering that person in his heart – he has the makings of a killer somewhere inside his timid watchful self.

Mr Shakespeare? He would do anything for a new sensation, perhaps even murder. When a man dulls his sensibilities with excess, the time always comes when he feels the need for blood, for violence.

For the love of God, how was one to know?

Detective Inspector Turpin was above suspicion, of course.

Yet why of course? Strategically, who could be better placed for murder than a policeman? The police constable on the beat could have done it. Who would a little girl trust more completely than a policeman?

The fire was dying, and it seemed to Asta that the bedroom was dark and cold as interplanetary space. The headlights of a passing car shot a streak of white light in at the window. She was alone, alone and helpless, a fat, foolish, obstinate, ageing woman; and everybody laughed at her as soon as her back was turned. They called her the Battleaxe, she remembered. Until this moment she had been rather proud of the nickname. It suggested the Crusader – Godfrey, Richard, Raymond; Bohemond roaring at the head of that last mad charge. That suicidal hopeless charge nevertheless smashed the gathered might of the Infidel.

Such thoughts as this had stirred her blood. But tonight it seemed that the darkness was full of sly little voices shyly sniggering. 'God, be kind to a foolish, fat woman who doesn't know what to do. Tell me what to do, please, Lord God!' she said aloud.

No answer came out of the dark. There was only the tired tinkle of the dead embers under the dying fire.

She willed herself to relax, ordered herself to pull herself together, and commanded herself to count slowly up to a hundred and go to sleep.

1... 2... 3... 4... 5... 6... 7...

– *It could be Milton Catt!*

No, none of that!... 11... 12... 13... 14... 15... 16... 17... 18... 19...

– *Graham Strindberg!*

Ah-ah! Keep hold of yourself, Asta!... 20... 21... 22... 23... 24... 25... 26... 27... (Be calm, calm, calm)... 28... 29...

– *Or little Mr Scripture, why not?*

No. Sleep, sleep Asta, you must sleep!... 30... 31... 32... 33... 34... 35... 36...

The world spun itself into a smoke-ring, and this ring spinning slower and growing greyer slid into the shape of a stretched-out heart; and this stretched-out heart pushed a pale tendril into a cold black wind, which took hold of the whole and sucked it away into nothingness, and then Asta was walking on something that felt like cotton. She was in a street. The houses were nightmarishly constructed of whorls and coils of creeping smoke. Amorphous, strangely flabby-looking clouds, or lumps, of this smoke pushed out tentacles. They writhed and heaved themselves into unimagined squidlike forms.

The belly of one floating vaporous octopus cracked open and disclosed four vacant black eyes… and the eyes became windows, and the tentacles, moving like the hands of a Javanese dancer, described the structure of a disintegrating house, an abandoned, crumbling house that danced and quivered like a mirage. But this mirage, in this desert of mist, was not born of light but of darkness; and not of heat, because it was deadly cold.

Asta was afraid. She wanted to go away, but she had to go on. As she went, she heard a secretive whisper, and she knew that if she looked back she would see that the street had closed behind her. But she dared not look back. Yet she knew that the dead house with Doric columns on the left and the ghostly house on the right with the Byzantine dome that palpitated as if it were alive had slid into each other and were following her. She knew that she was going to a certain house, ten paces down this hellish street. She struggled with all her might to stand still, but she was compelled to go on. The squat, four-eyed, fantastic houses slipped together behind her, cold and pale and quiet as jelly, so that she knew that if she turned – if she could turn – she would find herself stuck forever in a clammy wall of congealed mist that had the power to form disgusting shapes. There was no turning. And here was the House.

It was a sealed, silent house, solid in comparison with those shifty, house-shaped vapours that had crept behind her. Yet it looked sick – sick and bad. The spiked area-railings were rotten brown teeth. The basement was a mouth. The windows were veiled eyes under cataracts of fog. She had to go to the door and knock. She struggled, but something irresistible – something flabby and cold in the small of her back – impelled her forward.

There loomed the great grey door, blistered with age and dampness. There hung the iron door-knocker, red with rust. Behind her were gathered all the powers of darkness. They were whispering.

They were closing in, jostling her. Something dead yet alive, a gelatinous something that had the colourlessness and the coldness of twilight in deep water, wrapped itself around her right hand.

This Thing, so cold and so pale, palpitated like the heart of a bird, but mixed with the palpitation there was a sort of twitching and squirming.

She lifted the knocker and let it fall. As the reverberations and the echoes died, the door opened, and something she could not see reached out and dragged her inside and the door slammed –

And she awoke with a scream of terror, in her bedroom. The fire was not yet out. Something was rattling on the floor. Asta cried: 'Who is it?' and switched on the light. *It* was a little bedside table rolling itself still on the carpet in the debris of a glass cigarette-box. She must have struck out and knocked it down.

Laughing and crying with relief, Asta got up, put on a warm dressing-gown and made herself a cup of tea. She said to herself sturdily that there was no use trying to sleep again. In point of fact, she was afraid to sleep again.

She wandered about the house and waited for the dawn, brooding...

26

Milton Catt. Here, potentially, was anything in the world. He was a beautiful man, a masculine man, a man at whom every woman looked twice. He had the head and the body of an Apollo – a bronze Apollo exquisitely finished about the head in coppery gold. Imagine a shy, withdrawn, discontented and slightly sullen Apollo. He inspired in women a devouring passion; they felt that in his embrace they might experience the ecstasies of those women of the Ancients that had in unimaginable orgasms slaked the brief lusts of Olympus. Milton Catt was a physical culturist. He strove with the gods: he fought the earth – he wrestled with the law of gravity. He was a weightlifter. Twisting himself into strange attitudes he could get tremendous weights away from the ground by means of the 'dead lift', the 'snatch' and the 'bent press'. He never travelled half a mile without a pair of Patent Spring Crusher Grips in his trouser pockets, and as he walked he squeezed them rhythmically, breathing in and holding his breath until he could hold it no more and then letting it out in a fine trickle – all the time squeezing and slowly relaxing the grip of his hands on his Patent Springs. It was common knowledge that when he was at home Catt worked hard stretching a springy contraption called a Buster. He stretched and relaxed, stretched and relaxed, stretched and relaxed, building and building his body.

Now he had a sun-ray lamp. Recently he had married an elderly woman of independent means, the widow of a crockery manufacturer named Woodware, a half-sober lady with feverish eyes and tremendous eyebrows, at least thirty years older than himself. She had bought him the lamp. He owed his tan to her. Since their marriage, the eyes of the widow Woodware had grown even more feverish. Several widows, spinsters and unhappy wives in Asta's neighbourhood – lifting the corners of their mouths and exchanging glances – thought that they could guess why. They recognised frustration when they saw it.

Catt, despite his enormous muscles, was a humanitarian. He shuddered at the thought of slaughtered beasts, yet he ate steak because he believed that steak was necessary for the proper development of the Apollonian body. He loved lambs, and he loved lamb chops. He loathed offal on the butcher's slab, yet he was unable to resist fried liver or grilled kidneys. He adored Woman but was girl-shy. He had four albums of photographs of himself illustrating the development of his muscles. What did he want muscles for? To exhibit. But why?

Catt, surely, thought Asta, might find himself involved, one foggy afternoon, in a certain sort of crime. People had expected too much of this young man. He had been embraced as a bronze god and sent away with contemptuous smiles – less than a man. Could it be that Milton Catt, desiring to prove himself to himself, had chosen a certain moment to demonstrate himself to himself, using the body of a female child who expected nothing?

Asta sipped her tea.

How about little Mr Scripture? He was a nobody, indescribable. For a living he worked as an accountant and seldom went out without his wife, Oonagh, who was somewhat younger than himself.

He always wore glasses, never wore a hat, was getting bald and had a noticeably delicate way of politely insinuating himself into your company. There seemed to be no harm in the little man.

But Oonagh was a good deal taller than her husband; she went in for conspicuous hats and spoke in an affected way. Winter and summer she wore some sort of fur: in the winter a mink-marmot coat somewhat the worse for wear; in the summer the pieced-together bits of some sliced-up mink, real mink in a strip about three inches wide and two feet long. Oonagh publicly despised her husband. She laughed at the things he said. When he wanted to tell a story, her great glottal laugh sucked it away like a rusty pump, leaving the poor little man high and dry. It was easy to see that she dominated him, hated him, yet had no idea of how to live without him. As for her husband, a schoolgirl might perceive that she was a burden to him but that he needed her, as a buzzer needs a battery. Or he was afraid of her.

Such a man, it might be argued, would look for some way to make the most of his manhood. He might do evil in order to keep it locked up in his heart – to be able to smile to himself occasionally, between midnight and dawn.

'You think I'm nobody,' he would say inside himself. 'I am not nobody. I'm dangerous, but you'll never know.'

Asta remembered that a little man not unlike Mr Scripture had been convicted of firing ricks not far from where she had lived thirty years before. He was a tailor with a club foot, appropriately nicknamed 'Rabbits'; he really did look remarkably like a rabbit escaped from a snare, hopping and lamely bobbing, twitching its poor little nose. A convicted poacher had been suspected, but at the last moment Rabbits came forward with the pride of hell in his eyes and the terror of the magistrate in his quavering voice and confessed, offering incontrovertible evidence against himself. Asked why he had put a match to three haystacks, Rabbits had replied: 'Because I wanted to.'

Rabbits had been married to a big, noisy wife – like Crippen, or like Scripture. Mr Scripture might easily have killed Sonia Sabbatani. Asta could see the little man, prim and respectable, coming home an hour or two late on a foggy afternoon. Out comes Oonagh, sloppy in a sweaty old rayon dressing-gown, stuffing back into place a pale, pear-shaped breast, tightening her girdle, at the same time screaming: 'Where have you been?' 'Delayed by the fog, Oonagh dear.' 'And I suppose you expect me to sit and wait for you? Open yourself a tin of salmon, my Lord and Master, and bring me up a cup of tea when you've finished. And mind you wash the plate. I've got a pain. I'm lying down. You and your fog! *Ach*, you shrimp!'

And Mr Scripture with a couple of words of cringing acquiescence goes to the kitchen and puts on the kettle... and smiles at the dirty dishes. The kettle sings and bubbles, and so does his heart...

Why not?

Or why not Graham Strindberg? He was a plunger into strange depths. He believed that there was a God and that there was a Devil. But not knowing exactly how things stood he did not like to commit himself. Graham Strindberg saw everything from every viewpoint, all at the same time; and he saw himself as a self-supporting state, beautifully mountainous, elegantly painted with sunsets, traditionally neutral. He was a little Switzerland in an embattled universe. Equally protected, the agents of heaven and of hell sunned themselves by the placid lakes of his retirement. He was neutral territory, where the saints and the demons were all one, as long as they did not assert themselves by daylight.

Yet what queer contracts might be made under the blanket of the dark?

Good is a gentleman; Evil is a cad, a gentleman gone wrong. Good is a dog; Evil is a fox. Good, as a gentleman, tries to think well of the watchful enemy, but Evil knows all the tricks.

Given a certain midnight (thought Asta), such neutral territory might find itself possessed by the Powers of Evil. Shame and remorse might come with the daylight... but a strangled child would still be lying with a blackened face in a rotting house...

Impossible, impossible! cried the daytime mind of Asta Thundersley. *Why impossible?* asked the scavenging intelligence of the dark. *What has he done that is good? What has he done that is evil? He can fly into a rage. To which side of the frontier does his anger belong?*

Asta shook her head. Rain was falling; dawn was far away. She made herself some tea. The kitchen was warm: the stove was a good one – it never went out, and one dirty little shovelful of coke kept its fire alive for a day and a night. This was a comforting thought. So much kindly warmth out of a handful of slaggy cinders! Putting her elbows on the table she fitted her resolute chin into the cup of her joined hands. She was calmer now and drowsy; almost at peace.

If Asta had closed her eyes then she might have fallen asleep; but she opened them and saw, on the lowest rack of the dresser, a large oval dish, biscuit-coloured and patterned in high relief. This dish had not been used upstairs for many years. The pattern crept in and out around a lobster.

Mothmar! said Asta, starting up. The body of the lobster resembled Mothmar's nose, and the extended claws his eyebrows. Mothmar Acord had a baked, glazed, pitted face – a dish-shaped face, discoloured by oriental suns and high fevers and distorted by unholy passions. The oval dish might have been Mothmar's head on a pillow – only the mouth was not there. His mouth was difficult to describe and impossible to forget. The upper lip was a Cupid's bow; the lower was sucked away so that it radiated wrinkles like the ribs of a fan. Under heavy brows like frayed packing-string, his murderous little blue eyes stared you out of countenance and then withdrew into spider webs of wrinkles while the mouth smiled downward. He had lived most of his life in the tropics; drank soberly for hours and then suddenly got drunk and pinched you viciously, always smiling. Mothmar had the air of a man gone rotten without ripening in too much sunshine – the kind of sunshine from which a man tries to hide and so goes yellow and decays.

Why not Mothmar Acord? Why not?

But if it comes to the matter of that, why not Sinclair Wensday? There was a pleasant fellow, tall and popular, well-spoken, well-mannered, generous and good-looking in that tired, dissipated way which makes women interested. Sometimes he was gloomy; sometimes he was hilarious – it was whispered that Sinclair Wensday took drugs – he had what they call a 'cocaine personality'. Nothing was proved. It was known that he had had love affairs with two or three girls of the neighbourhood. Men wondered how Sinclair Wensday could have anything to do with anyone but his wife, Avril, who was extremely beautiful. Women wondered how Avril could have anything to do with any man but Sinclair, who, they were agreed, was terribly attractive. He looked like Galahad gone to the Devil. When she was sullen and quiet Avril might have sat to a painter of biblical pictures: she was a martyr with dull red hair and half-closed eyes, seeing Paradise between the bars of black lashes. Then, when she smiled – which was seldom – she looked like a whore. Everybody knew that Avril and her husband loved each other. Yet they could not live together – they separated forever about four times a year. Sinclair Wensday would come into the Bar Bacchus with wild eyes, his collar unbuttoned and a drying scratch on his cheek. He would look left and right with desperate expectation then lose a couple of inches of stature as he sank into himself at the bar. 'Well, *this* is it,' he would say, gulping liquor, 'once and for all, this *is* it...'

Soon he would vomit unassimilated miseries. Avril slept with this one, Avril slept with that one, Avril went to bed with the other one... but he loved her, loved her!

At the same time, in the Firedrake two streets away, Avril would be rolling a sleeve to show a bruise or pointing to a black eye and sobbing: 'This is *it*. Definitely, this is *it*.' And she would describe how Sinclair slunk out to make love to half the women in town.

In a week they would be together again in the Bar Bacchus, squeezing hands half in love and half in loathing, exchanging glances, and sighs, and snarls.

Who could say how such savage love might end? It was nothing but hate and lust, thirst for power and the desire to be hurt and to hurt! Why *not* Sinclair Wensday?

Asta sighed in the middle of a yawn, or yawned in the middle of a sigh, whispered 'murderers, murderers' and fell asleep.

Mrs Kipling came down at half past seven next morning and saw her bent over the table with her stubborn forehead in the crook of her left arm. An end of her grizzled hair was floating in a cup of cold tea, and her right hand clutched a teaspoon.

'Tea, Kipling!' shouted Asta, starting up.

Mrs Kipling screamed. She had thought – almost hoped – that Asta was dead.

27

At eight o'clock the first post came. The postman had to ring: one of the envelopes was too bulky to pass through the slot of the letterbox. It came from Schiff and was stuffed with samples of carnival novelties: paper hats, coloured streamers, coiled toys designed to stretch out squeaking and tickle your neighbour, uninflated rubber balloons of unconventional patterns, red cardboard noses, masks, balls of pith for throwing at people and all kinds of amusing invitation cards.

Near the bottom of the second page Schiff had written:

To be for the present unhappy in the position to not on account of certain circumstances over which I have no control be, as I ordinarily would, in a position to gladly and with my hand on my heart as one friend to another offer you free of charge my services, gives me grief and unhappiness. My Formule I give freely and hope to, in happier circumstances over which I trust I shall have the fullest control, give more as it is in my nature to ordinarily do. I at, however, the present sad moment, am by the circumstances with grief compelled to ask Consultant Fee £5.0.0 (Five Pounds Exactly.) The Formule, which I baptise in the name of BATTLEAXE, is as research has made clear a psychic laxative and brain cathartic of the first order. Put on the Market it could not fail to succeed, in which case I have a cheaper formula almost equally as good as the one that I have with all possible admiration and respect pinned to this note...

The Formule, on page three, was as follows:

THE FORMULE
According to Quantity, in the Following Proportion
Take 1 Bot. ORANGE CURAÇAO
 1 Bot. VERY DRY GIN
 1 Bot. MANDARIN
 ¼ Bot. BRANDY
 ¼ Bot. ABRICOTINE
 ⅛ Bot. COINTREAU
 A Dash of ORANGE BITTERS.
Mix the above very thoroughly.

Now, squeeze out and carefully strain the juice of twenty-four fresh oranges. Mix this juice with the above Mixture very thoroughly. Put in icebox and freeze very cold.

WHEN READY TO SERVE:

Fill a large tumbler ⅝ (five-eighths) full with the Mixture as above.

Almost fill your tumbler then with Champagne.

It need not be Vintage Champagne.

Add a slice of orange, a slice of fresh peach, a finely cut curl of orange peel.

Serve Bitterly Cold.

If the Formule is preferred weaker, dilute with Champagne.

I recommend ROUSPETEUR FRERES, which I can get for you at not disadvantageous prices. Many people prefer it weaker. It is argued that the Formule is better in the following proportions:

⅜ (three-eighths) Mixture

⅝ (five-eighths) ROUSPETEUR FRERES CHAMPAGNE

Swizzle with swizzle-stick.

This tastes like fruit-juice and is good.

After that she opened letters from the National Society For The Prevention of Cruelty to this, that or the other.

She was tired and sad. Her thoughts were wandering... Whosoever kicks a dog kicks a man by proxy, that was her opinion. A blowfly is an evil thing, better dead.

Kill the blowfly and have done.

Find pleasure in tearing off the wings or the legs of that fly, and the time will come when you will have graduated from fly to mouse, mouse to rat, rat to cat, cat to dog, dog to child –

Enough. Enough is enough! (Asta shuddered). Pull a fly's wings off, and you rip off the wings of a bird.

Pluck off the fly's legs, and you tear a man between four wild horses.

Kill if you must, but kill clean! That which you must kill so that you may live is your adversary. Then kill it quickly and have done; the longer it lives in pain, the greater its power in the end.

The tormented beetle takes a terrible revenge at last... the imprisoned goldfish rounds up its jailers in hundreds and thousands... the gamecock or the terrier dying in the pit sets man against man in vaster pits at long last: the tortured beast is master of the world when all is said and done.

All cruelty is one.

'Down with it!' cried the spirit of Asta Thundersley, as she plunged into the day's correspondence, most of which referred to the case of a woman in Buckinghamshire who kept underfed ducks in a basement. Eagles, chickens, ducks... aviators, infantrymen, sailors... heavens above, earth beneath and waters under the earth – all cruelty and oppression were one. There was only one calloused heart in the universe and only one good heart. There was only the Devil on one hand and God on the other.

'*Ha!*' said Asta. The hairs at the nape of her neck bristled and grew damp. She was about to make a fool of herself again – this time about ducks.

At four o'clock Thea Olivia, who had eaten three-quarters of a pound of meat, some vegetables and a bit of cheese as big as your fist off a tray in her room, came down in lavender-and-grey for tea.

'My inky fingers?' she said to Asta, who was licking an envelope. 'How is my little inky fingers?'

'Hello, Duck,' said Asta.

28

The man who had murdered Sonia Sabbatani dressed himself with care. He was an extremely sensitive man, dainty in his habits, sensitive to harsh words and given to misinterpreting sidelong glances. His nostrils, also, were uncomfortably sensitive. If he had not been smoking too much – ten cigarettes in a day were too much, for he smoked only to defend himself against other people's breath – he could shut his eyes and recognise people he had met by their smell. He was, therefore, considerate of other people's nostrils. Anxious not to give offence, he scoured his body, especially his feet, as thoroughly as a surgeon scours his hands, twice a day. He detested above all things the odour of breath. It offended him profoundly. He had the nose of a tobacco-blender or a tea-taster and could tell with reasonable accuracy at half a yard what anyone had eaten since breakfast time. Radishes disgusted him; cheese turned his stomach; beer caused him to retch. At the same time this man liked to meet people. He was a young man with his way to make in the world – a man with ambition – and it was necessary for him to make contacts, as the saying goes. So he had developed a remarkable knack of controlling his breathing. He never in any circumstances inhaled through his nose while anyone in his immediate vicinity was breathing out through the mouth. His sensitivity cut both ways: it seemed to him that he must offend others as others offended him. So he had cultivated a trick of holding his breath. He had been holding his breath, off and on, for nearly twenty years. Thus, his shoulders were drawn back and his chest thrust forward: he had acquired the lungs of a pearl-fisher. His trepidation in relation to bad smells had given birth to highly individual ways of standing, looking and holding his head. He was of normal height. In talking to a short man he held his head high with the chin thrust out. And if he happened to be in intimate conversation with a tall man he kept his nose down, tucking in his chin and still contriving to look the other straight in the eye. So he had what might have been mistaken for a military carriage, only he leaned backwards. His distinctive erectness contrasted oddly with the expression of his face. The nostrils appeared to be struggling between a tendency to expand in an interested sniff and snap shut in a spasm of distaste. He kept most of his mouth closed when he talked, using only one side of it – the side farthest from whoever he was talking to. He knew that this habit might lead people to believe that he was trying to make himself look tough, so he made his expression affable by means of his eyes and eyebrows. The Murderer's eyes were singularly unexpressive, but he could force his eyebrows into a whimsical, almost apologetic expression. He had one devouring fear – that somebody with bad teeth or bronchitis (he could diagnose a bronchial halitosis at three-and-a-half feet) might come up to him and talk right into his face. So, when anyone came near him he put out an anxious hand. If the person speaking to him was a man, The Murderer took him by the lapel; if a woman, by the elbow. In any case, he kept people at a distance. And still he wanted to be with people.

He had bathed fastidiously. Now he knotted his tie. He was pleased with himself and smiled at his reflection in the mirror. The reflection smiled back at him slyly and knowingly and nodded as if to say: We two have something on each other, but we are in accord. You keep my secret and I'll keep yours.

The Murderer looked at his little clock. It was twenty-seven minutes past six; too early, much too early. He did not want to hurry. He would sit, perfectly calmly, and then – say in an hour – go out and walk slowly to Asta's place. And there he would sit very quietly in one of those deep, cool chairs with the linen covers... the cool, clean linen covers that did not in any circumstances provoke perspiration... sit and be nice to people and let people be nice to him, and eat canapés and drink one or two drinks, and make a gentlemanly evening of it. A party was always useful: one never knew whom one might meet. Asta Thundersley was a lady; eccentric but unquestionably a lady. It all helped. In any case, the cost of an evening meal was saved.

The Murderer was in a pleasant humour, in love with the world. He shook open the evening paper. EMERALD – INSURANCE CO. FIGHTS WIDOW'S CLAIM. The unhappy burglar had paid up his premiums, but the Comet Fire And Life maintained that Emerald had committed suicide.

Too bad, too bad…

Near the centre of the third column smaller type said: Girl Sonia. Killer Still Free. The police had a clue.

He laughed: at least, his face remained unchanged, and his stomach laughed.

Who could swear to me? he asked himself. *Who could swear on the Book? Clue! What clue? There is no clue, and they know it. Otherwise, why do they squeeze the story down and away? Their argument is, of course, that they have more in their minds than they want to say. But in our case, exactly what have they got? There was a black fog. If ten witnesses saw me pick the child up outside the school – what would their oaths be worth? In that fog, nothing. It happened to Sonia Sabbatani. So what? She might have been any of two or three hundred children. Clues? Hah! What clues?*

I am standing on the corner of the street, and the girl happens to come by. 'See you safely home?' I ask her, and she says: 'Thanks very much, Mister So-And-So.' She knew my voice. Face, figure, walk, anything at all – I didn't recognise her myself in that fog until she spoke! If I didn't even know it was her until I heard her voice, how is anybody to know that the man is me?

Be calm, be reasonable – no nerves, no jitters; nothing but calm, calm! Black fog and the night coming: what would anyone's testimony be worth? Anyone's oath, anywhere? And who was there in that dead old street? Nobody. Why should anyone be there? No property to protect – condemned houses, nothing more – why should a policeman, even, be there?

No reason at all. And there wasn't anybody anywhere.

Yes, I was naughty. I was very naughty indeed…

The Murderer shook his head, got out of his chair and carefully brushed his teeth.

... I deserve to be hanged. But even if they caught me, they wouldn't hang me. They'd say I was insane. But I'm not. And they won't catch me anyway. It wasn't a nice thing to do. But the only alternative would have been to take Sonia to her home, and that would have been the end of that: she knew my voice. You can't safely loiter about the same place twice. In that kind of weather you're as good as masked like the Ku Klux Klan. Kill and have done. In any case, what did I mean to do? To kill? Simply to kill. It is a pity that it had to be little Sonia Sabbatani; but it had to be someone. Next time (he had not the slightest doubt that there would be a next time), next time, he would see...

But this was the first kill, and he still thrilled with a curious mixture of pride and of shame at the thought of it, like a young girl who has gone out and lost her virginity on the sly. He knew now what Zarathustra meant when he spoke of the murderer who 'thirsted for the pleasure of the knife'. Of course, he had not used a knife. He owned several knives but used them only to sharpen pencils or to play with; their lean, cold blades, honed sharp and brightly polished, gave him a sense of power, made him feel dangerous. He liked to open and shut them – especially one wicked Spanish knife with an engraved blade that might have been designed for cruel murder. This blade locked back by means of a primitive yet efficient device consisting of a perforated steel spring and a ratchet. It opened with a noise like the grinding of iron teeth, and there it was, ten inches long; the very sight of it made the blood stand still. It amused him sometimes to stand before a mirror, knife in fist, making quick, ferocious passes at himself and dreaming dreams... always dreaming dreams... dreams of blood and death.

No, he had not used a knife this time.

There was, he thought, the Pleasure Of The Thumbs; the Pleasure Of The Strangler. '*Under my thumb.*' How apt some of these metaphors were. There was power, absolute power, power over life and death. Your thumbs sank in. You felt the heaving and the writhing of the little body. But it was doomed. You were DOOM. You were the Angel Of Death. You were God. You could take life or give it back. You could – and did – let the little creature breathe again for a second or two. Why curtail a pleasure by gluttonous haste? You are a gourmet – you prolong your pleasures, tease yourself a little, and so increase your enjoyment of things. So you let the victim, the sacrificial offering, come back to life a little – not sufficiently alive to scream: that would never do. Just for two or three gulps of breath. Then – *under the thumb, under the thumb!* Who could have imagined that a child's heart could beat so hard? Well, all good things must have an end. You finished it off at last.

All the same, next time he would use a knife. This might be a little dangerous, because of the splashes. Still, did they ever catch Jack The Ripper? And how many crimes did Fritz Haarmann get away with before he had the bad luck to be caught? Or Peter Kürten. These two men ended on the gallows, it is true. Yet how calmly they died! Why? Because they had died in the knowledge that they had lived, and lived, and lived – lived more red-blooded life in their forty-year lifetimes than your ordinary respectable law-abiding citizen could live in a hundred years. It was dangerous, yes. But the danger that followed the kill was, so to speak, the savoury that rounded off the roast.

Next time the knife. Not the nice Spanish knife, the knife christened 'Dago Pete', but a very ordinary knife, a bread knife, a sixpenny vegetable knife, a kitchen knife, a shoemaker's knife.

And after that, if only to baffle the police by a variation of the *modus operandi*, a piece of cord. And after that... well, it would all depend upon circumstances.

29

Soon, having fallen into a reverie, The Murderer began to be sorry for himself. The ecstasy was passing. He told himself again that he had been 'naughty'. Somewhere inside him a snivelling voice said: *It isn't my fault. I couldn't help it.* He reasoned with himself: *It isn't my fault. Look at Peter Kürten.* He said: *'The woman who took me up when I first came out of prison was one whose temperament was the very opposite* of my own. She liked cruel treatment.' And then the Public Prosecutor said: 'That, of course, will have increased the sadistic leanings.'

There you are! Lots of boys have the impulse to be cruel, to kill. Lots of boys want to hunt down animals in jungles and kill them, be detectives and hunt down men and hang them – which amounts to the same thing. But they don't all go out and be naughty in the same way as I have been naughty. I shouldn't have been encouraged – given a big sexual thrill in that way...

I would still be a nice shy boy, doing nothing wrong – I mean to say nothing actually illegal – if it hadn't been for Her.

She enjoyed being ill-treated. I would have been too timid even to suggest that kind of game. She suggested it. She made me feel that my manhood depended upon my power to hurt. If they hang me, they ought to hang Her. They cut Peter Kürten's head off for seventy crimes of violence. What did they do to the woman who brought out what was in him? Nothing. Is this justice?

The Murderer went to his bookshelf and read what Professor Hübner had said:

Sadism is infinitely many-sided and comprises a wide field, including anything from dreams of torturing animals, the exaggerated punishment of children, or fire mania, to lust murders, which are generally arrived at by a series of progressive actions. A certain tendency to cruelty was born in Kürten. Everything else has been acquired. In his case the meeting with the woman twice his age with the masochistic tendencies; the reading of works of sexual pathology, combined with his egotistical megalomania, were responsible for the extent of his sadism. This developed gradually.

'And what about me?' said The Murderer. 'What about me?'

The best thing was to put it out of his mind for the time being. The thing of which he had frequently dreamed with pleasurable shudders had happened. It was going to happen again. But he felt a certain delicacy about it. If anyone talked to him of it, he would feel embarrassed.

But he thanked God that his mind could focus itself upon big, noble issues.

Almost with tears in his eyes, The Murderer thought of mankind, for he liked to think of himself as the kindest and sweetest of men, full of noble sentiments and motivated by a desire to benefit mankind. He devoted a considerable proportion of his daydreaming to fantasies of conquest, or sometimes of self-immolation.

Sometimes he saw himself as a martyr.

Down in the smoky torture-chamber behind his everyday mind he stretched himself on an imaginary rack by the wild, leaping light of flaring flambeaux. The winches creaked; the ropes snapped taut and shrieked as they strained over the blocks. The torturers gasped and grunted as they threw their weight upon the windlasses. But he, the hero, made no sound, except for the snapping of his dislocated joints. He just smiled quietly into the faces of the executioners. 'Now will you talk?' He only smiled. The Hooded Inquisitor made a sign. The torturers put out their strength. In the dancing torchlight the strong muscles of their shoulders and backs seemed to jump and tremble like imprisoned things that wanted to burst their way out. The agony was unbearable, yet he bore it. 'Now will you give us the names of your confederates?'

He smiled. At last, as he lay dying (one of his legs had come off), the Inquisitor said to him in a voice of awe: 'You're an obstinate heretic, but, by all His Saints, you are a *man*!'

Sometimes – it depended upon his mood, which, in turn, depended upon the events of the day – he was riding into a conquered city upon a great white horse.

From head to foot he was encased in sombre, black armour. The lurid light of a blazing building writhed upon hauberk, gorget and cuisse. His visor, thrown back, left uncovered his face, which was noble and proud, stern but pure. Behind him rode his knights clad all in steel, and behind them marched his men-at-arms under a forest of gleaming spears. As he rode, thousands of the townsmen he had liberated came thronging about him, weeping with gratitude, fighting for one little bit of the dung of his horse which they would preserve as a holy relic.

'God bless the Liberator!' He rode on, stern, preoccupied. In the great castle taken from the Tyrant he sat upon a great velvet chair, magnificent in a robe of velvet blacker than night, embroidered with gold arabesques, and did justice. Cold and clean but terrible was the justice of the Liberator! The Baron Otmar starved the poor? Then let him be bound with silken cords and left to die of hunger in sight of a table laid with innumerable dishes of savoury meat... but give him a cup of water every day so that he may live long enough to know the meaning of hunger.

The Baron Something had worked his vassals to death? Then let him be imprisoned in a cell in which there was a cage containing ten thousand starving rats, and let this cage be devised so that only by the forward and backward movement of a stiff, heavy lever, could the rats be prevented from escaping. Let him work *that* one out! And in the streets oxen were being roasted whole, wine spurted from the fountains and everyone cried: 'God bless the Liberator!'

Again, he was the captain of a great liner. In the middle of one dreadful night there was a grinding crash. The ship had struck an iceberg and was sinking fast. Women and children first! He brandished a big, blue revolver. 'Back there, you dogs, and let the women and children get into the boats first!' A man – an enormous, handsome Greek god of a man, who had always showed off his superior muscles and weight – leaped forward, mad with panic. The revolver spat yellow fire, and the handsome face became, abruptly, like strawberry jam. All the other men stood, cowed, while the women and the children got into the boats. Everyone on deck got off. Only he, the captain, was left. 'For God's sake, Skipper, come down.' No, the weight of one more passenger might sink the boat; he would go down with his ship. But, as the boats pulled away (he could hear everybody saying that the captain was a saint and a hero), he heard a little whimpering cry. Somewhere a girl was imprisoned. He lifted beams of a ton weight, tore down barriers of broken iron, smashed bulkheads with a blow of the fist, and there she was, radiant and beautiful but terrified. The fear of death was upon her. 'There, there little woman...' The shock of the collision had torn off all her outer garments. He took her on deck. The ship was settling. The boats had disappeared. 'This is the end,' he said. They locked in an unbreakable embrace as the ship went down...

The Murderer was always thankful that he was not selfish like other men and rejoiced in his social-mindedness. He could not meet a beggar in the street without giving away a coin or two and saying a few sympathetic words. He was a member of two or three societies devoted to the abolition of corporal punishment, and whatnot. He would have been among the first to protest against the use of pigs and goats in the atom-bomb test at Bikini. There were occasions when he saw himself as a great militant humanitarian. He was something of a Socialist. He knew that Good must be pitiless. In fantasy, he was the man who, with his own hand, cut to pieces the Justice Of The Peace who ordered the birching of a small boy; and, although it was not expedient to say so, he saw Herr Hitler's point. The pure man must be strong. Purity and strength are correlated. He must be like pure iron – malleable yet the strongest thing in the world. Out of his malleability must be forged... for the sake of example, a knife... a knife to cut the throat of Evil.

And then he was in a quiet town. Once again he was the Liberator – pure and passionate yet cold, a Leader, a god. Under the cover of the law-protected roofs – here, there, everywhere, waiting for his word – his legions waited. He gave the Word. From Ealing to Barking, from Enfield to Harrow, the mob arose. The screams of the evildoers rose high above the thunder of applause. This was The Night Of The Long Knife... and, in due course, he sat in judgement. Lisping, shrugging, gesticulating, shuffling, the Ringleaders Of The Adversaries were brought before him. Should he kill them? Yes, but not immediately. They and theirs must be stamped out, stamped out utterly forever. 'Question them!' And then he was looking down, while stretched upon a rack someone gibbered and told everything out of a bleeding mouth.

And later, there was peace in the world, *his* peace, and the world cried: *'Hail, Peacemaker!'*

His peace, the Peace Of The Murderer, had necessarily to be preceded by violence. *His* world would give birth to a new baby; but, first of all, there would be plenty of birth pangs. *His* peace would be something like the exhaustion of the mother of the first-born; a little death, the blood washed away. And in ten thousand places new grass would be growing. Loving mankind as he did, he had persuaded himself that people needed to be thinned out – above all, that the world needed the guidance of a leader of steel-clad knights, a man with a pale, set face, riding that white horse.

Here was his Ideal Man – the Leader. Sometimes he felt that, circumstances being favourable, he could have achieved such leadership. Then he saw himself walking along an interminable avenue of waving hands towards a great wreath-hung platform, while a hundred thousand voices thundered: '*Hail, Peacemaker! Hail, Liberator!*' His face was even paler and more firmly set than usual as he climbed the steps. One lock of hair (the only good thing that ever dared to rebel against him) fell across his forehead. He let it stay where it fell and raised a hand for silence. With one flick of the wrist he stilled that storm of approbation. Then he spoke, standing in a floodlight; the vast hall threw back thunderous echoes. Then his terrible, urgent voice dashed the echoes back where they belonged and silenced them. He was a tempest, a raging torrent. Two hundred thousand eyes were fixed in adoration upon his face. His wild, incandescent eyes were holding hypnotically the gaze of a multitude a hundred thousand strong. And how he talked! With what fire, with what passion! Whenever he paused for breath, the pent-up breath of the listening multitude let itself out in such cheering as had never been heard before in the whole history of the world. He raised a hand again. Then he continued. His arguments clamped down hard, inescapable… like the thumbs of a strangler. His phrases were incisive; they bit deep… like Spanish knives. And the end of the speech was the beginning of a new world…

Still, always, when the daydream had spent itself, he knew that he was not a leader of men; he remembered that he was shy of men. He knew that he would never shout his will into the face of mankind because he shrank away from mankind and feared a defiant reply. A bus conductor, a taxi-driver, a shop-walker or a beggar in the street could abash him with a nonchalant rejoinder. He dreaded the rough, rude answer. For this reason, as he was well aware, he was invariably kind and gentle with people, full of understanding. He had almost persuaded himself that there was a good deal of the saint in him. All the same, he knew that if he could have had his way some insolent man or woman would have gone crashing down with splintered teeth, more often than he could remember.

No, he could not actually *lead* men. But he could, he was convinced, have been a power behind a leader… if he could have cultivated a certain courage of the subtle Machiavellian sort. But all his courage, Machiavellian or animal, was a dream dreamed in a furnished room in front of a gas fire. Black armour? He would not have the strength to walk in armour, black or white, to the end of the street. As for the high-stepping white horse, he would be afraid to lay his hand on the pommel of its saddle. If he could have brought himself to sit astride the humblest old hack of a horse, he would have patted its neck with an uncertain hand and said: 'There, there, poor old fellow,' like Mr Winkle. He did not even have a pale set face – except when he saw himself in a glass in the privacy of his bed-sitting-room.

Yet he felt that he could have been a Leader, a Liberator, given luck.

30

He was constantly thinking of everything and of nothing. There was such a woolly hood of preoccupation over the eyes and ears of this man that occasionally he seemed to be blind and deaf – the absentminded uncle with his *'Ha! Where was I?'* and *'Uh? What was that again?'* Once, visiting a newly married friend who had set up house on the fifth floor of a block of flats, he fell into a typical state of abstraction…

He saw himself as married to his friend's wife and installed in this apartment. His wife found him somehow unsatisfactory; she took a lover. He knew that she had her lover but said nothing. He was the quiet man, the Watcher By Night – he could wait. Oh, he knew all about the agonised embraces, the desperate meetings and anguished partings! He knew. But he could wait. He was the Schemer, the Patient One. At last the moment was his. There came a fragrant night in late spring. The sitting-room window faced westwards. Clouds like Spanish knives had shaved red slices out of the grey-blue sky. Nana was in the bathroom. 'Ah, dear dear!' he murmured. 'Look at the grey of the pavement below! Look.' (There was little time to lose.) 'Look at the people like ants below – down there, just look!'

And then a quick stoop – hands to the ankles, heave up, thrust out hard, and back to the easy chair, flipping over the pages of an album as the cistern went *ha-hoosh* and the lady came back with an air of abstraction…

Calm, brother, calm, in anticipation of the buzz and twitter from below! 'Where's Tom?' The Murderer is bewildered: 'Here, surely?'

Then the scream, the stampede in the passage and the thumb squeezing the life out of the battery of the electric bell.

'He fell, sir – fell down, smack at my feet!'

'Now take it easy. He fell at your feet. Then what? You looked where? Upwards? You did. And you saw what? What did you say? You "sort of saw the gentleman take a jump"? Think again, my friend. The gentleman was looking out of the window while I was in the room. Come, now – "take a jump", you say. Let's get this clear. Are you telling us the gentleman jumped out of the window?'

'Yes, sir. That's how it looked to me.'

'I can scarcely credit this, my friend… No, no, Nana – please don't look! One thing only – one very little thing – how long were you in the bathroom?'

'A few minutes; not more than four or five: probably less than five minutes.'

'Pray be calm, my dear – relax and be calm, my dear!'

He, the deceived husband, was wet with anguish. Nana was looking at him: *she knew*! He gave her a look out of the left-hand corners of his eyes, indicating that he knew she knew. Then her eyes changed: she worshipped him…

'A penny for your thoughts,' said his host.

The Murderer started. '*Hah?*' Then he laughed, and the company laughed with him – that dreamer, that man of dreams. Nana was rubbing her cheek against her husband's shoulder.

'Oh-oh, please, please excuse me,' The Murderer said. 'I seem to go into a trance these days. Do please forgive me…'

A roar of laughter, a replenishment of glasses, a slapping of shoulders, an offering of sandwiches. But The Murderer wanted to go home and dream some dreams… He was still blinking in his dazed way.

'What a dreamy fellow you are!' said his host.

Soon he excused himself, saying that he had some work to do, and walked slowly homewards. He resented a spatter of rain that forced him to run for a bus. How can a man dream dreams while he is running? Still, it would never do to get his suit wet. His grey suit was the only presentable one he possessed.

When he was gone the others talked about him. The newly married wife said: 'I suppose he's all right, but I'm not sure that I like him.'

'Why, what's the matter with him?'

'I don't know. Nothing, I suppose. I don't know what it is, but somehow there's just something… I don't know what… something creepy about him.'

'Creepy? What, him? Oh come, come, darling! He wouldn't hurt a fly.'

'I didn't say he would. I only said that he gave me the creeps – why, goodness knows. It's just a feeling.'

'You know what it is? It's that dreamy look of his,' said a girl named Muriel. 'Like a zombie.'

'And what's a zombie?'

'Isn't it a sort of walking corpse?'

'Well, I see what you mean,' said the host. 'I must admit that he does, as it were, look as if he was walking in his sleep. But he's all right. I've known him for ages. Gentle sort of creature, terribly fond of children.'

'Is he married?' asked Muriel.

The host laughed; this question amused him. 'Married? Good Lord no! I couldn't imagine him marrying anybody, could you?'

'Why not? Is he impotent?'

'How the devil should I know?'

'Is he queer?'

'No, I should say definitely not queer. I don't think he's got much interest in sex at all. At least, I don't associate him with anything of the kind. The peculiar thing about him is that women find him attractive. What they see in him I can't imagine. But I know quite a few girls who have more or less fallen for him. I wonder why?'

Muriel said: 'Oh, I don't know. He isn't so bad really. I think he's rather interesting.'

'In what way interesting?' asked Nana.

'I don't know. Just one of those things. Sort of interesting.'

The host said: 'I know what it is. It's the same as with those professional polygamists. They're irresistible to women because they'd so obviously make good, faithful, docile husbands. You couldn't imagine him, for instance, rushing from pub to pub or brothel to brothel night after night, could you? No; security, nice quiet devotion, the pay envelope intact every Friday night, that's what you'd expect from our old pal. House-trained, obedient, born to be henpecked. That's what most women like, especially widows with a little money of their own.'

Nana said: 'You know too much about women. If you're not careful, I shall henpeck you.'

'Then I shall lock you up in a dark room and feed you on bread and water and break your spirit that way.'

The girl Muriel asked: 'What does he *do*?'

The host looked blank and then said: 'Well, as a matter of fact, I think he writes.'

'Well, everybody writes nowadays. What does he write?'

'He's very cagey about it. But once I caught him reading the *Weekly Sweetheart*. You know, that tuppenny rag that has stories about mill-girls and baronets and all that sort of thing. It's my theory that he writes that kind of stuff, but I couldn't say for certain.

I shouldn't be surprised, though, because he doesn't seem to want to talk about it.'

Muriel nodded and said: 'Well, I don't blame him. I wouldn't want to admit that I wrote tripe like that, would you?'

The wife said: 'I don't see why not. What's the matter with it? There's nothing shameful in it, is there? I'd just as soon write stories about mill-girls and baronets as go about in corduroy trousers writing highbrow poetry. It's an honest living, and –'

Her husband whooped with laughter and shouted: 'Ah-ha! Here speaks the married woman! Honest living! Ah-ha! Ah-ha – the pay envelope, the pay envelope! There you are, you see – the irresistible fascination of the pay envelope, eh?'

'Darling, don't be such a bloody idiot,' said his wife.

'I wasn't saying there was anything wrong in writing that sort of stuff,' said Muriel, 'but if a man happens to be shy and sensitive... you know what I mean.'

The husband said: 'Oh sure, sure, we know what you mean all right, we know what you mean, Muriel, my dear. You and your *Weekly Sweetheart*.'

'I wonder –' said Muriel and then stopped.

'You see, darling, she wonders. She wonders,' said the husband, affectionately patting the hindquarters of his wife. 'There's the secret of that fatal fascination. He gets them wondering, my poppet, he gets them wondering. He gives them food for thought.'

'All he gives me is the creeps,' she said, toying with the lobe of his ear.

'Oh, forget him, my poppet!'

'With pleasure, my own!'

31

While this conversation was in progress, The Murderer was back in his bed-sitting-room. He had switched on the light, drawn the curtains, taken off and carefully hung up his only decent grey suit and put on a tired-looking old blue woollen dressing-gown. He had work to do. The idea of work was distasteful to him: he just wanted to dream. But a man must eat, keep a roof over his head and dress respectably. He had a craving for new suits. Once in a while he saw himself as Beau Brummell swaggering in impeccable coats, immaculate linen and cravats that took an hour to tie – the haughty, the intolerably insolent, the fastidious buck whose wit was more to be feared than… say, a Spanish knife – an elegant Blade.

He caught himself on the shadowy verge of another daydream and dragged himself to his little table. He had to work. The Ubiquity Press paid him a guinea a thousand words. There were men who made fat livings out of Ubiquity at that rate, but they could work like demons: words seemed to pour out of them like sugar from a torn paper bag. The Murderer was something of an artist: he laid out his second-hand sentences with the meticulosity of a rag-picker sorting rubbish; by hand, with a fine-pointed pen. At present he was working on a new serial for *The Knuckleduster*, a boys' paper that specialised in tales of violence. He had invented a character named 'Ironskin Obst' who had discovered a serum that gave his skin the impregnability of fine steel without impairing its flexibility. Fire a gun at Obst, and the bullet flattened itself against his forehead; throw him off a cliff, and instead of smashing himself on the rocks below Obst smashed the rocks. Hit him, and you beat your hand to pulp. The only way to get at Ironskin was with a blowlamp – and an extra-special blowlamp at that. The Villain had such a blowlamp.

The pity of it was that words came so slowly. He had to exert himself to make five pounds a week, and he detested exertion. He wanted to dream.

He sat down sighing, dipped a long, sharp, shiny nib in the inkpot and began to write:

IRONSKIN OBST!
by
DASHWOOD STEEL

He liked this nom de plume even better than the one with which he signed his stories in *Young Detective Weekly* – 'Dirk Pike'. Readers of *The Thunderbolt* knew him as 'Lance Stockmar'. Sometimes he contributed to *The Smasher* under the pseudonym 'Carver Riddle'. When he wrote for the *Weekly Sweetheart* he took pleasure in signing himself 'Rayon Knickerbocker'. But 'Dashwood Steel' was the name he liked best of all – the name he would have chosen for himself if he had had any say in the matter.

Ironskin Obst laughed as the red-hot iron seared his eyeballs, he wrote. Then he nibbled his penholder. If only such things could be! But no, no dreams just now! Work…

Nothing could hurt him. Knives broke and bullets rebounded from the serum-strengthened body of Ironskin Obst. Even fire was powerless to hurt him.

But oh, oh, oh if only such things *could* be! Oh for impregnability and the attributes of Samson Herk, who could poke his finger through the side of a submarine! Such physical strength, combined with the powers of Svenska Agali, the schoolboy hypnotist…

But the sneering oblong mouth of the gas fire asks for shillings. To work!

Genius is ninety per cent perspiration… which smells. The world is grim and hard and stinks. What can a sensitive man do?

He wrote.

32

His landlady, who spoke of him as the nicest gentleman she had ever let rooms to, had put flowers on his dressing-table. The Murderer selected a small yellow chrysanthemum and stuck it in his buttonhole.

Then he went out. He walked slowly. It was not that he did not know where Frame Place was: he wanted to give himself the thrill that came of talking to a policeman.

'Oh, officer…'

'Yes, sir?'

'I wonder if you could tell me the best way to get to Frame Place?'

'Well now, Frame Place, let's see. Go straight along as you're going, and when you get to the end of the street turn right, take the first on your left, go straight on and bear right left and there you are. It's a kind of a crescent, sort of.'

The Murderer went on his way. He was laughing to himself. If that poor fool of a policeman had lifted out a hand and grabbed him by the collar, he would have made himself a sergeant. And there he was, pounding a beat while he – The Murderer – was at large.

On the next street corner he asked another policeman for a light.

'You're welcome, sir, if I've got one.'

The Murderer walked steadily up the long shadowy street. He was thinking, incongruously, of his father, who had died in the war; of his mother, who had come of a good family; of his uncle-by-marriage, who was an ironmonger; of his mother's sister, who was remotely related to a baronet; and of his brother, who was a corn chandler...

He reached Asta Thundersley's house in Frame Place by the river.

Another man in a grey suit had just rung the bell. The Murderer said: 'I'm rather afraid we must be a little early.'

The other man, who seemed also to be of a quiet, reticent disposition, said: 'Oh, yes. I shouldn't be surprised if you weren't right. Early, yes; I'm rather afraid we must be.'

They looked at each other. After what he thought was a decent interval The Murderer approached the bell-push with an extended forefinger, whereupon the other man retreated several paces – obviously he did not want the people of the house to think that he had had the temerity to ring twice. The Murderer saw this and paused. They avoided each other's eyes. But just then a man and a woman came up. The man looked crushed and angry, as if everything had been squeezed out of him except one deep, dark hate. And it was easy to see that the woman was the object and the inspiration of this hate. She was a big blonde, with little pale eyes set too close to a nose shaped like a potato. Her face appeared flat and powdery as a flounder dusted with flour before it is thrown into a frying pan, and her mouth protruded like the scalloped edge of a pie. Without hesitation she thrust a hand forward and held her thumb on the button of the bell for a good five seconds. Then The Tiger Fitzpatrick threw the door open and, muttering something that sounded like an apology, uncouthly bowed them in.

But as the door was closing someone pushed it. Another guest had arrived, the whites of whose eyes were yellow and bloodshot, and he carried a curiously carved stick of some brown-and-yellow tropical wood.

The guests exchanged glances but did not speak to one another. The Tiger Fitzpatrick conducted them to the sitting-room.

This room was divided by tall green folding doors, which had been thrown back. At the far end, Asta Thundersley's caterers had laid out an immense table on trestles, covered with a pure white cloth, and upon this table stood three massive five-branched candlesticks. Between the candlesticks there were two immense punch bowls, each of which contained at least two gallons of a turbid orange-coloured mixture, the pungent smell of which filled the place. To the excited eyes of The Murderer it seemed that there were five hundred glasses in the foreground, five hundred bottles of champagne in the background and five hundred dishes of rare and complicated canapés on the left and the right. Asta Thundersley came forward, roaring words of welcome and gripping hands.

She was dressed in brocade. Her strong, meaty shoulders were bare. Her square nails were painted light red; she seemed to be a little ashamed of them. From time to time she put her hands behind her and picked off a flake of varnish. Her sister, Tot, on the other hand, looked cool, sweet, calm and comfortable.

She had placed herself advantageously near the fireplace, with the light behind her, and was dressed in lavender-grey. About her throat she had tied a velvet band, to the front of which was pinned an amethyst – no other jewellery, only an antique watch in a double case with a fern-leaf pattern in amethysts and tiny diamonds. Thea Olivia's hands were small and exquisite, and she knew exactly what to do with them. Whenever Asta saw her, she shook her head in an involuntary gesture of admiration. That sister of hers was perfect – whatever she did was right – her hands, her feet, her knees, her chin, every hair and everything was in its proper place. Asta was convinced that beside her sister she looked as she felt – a clumsy idiot. Her admiration was not unmixed with resentment. She had spent three hours and three guineas on her appearance that day.

She puffed away uneasy speculation in one great snort and, as the bell rang again, said to The Tiger Fitzpatrick in a whisper which might have been heard three doors away: 'Keep on your toes, you punch-drunk idiot, or, as God is my judge, I'll knock your head off.'

Shocket The Bloodsucker arrived with Titch Whitbread, a boy of twenty with a complexion of blood and cream and thick blond hair. Titch Whitbread would have been conventionally handsome if the bridge of his nose had not been beaten in and his left ear knocked out of shape. But he had a full set of strong white teeth which he displayed in a tireless grin of spontaneous delight. Everyone took to him immediately. He was engagingly boyish; there was something about him that made women want to look into his round blue eyes and talk baby-talk. Titch Whitbread was overwhelmed by the magnificence of the house and by the accents of the people making conversation. Here was Class.

He grinned over a glass of ginger ale, answered if he was spoken to and looked so happy that hardened victims of boredom, seeing his radiant face, felt a tenderness for him – a small, sad glow of nostalgia for youth and innocence.

But Shocket The Bloodsucker talked for the two of them. When Shocket opened his mouth, which he did continuously, you were reminded of a piece of steak in which a butcher has made a preliminary cut. Out of this red, glutinous gash came a mono-tonous, husky voice with the penetrative quality of a cowbell in a mist: '... and this is Titch Whitbread. He's a killer. He's a murderer. Do you see that left hand? There's a dose of chloroform in it. And do you see that right hand? I'll tell you something. One poke with that right hand and your face is nothing but the place where your teeth used to be. No, no! Don't give Titch anything to drink. *He* won't drink it. He's a good, clean boy. *I* don't mind if *I* do! I'm a father to 'em – isn't that right, Titch? I never let 'em out of my sight. You ask Scotty Landauer. Who got Scotty into the running for the middleweight championship? Me – old Shocket. And, by God, Scotty would have taken the championship off of Joey Hands, only Scotty wasn't a clean boy. Broke training – late nights, beer, women (if you'll excuse the expression) – that was the ruination of Scotty. Nothing like that about Titch, I swear it on my mother's grave! No, may I be struck down dead this minute – no, may I never see my daughters alive again! I should be paralysed and may my children be paralysed and my wife should choke on the next piece of bread she eats, Titch Whitbread is the next champion! I should be knocked down by a taxi, and it should squash my guts out the next time I cross the road – may I go blind and beg in the streets – Titch is the next champion! He can hit like Sam Langford, he can take punishment like George Cook, he's a lion – he's a tiger – he's a clean-living boy – he's got more science than Einstein! And if *I* tell you that left hand is a dose of chloroform, *that* left hand *is* a dose of *chloroform*! All I want is for somebody, so they should guarantee Titch thirty thousand pounds in the next ten years, and – may I die a lingering death of cancer if what I say isn't as true as fifty Bibles – they'd make sixty thousand pounds! On my dying oath!'

Cigarette, who was watching Titch Whitbread with hot-eyed, dreamy abstraction, said: 'Why, I think that's wonderful!'

Shocket stopped talking, blew his nose into a handkerchief which he afterwards unfolded and scrutinised with the air of a man who is reading a threatening letter from a creditor and watched her closely. She had already emptied two glasses. It had brought out a smoulder on her cheeks. She was beginning, in her avid way, to look from face to face among the gathering guests. She wanted to recognise somebody, to make new contacts. Tobit Osbert and Catchy were engaged in polite conversation with Thea Olivia, behind whom hovered Sir Storrington Thirst, leaning familiarly upon the shoulder of Graham Strindberg. Cigarette sauntered over with her glass.

Thea Olivia was saying: 'I know I'm a silly old woman and you'll laugh at me, but I simply don't understand. I admit that I simply *don't* understand why these people *do* such things. Why do they? What benefit do they get out of it? It all seems so useless.'

Graham Strindberg said: 'They're made that way.'

Sir Storrington Thirst said: 'They get a kick out of it. I knew a man in Kenya –'

'It's so horrible, vile!' said Catchy. 'Hanging is much too good for anyone who does a thing like that. Much too good. He deserves – why, I don't know what he deserves. He deserves to be cut into little bits.'

'Hear, hear,' said Sir Storrington, 'little bits, quite right.'

Tobit Osbert shrugged a non-committal shoulder and said: 'No, I can't say I agree with you altogether there, Sir Storrington. One simply doesn't *do* that sort of thing. Find him out, try him properly and hang him quickly if he's guilty. That's the only thing to do. But no little bits. Certain people have no right to live among their fellow men. It seems to me that the thing to do is to stop them. I mean, to put an end to them.'

'How do they get to *be* like that?' asked Thea Olivia.

'Environment, upbringing,' said Catchy, 'that's the root of it all.'

Sir Storrington said: 'I don't quite get what you mean.'

'Well,' said Catchy, 'what I mean to say is, the way you're brought up. I don't quite know how to put it. I know what I want to say, but I don't know how to say it.'

In an ingratiating growl Sir Storrington said: 'Can't say I see eye to eye with you there, my dear. Look at me. Why, for the slightest word, I got hell. Why, if I failed to call my father "sir", he knocked me down. Remember once, I was accused of stealing pears. Didn't steal pears. Naturally denied stealing pears, was horsewhipped twice, once for stealing pears and the second time for lying. Couldn't sit, stand or lie down for a fortnight. Went into a high fever. Then my young brother owned up – *he'd* stolen the pears. I may say that I'd known it all along but had said nothing; brothers stick together, what? I went to my father and said: "Hope and trust you're convinced that I'm not a liar now, sir?" Father said: "Yes, my son, I'm convinced. But take this for your temerity – for daring to address me in that tone of voice." And gave me about three dozen with a malacca walking-stick that had a silver knob carved to look like an elephant's head. Upbringing? Environment? Never had any worth mentioning. Can't say I believe in it. Father used to grab me by the ankle and hold me head down out of a four-storey window, supposed to give one a horror of heights. Have *I* a horror of heights? Once, for a bet, I walked blindfold around the top of the Flatiron Building, New York. Do *I* go about killing little girls on account of environment? Stuff!'

'Oh Christ!' said Cigarette. 'Is everybody still talking about this Sonia Sabbatani business? Everywhere I go, all I hear is Sonia Sabbatani, Sonia Sabbatani, Sonia Sabbatani: murder, murder, murder. Can't anybody talk about anything else, for God's sake?'

Tobit Osbert said: 'But it really is a bad business. I knew the Sabbatanis. Sam did me more than one good turn. It brings the real monstrousness of the thing home to you, in a case like that.'

'I never saw Toby cry before,' said Catchy.

'Did you really cry?' asked Thea Olivia with tender coquetry.

'I didn't actually cry. I saw the grief of the others, and it may be that tears came into my eyes.'

'Yes, Toby, and ran down your face,' said Catchy.

'You mustn't be ashamed of having cried. It does you credit,' said Thea Olivia.

Graham Strindberg muttered: 'Where was God? Where was God?'

Suddenly Cigarette's eyes became narrow and hard. They were focused on the face of a man who stood talking to Asta Thundersley in another corner of the room. 'Look,' said Cigarette, 'look who we've got here. Dicks!'

'Dicks?' asked Thea Olivia. 'Who is Mr Dicks?'

'I mean detectives,' said Cigarette. She was looking at the man who at that time was Detective Inspector, but now is Chief Inspector, Turpin.

BOOK THREE

33

The affair of Chicken Eyes Emerald having been resolved, Turpin was taking time off. Now, in his strenuous, jerky way, he was resting.

Normally, after a long-drawn-out job of work, Turpin took his wife to a cinema and spent a calm hour or two, smoking an inexpensive cigar and admiring the footwork of Fred Astaire. He laughed until he choked ('laughed like a lavatory', as the Bar Bacchus crowd would have said) at Mickey Mouse and could give a tolerable imitation of Donald Duck. After the pictures, Turpin and his wife went home arm in arm, in perfect accord, never exchanging two words until they reached their doorstep, when she said: 'I hope you've got *your* key...' Then there would be supper. The implacable manhunter loved his long, lazy evenings at home, where there was always something to be done – a nail here, a screw there, a dab of glue and a firm hand at such and such a joint – something to be done, which he seldom did. He was the laughing-stock of the family. The children called him *In-A-Minute* – he was always putting things off. In the end it was Mrs Turpin who unstopped the sink or fixed the rattling window.

But she had gone to visit her mother. He was alone. Turpin found no pleasure in the cinema if his wife was not with him: there was no one to whisper to. Asta Thundersley's invitation intrigued him. There was no harm in paying half-an-hour's visit. He had met Asta twice – call it three times – and considered her as a lunatic, wrong-headed in a good direction, but not quite right.

Officially, he could not approve of Asta, yet she was a person after his own heart. She was angry and rebellious: that was silly. She knew exactly what she hated: he could not blame her for that. Her heart got into her throat: he was not out of sympathy with the noise she made. There had been occasions when Turpin had teetered on the verge of an outburst in the high, wide and handsome manner of Asta Thundersley. But the sort of scene she was capable of making over the impoliteness of a bus conductor would have cost him his position: detectives may not make scenes. They should not even express anger. Two or three times in his life Turpin would have given anything but his job for the joy of exploding like an overstrained boiler. But he was bound by the cold white bands of legal dialectic. Still, he envied Asta, who, privileged as a woman and a popular eccentric, could push open doors marked *Private*, grab terrified officials by the collar, beat people over the head with her umbrella and shout at the top of her voice wherever she happened to be. She had guts where her brains ought to have been, he thought; but he liked guts.

He was not in the habit of accepting invitations and not much of a man for drinking parties. But it is a good thing for a man in Turpin's business to see a little of everything. Everything was experience; and experience sharpened the wits. The world was a great whirling grindstone upon which Turpin unostentatiously ground himself keener and keener like a headsman's axe. It was interesting, a bohemian party like this: you never knew what you might find.

He was saying: 'If it's all the same to you, miss, I think I'd just as soon have a glass of beer, if it's not putting you to any inconvenience.'

Asta poured out a bottle of Bass, filling a glass with froth so that Turpin, wishing her good health and taking a polite sip, appeared for a moment to have become venerable yet dandified, with a neat little white moustache such as used to be worn by Mr Lewis Stone. Then she took him aside and whispered: 'You know, I think the man who killed little Sonia Sabbatani must be here tonight.'

Detective Inspector Turpin said: 'Oh, yes? Is that a fact?'

'I'm sure of it.'

'What makes you think so?'

'I've been working things out. Practically every man here tonight is a suspect. Practically everyone.'

Smiling, Turpin glanced at the crowd. At least sixty people were drinking great glasses of Schiff's cloudy orange-coloured mixture.

'While you're about it, you might have invited the rest of London,' said Turpin.

'Why be more of an idiot than God made you, for God's sake? Do you take me for a fool? The man who killed poor little Sonia was one of the Bar Bacchus crowd.'

'You know that for a fact, I dare say?'

'I'm absolutely sure of it.'

'Well, no doubt you've got your very good reasons.'

'Look here, Turpin, work it out for yourself –'

'I wish I could work it out for myself, Miss Thundersley, but it isn't my department. All the same, I'd like to hear what I've got to work out for myself, if you know what I mean.'

'That poor little girl was enticed – lured – inveigled into the filthy coal-cellar of that horrible house. I've been a little girl myself. You've never been a little girl, Dick, so let me tell you. There isn't one girl in a million who'd go with a stranger into a deserted house, so she must have known him. Well, how could she have known him? Through her father's shop. Sam Sabbatani is one of those homely little tradesmen: his wife and kid were always in and out of the shop. Everyone who set foot in the place was one of the family. Poor Mrs Sabbatani is forever bringing in cups of tea. She's made that way. You know the type of person I mean. Well, as it happens, Sam made a bit of a connection at the Bar Bacchus. He's still got a little advertisement hung up there – done in red-and - black lettering in a little brown frame. You know Gonger, the barman? Well, Sam Sabbatani made an arrangement with him – Gonger displayed Sam's showcard, and Sam pressed Gonger's suits and kept him in white jackets. You ask Gonger, you ask Sam Sabbatani. Most of Sam's customers came from the Bar Bacchus. Work it out, Turpin, work it out!'

'There isn't anything to work out,' said Turpin, smiling.

It was then that Cigarette, looking hostile, spoke of Dicks, or detectives.

A waiter, observing that her glass was empty, paused with a tray of full glasses. Cigarette took one and put back the glass she had emptied, saying: 'There's more in this stuff than meets the eye, comrade.'

Then she gulped about a quarter of a pint of Schiff's *Formule* and became angry. She strode over to Detective Inspector Turpin, knocking down a little three-legged table on her way, and cried: 'How dare you come here? You copper's nark, you dirty little bogey! What are you doing in the company of decent human beings! You filthy bloodhound, why aren't you out? Why aren't you out hunting; why aren't you out hunting better men to death, you stinking dirty wolf? You murdered Chicken Eyes Emerald. You murdered him! You dirty coward! You wouldn't have dared to meet him face to face as man to man – no, no, you had to be mob-handed, you beast, with thousands of coppers behind you, all hunting down one man. You hound! And I suppose you've come here to gloat, to show off! You –'

'Cigarette, shut up,' said Asta.

'I'm sorry. I know I'm your guest,' said Cigarette, 'but I won't shut up! Christ Almighty, instead of hounding better men to death, why don't these bastards go out and find out who killed that little girl?'

'All right,' said Detective Inspector Turpin, 'take it easy, just take it easy.'

He took a full glass from a passing waiter, handed it to Cigarette, and said: 'Let's have a drink.'

She drank, and she melted. Looking sideways at Turpin through her eyelashes she said, in a different voice: 'I'm sorry. I behaved like a perfect pig. You won't believe me, but ordinarily I have quite good manners. I don't know what came over me. Will you forgive me? Do, please, say you forgive me.'

'Nothing to forgive, I'm sure.'

'Call me Cigarette. Everybody calls me Cigarette. Do please forget what I said. I didn't mean a word of it.'

'That's all right.'

'Do you know me?'

Turpin knew her, but he said: 'I can't say I've had the privilege.'

'I was Chicken's girl. Does that convey anything to you?'

'Ah-ha?'

'He was a rat, you know.'

'So?'

'But I loved him. I loved him, Turpin!'

'It's all over now,' said Turpin. 'Be sociable, eh?'

'I like you, Turpin. Turpin, tell me all about yourself.'

'*You've* just told *me*.'

'What's your wife like?'

'What makes you ask, miss?'

'Do you make love to her often, Turpin?' asked Cigarette.

'Why don't you finish that nice drink?'

'Oh, Turpin, Turpin, I *do* think you're pretty terrific! You know, for a little while I hated you, but now I think you're pretty damned fine. Do you know what? My father used to hunt silly little foxes. But you, you hunt real live men. My God, Turpin, it takes something to hunt down a man like the Chicken – it does! He was a man! …And you're a better man…' said Cigarette, with certain inward explosions that presaged hysterics. 'You're a – *ha-hup, ha-hup* –'

'You can cut that out,' said Detective Inspector Turpin, in an undertone like cracked ice made articulate. 'I've heard it all before. Have another drink and get properly drunk, and go home and sleep; and get up, and get drunk again tomorrow, and go to sleep again. But just for now be quiet. Is that clear?'

'Yes,' said Cigarette, quietly crying.

Turpin sidestepped like a boxer and disappeared into the thickening crowd.

'Turp! …Turp!' cried Cigarette, in a gulping voice. 'Stand by me, Turp! Let's play games, Turp – I'll hide, and you've got to find me –'

A waiter was passing. She exchanged her half-empty glass for a full one. There was a numbness in her cheeks. None of Asta's guests was quite sober now.

34

Oonagh Scripture was leaning upon Sinclair Wensday, who was caressing her shoulder and exchanging glances with a fat, tow-headed girl whom nobody knew. His wife Avril was watching him with her right eye and ogling Alan Shakespeare with her left; from time to time they exchanged a look of quiet hate. Muriel, having recognised The Murderer, had rushed across the room to embrace him, but he was deep in conversation with Thea Olivia now, together with Hemmeridge, Graham Strindberg and Mothmar Acord. Milton Catt intercepted her; they embraced. Tony Mungo clutched her wrist and kissed it; Geezle bowed. Roget, demonstrating a trick with a tray and three glasses, made a clang and a clash, and then Sir Storrington Thirst made noise and mess scraping up glass and drink with a fire shovel. Ayesha Babbington had interested herself in the trapezius muscles of Milton Catt, who at the same time was being palpated by Shocket The Bloodsucker, who was saying: 'Train! Train! May my mother, God rest her dear soul, rot in hell, may my children, God bless them, be given to Narzy degenerates, I'll make you light-heavyweight champion. It's an offer. May I go blind and paralysed if I lie! May my wife and children go deaf and dumb and blind and paralysed! ...Would I say this if I didn't mean it?'

There was a silence. 'Titch!' cried Shocket, looking wildly about the place. 'Titch, did I done you harm? If so, when?'

'Never no harm to me, Bloodsucker.'

'There you are then, you see?' said Shocket to Milton Catt. 'You see? I never did no harm, not to nobody. I tell the man I can make him a light-heavyweight champion already, and he looks at me like I done a murder. Gratitude!'

At the sound of the word 'murder', conversation clicked back to the topic that had occupied everybody's time for the past ten days: Sonia Sabbatani. That crime was still interesting in the locality. The corpse was still fresh. In a few more days they would have talked it stale, then it would begin to bore them, and they'd drop it and forget it.

'Still no news of that awful business?' said Ayesha Babbington. 'God above, what do we keep the police for?'

'Just so. Is it for this sort of thing that we ruin ourselves paying taxes?' said Sir Storrington.

Hemmeridge, in his sibilant, simpering, effeminate voice said: 'Of course, there'll be lots more now, you know.'

'Good Lord, what a horrible thought!' said Tobit Osbert. He was holding Catchy's hand. Catchy squeezed his wrist.

'Why, don't you see, one murder makes many,' said Hemmeridge.

'I've heard that said about marriage,' said Mothmar Acord with a lowering look, compounded of low cunning and secret scorn. This man seemed always to be on the verge of an outburst of mad rage or contemptuous laughter.

'Well, it's pretty much the same sort of thing, don't you see?' said Hemmeridge, with a titter. 'None the less, people go to a wedding and it puts ideas in their heads. They think it would be really rather nice to go and have a wedding themselves and some of them do go and have a wedding themselves. Same with christenings. Girl sees pretty little pink ready-made baby going 'goo goo' and thinks that she would rather like to find a delicious little living doll like that under her own cabbage leaf or in her own doctor's little black bag – according to what her mother has told her – don't you see, and up goes the birth rate. And as I think I was saying, it's much the same thing with this affair. Man kills little girl. Man gets away with it. Lots of people want to kill little girls only they need a little encouragement.'

'You're perfectly right,' said Schiff. 'It's perfectly natural. It's fundamental. Read *Das Buch Von Es.*'

'If you'll have the goodness to allow me to finish my sentence,' said Hemmeridge petulantly, 'lots of people think it would be really an awfully nice thing to go out and kill somebody. Only most of us, thank goodness, do our killing in our dreams. I mean, we get someone else to do our killing for us. I mean, we go out and buy a nice bloodthirsty detective story or one of those Americanish tough-guy books in which the hero is a bit of a murderer thinly disguised as a private detective and goes about slapping glamorous female poisoners in the face or tearing their clothes off or something.' He giggled, swallowed a mouthful of his drink and continued: 'Thank goodness, what? Look at me. Here I am, in the land of the living, not quite dead of malnutrition, neatly dressed and in clean linen. For this I must thank the general public's enjoyment of murder. Since, as you may or may not know, I write crime stories myself – when I happen to think of a good bloodthirsty plot. Do you see this grey suit I am wearing? It was bought out of the blood of a dismembered heiress in a trunk at Waterloo station. Do you see this rather nice silk tie? I got it out of a mad surgeon who loved to vivisect people and make them into peculiar shapes. It was all that was left over after I had paid certain arrears of board and lodging. I do like to have something to show for money received on account of my crimes – I always buy myself a little something or other: a tie, a card of bachelor buttons, a pair of sixpenny cuff-links or even a pair of gloves. But what was I saying? Oh yes. One murder makes many. That, by the by, would be a goodish title for a story, wouldn't it? The sort of fellow that goes out and kills little Sonia What's-Her-Name is, actually, not at all rare. He nearly always gets away with it, don't you see? It's like diving into ice-cold water – you only have to make your mind up to it, and once the first shock is over there is a pleasant tingle and glow. It gives you a certain sense of power, don't you see? Something like well-being, having done it once, you'll do it again, and then again, and yet again. You mark my words, one murder makes many, I repeat. And, furthermore, encouraged by the failure of the police – poor things – to find the perpetrator of this much-publicised atrocity, someone else will find his nerve and take his quick, wild plunge through the thin ice into those strangely stimulating dark, still waters of death.'

Hemmeridge drained his glass. A waiter gave him a fresh drink. Mr Pink, who had been listening and nodding, said: 'But look here, sir! This is dreadful! No, this really is dreadful! You know that what you're doing isn't nice – I mean, writing that sort of nasty story and putting nasty ideas into people's heads – you *know* what you're doing and still you go on doing it. Why? You ought to stop doing it at once, as soon as you realise that what you're doing is wrong. Oughtn't you now? Be honest, eh?'

'Oh, my dear fellow!' cried Hemmeridge, laughing. 'What

difference can it possibly make? People *like* that sort of nonsense. If there had been no murder, we should have had to invent it. Besides, if – te-he! – if I may coin a phrase, a man must live, and please don't say: "*Je ne vois pas la nécessité.*"'

'Oh, but I know that a man must live,' said Pink. 'I do, I do indeed, I honestly and solemnly assure you, but a man can live in all sorts of ways.'

'Ah, yes, Mr Pink. But I happen to be in my little way a writer.'

'But, Mr Hemmeridge, so was Thackeray, so was Tolstoy. So is the great Ernest Hemingway.'

'And so are you, Mr Pink.'

Mr Pink blushed like a fourteen-year-old girl and said: 'No, no, really not. Not a writer, only an interpreter and, by the way, Mr Hemmeridge, you are a literary man and may perhaps advise me. Last night I had an idea.'

'A revelation surely?' murmured Tobit Osbert.

Hemmeridge giggled into his glass, but Mr Pink went on very seriously: 'You know, I believe, that I have been trying to put the eternal truths into everyday language. Well, last night it occurred to me that it might be possible to translate some of the writings of St John Of The Cross into popular songs. Take this for instance: "*As to my affairs, daughter, let them not trouble you, for none of them troubles me... These things are not done by men, but by God, who knows what is meet for us and ordains things for our good. Think only that God ordains all. And where there is no love, put love, and you will find love.*" Now what do you say to that as a kind of dance-music song? Title: "You've Got To Put What You Want Where You Want It". Or, again, take this passage: "*For, in order to pass from the all to the All, Thou hast to deny thyself wholly in all.*" Now that is, if I may say so, a little elusive to the modern mind. Might one not transcribe it as – "*Go chase yourself and catch yourself?*" What do you think?'

Before Hemmeridge could reply, Mothmar Acord said: 'I don't really see what all the kerfuffle is about. What is there so extraordinary in a kid being killed? One of these days I dare say there will be a war, and then we'll knock over millions of 'em and congratulate ourselves.'

Thea Olivia, with a little cry of horror, said: 'You mustn't say such things!'

Looking down at his freckled hands Mothmar Acord lifted a shoulder and a corner of his mouth and sauntered away to talk to Avril Wensday.

Tobit Osbert said: 'It seems to me that Mr Acord isn't quite right in what he said. Dropping a bomb is one thing. Getting hold of someone by the throat and choking them and – excuse me, madam – raping them, is another thing. Look down from a very high building. Look down from the Monument in the City, and even from that little height people don't look like people any more. You know how it is when you live in a high building. The higher you live, the more you get into the habit of throwing things out of the window. It seems to me that a man in an aeroplane thousands of feet above the ground can throw down bombs, or germs, or anything horrible that you can think of and still be quite a nice young man.'

'Until he comes to think of it,' said Hemmeridge.

'He knows not what he does,' said Mr Pink, laying one of his nervous hands upon Osbert's left shoulder.

'Yes, Mr Pink, that is more or less what I meant to say. He should be, as it were, *forgiven*, because he sort of does *not* know what he does. He presses a button or pulls a lever, and he's a mile away from the scene of the crime even before the crime is committed – I mean, before the bomb goes off and kills men, women and children. But a man who stands about on street corners in the dark and waits for a little girl to pass and takes advantage of the fact that she knows him and trusts him in order to do what that man did who killed Sonia Sabbatani – he *is* a murderer.'

'Yes,' said Mr Pink, biting his nails, 'but having learned of the effect of a bomb, is your bomber? I wonder…'

He paused, and Graham Strindberg said: 'Yet why should such things be? Why should Evil be? If evil exists and is powerful, is God all-powerful? Since there is evil, if God is all-powerful how can he be all-good? If God is all-good, how can he be all-powerful?'

With something like irritation, Mr Pink replied: 'I don't know,

Mr Strindberg.' He was by this time quietly drunk, and his eyes were like stars reflected in the rippling surface of a puddle. 'I really don't know, my dear sir! How can I know? God doesn't tell *me* his business, does he? Who the deuce are you that you must know everything? Do your toenails insist on knowing what your head is doing? Does the body of the martyr understand the soul that tells it to burn at the stake? In Macaulay there is an account of an old Puritan after Sedgemoor: he had had his arm smashed and was cutting it off himself with his own knife, sternly repeating the Lord's Prayer, with a face of iron and no expression of pain. What was *that* arm to question the will of that *man?* It was hurt? It was crushed? Its nerves cried out, yes? Yet I tell you that because of the unyielding spirit of that old man to whom God gave that arm, the misery of his poor flesh brought forth something good and beautiful. You must do what you *know* is good. Ask no questions. Expect no answers. Have faith. Believe me – do please believe me – God is good. He is! He *is!*'

'If he is *good,* is God all-*powerful,* then?' asked Graham Strindberg.

'Yes!' shouted Mr Pink.

Tom Beano appeared from nowhere in particular and roared: 'Don't make a fool of yourself, Pink! …Is Pink at his old games again? Godding and Christing? Gooding and evilling? Everything is for the best in this best of all possible worldsing? …Cut it out, Pink. This is a sociable party. Face facts. Who burned Giordano Bruno?'

Beano flourished a half-empty glass. He was red in the face, and his eyes were narrowed.

'I don't know, I'm sure,' said Thea Olivia.

Tobit Osbert started to say: 'We were talking about –'

'– I know, I know, *I know,*' said Beano. 'And there you are again, Pink. Where's the good in *that* business?'

'Beano, you know as well as I do that there isn't any good in it.'

'Is there bad in it, Pink?'

'I should jolly well think so!'

'Why, then? Come on, Pink. Why? Tell us why!'

'I don't know, I don't know why *anything*!' cried Mr Pink, with tears in the corners of his eyes. 'I know *what*. I don't know *why*. And so do you, Tom Beano, so do you!'

'So do I what, Pink?'

'Beano, you know right from wrong.'

'Aha?' said Beano, closing one eye. 'And what if I do?'

'Oh *dear* me, dear *me*!' said Mr Pink. 'All this is vanity, Tom Beano, and you know it. How dare you talk the way you talk? How dare you do it? How dare you ask me "where was God?" Where were you, Tom Beano? Where were *you* when that deed was done?'

'All right, then, and where were *you*?' asked Beano.

'I was spoiling sheets of foolscap paper,' said Mr Pink slowly. 'Scribble, scribble, scribble...' The tears in his eyes pushed themselves forward and came out.

'I didn't mean to upset you, Pink,' said Beano.

'You didn't upset me, bless you, Tom.'

'Then what the hell are you crying for?'

'Beano! Does some crazy conceit make you believe that anything you could say might get a tear out of my eye? God forgive you!'

'Ah? God forgive me, eh? Now listen to reason. Is God all-powerful: yes or no?'

'Yes.'

'Yet you ask God to forgive me. Is that so?'

'Yes.'

'Now listen...'

'Oh, please!' said Tobit Osbert. 'Do stop it!'

Sir Storrington slapped every back within reach and stammered: 'Kiss and be friends, what?' Thea Olivia, in her satisfied way, glanced from face to face. Hemmeridge, who was annoyed, looked away. Shocket The Bloodsucker was leering at her. The word had already got around that Thea Olivia was very wealthy and had, as people said, 'Ideas'.

She knew that everyone believed that she wanted a husband and smiled inside herself. She wanted someone with a bronze head and a chiselled mouth, a few inches taller than herself; diffident, with a suggestion of passion; impecunious yet proud – a terrible but sensitive man, intellectually isolated, envied by men and adored by women; a man into whose reluctant hand it would be necessary to press (with conspiracies and blandishments) the occasional five-pound note when the waiter was not looking.

He would be honourable: his sufferings would know no bounds. From time to time he would try to commit suicide – but she would be there in the nick of time to divert the pistol or catch his ankles as he dived over the edge of the sixth-storey penthouse roof. (He was not the sort of sneak that crawls into a gas oven or opens a vein in a hot bath.) He would need looking after. There would be important papers... documents... perhaps somewhere or other an importunate wife.

She would alter all that.

Gently, coolly, caressingly – cheek to bronze cheek, hand to fevered forehead – Thea Olivia would coax out folly like a blackhead and cream the pitted surface of his soul.

One day he would leave her. But she would wait. He'd come back – sheepish, stinking of Chanel Number Five, red-eyed, gulping, repentant – and she would receive him quietly yet with something like ecstasy, everything having been forgiven. Later, looking down at his handsome, exhausted face, she would say to herself: '*Poor wretch. All men are alike...*' After all, he was only a man... will-less, maculate, hungry for forgiveness.

Thea Olivia could have made do with Sir Storrington, Tobit Osbert, Hemmeridge or Tom Beano: there was plenty in them to occupy her great capacity for forgiveness, and Sean Mac Gabhann might have done at a pinch, or Graham Strindberg. It would, in fact, be rather pleasant to give Mac Gabhann money. She would know what he was after when he became sweet, attentive and full of charm, when his fascinating Irish brogue cooed and purred at double pressure. She would see through it, and, knowing that she was going to give in in any case, pretend to be adamant. No, not another shilling, you naughty, improvident man! Then he would turn his charm up like a gas jet: he would glow with charm as he set himself the task of wooing the chequebook out of her little papier-mâché-and-mother-of-pearl desk. In the end, when he thought that he had failed and was on the verge of an attack of the sulks, she would hand him an envelope and tell him with a little silvery laugh that she had written him the cheque the night before.

It would be fun, too, with Graham Strindberg. He was so tolerant; they could spend their days being tolerant together. As for Sir Storrington, he was a naughty boy also. He drank. She would try to cure him of that, to wheedle him out of his bad habits; be a mother to him; wean him from the black bottle. In that case she would be Lady Thirst, which would sound very pleasant indeed.

Or she could take Tom Beano in hand, reason with him and bring him to God. To Tobit Osbert she would be a kind, clever, beloved mama – a guiding star. She would pull that loose-knit personality together and make something of him, and then how grateful he would be!

Of course, there would be no sex in it; Thea Olivia had never thought much about that kind of thing. She was pure in her dreams of marriage. In point of fact, she would not have married the best man in the world to save his life. She had her dreams; they were enough for her. She was taking no chances. If anything happened to break those dreams, what would be left? The dirty realities of a sordid world. It was better to dream. She looked again at the animated face of Sean Mac Gabhann and smiled at him in her immaculate, maternal way. But he was in conversation with Monty Bar-Koch Ba. It was an uneasy conversation. The Zionist and the Irish Nationalist found themselves in complete accord. This had never happened before, and the novelty of the situation struck them both tongue-tied.

Monty Bar-Koch Ba looked at Mac Gabhann with suspicion. But then, he looked at everybody with suspicion. His soul was a fine filter that could separate from the current of any conversation a little muddy residue of unsuspected insults. You have, no doubt, blown a mouthful of cigarette smoke through a stretched handkerchief in order to demonstrate to your friends the sticky, tarry muck that comes and goes with a whiff of soothing, innocent tobacco. Bar-Koch Ba was that handkerchief, stretched taut and breathed.

He had said: 'I can't understand what all the fuss is about. A lunatic here, in this city, has raped and murdered a girl. One little girl, one little Jewish girl is raped and murdered. And there you are, all of you horrified, up in arms! Yet is it not a fact that in Germany Hitler has been in power for over two years and has raped and murdered thousands and thousands and thousands of Jewish girls? And there you are up in arms? No! You recognise Hitler, you honour Hitler, you send ambassadors to Hitler! One Jewish girl is raped and murdered on your own doorstep. Oh yes, that makes you indignant because it might be your own daughter! But ten thousand Jewish girls raped and murdered in Germany mean nothing to you. Hypocrisy! Smuggery, humbuggery!'

Mr Pink, who was ambling from group to group on uncertain feet, said: 'Just so, friend. It's all the same thing.'

'How do you mean – same thing?'

Sean Mac Gabhann, with something of a sneer, said: 'Will you be after telling me if any of you horrified people were half as horrified by what the Black And Tans did to us in Ireland?'

'It's exactly the same thing,' said Mr Pink, and slurring some of his words, 'zactlythesamething. People like to be on the safe side. People want to go on living. Yes? Well. People wait for murder to become leg-leg-legitimatised. When murder is leg… – made legal – everything's all right for murderers. People can serve the Devil in the name of God. They can find, as the Americans say, *new angles*. Convince themselves that in torturing and raping and killing they are working for the good of the Race. False! False! Mark my words, lots of people everywhere would do what that man did to Sonia Sabbatani, if only a few hundred people were doing the same sort of thing at the same time. Look at lynch mobs in the southern states of America. All of a sudden, up jumps a führer and shouts *"Let's lynch this nigger!"* And all sorts and conditions of men throw down their tools, and rush together, and make a mad, murderous mob that wants to break places open and tear poor human beings out, and march by torchlight, and hang unhappy wretches on trees. All of a sudden, in a small town, up jump two thousand red-handed murderers. They are everywhere all the time, friend, everywhere! In every man there lurks a hungry beast. Mr Whatever You Call Yourself, there isn't any difference at all between that poor little girl who was murdered the other day and the tens of thousands you were telling us of. Given the opportunity, Catholics murder Protestants, Protestants murder Catholics, Catholics murder Jews and Jews slay Amalekites. Given a mullah, the Moslems murder the Christians. In everyone there is a little egg full of murder waiting to be hatched. Crack it! Crack it and throw it out! Individual regeneration is everything. Christian girl, Jew girl –'

Bar-Koch Ba said, in a dangerous voice: 'You'd better mind your language.'

'My language? How has my language offended you, sir?'

'I didn't quite like the way you said that. What do you mean by "Jew girl"? You mean "Jewish girl", don't you?'

'I mean exactly what I say, sir, and I'll thank you not to grip me by the arm.'

'You're all the same,' said Bar-Koch Ba, and he went into one of his silences – one of those grey silences in which he seemed to lose all colour and become one with his clothes. He talked to people without looking at them.

35

The Murderer, who appeared to be half asleep, was looking for Turpin, who had sidestepped and slipped away when Cigarette had begun to hiccup herself into hysterics. When, at last, Turpin's face appeared again, between the beefy red face of Asta Thundersley and the tightly waved head of Mrs Scripture, The Murderer found it impossible to look away from the man. The thick, cloudy, ice-cold, orange-coloured drink was creeping around in his head. He felt happy and reckless. He believed that if he had a pen and some paper he could, at this moment, write formidable prose. He would describe Detective Inspector Turpin as a man made of mysterious grey squares, whose eyes alone were conspicuous – pale, bright, white-grey eyes, so similar in colour to the flame of burning sulphur that one expected them to give out a choking stench. No detail escaped him: he noted the narrow, soft collar held, under the knot of the three-and-sixpenny tie, by a fourpenny gilt pin; the severe grey suit; the old-fashioned gold watch-chain (obviously a legacy from his father) that hung between the lower pockets of his waistcoat. The pallid, puffy face of Turpin indicated that he needed sleep. The Murderer liked to think of himself as a detective. Turpin's suit, he calculated, could not have cost more than four pounds. Yes, the suit had been bought for about four pounds; the shoes were procurable at nineteen shillings; the shirt – with two collars thrown in – could be got for about six-and-sixpence in the City. The Murderer smiled inwardly. Here he sat, ten feet away from a Scotland Yard man, a full-blown detective inspector, who, if he only knew what was what, could put out a hand and, simply by grasping his shoulder, hurry himself towards a chief inspectorship.

He took another drink. In the five seconds that passed between the swallow and the gentle clink of the carefully-put-down glass, The Murderer found himself in the clutch of an irresistible yearning to get up, walk over to Turpin and give himself up.

He drank again and, as the stuff that tasted like orange juice went down, determined to make an end of the matter before Turpin left the house.

He slid everyday prudence into the pigeonhole of another daydream. Now he saw himself as a nonchalant man of ice and fire, making as great a sensation as any man had ever made in that locality by means of a gesture.

He would save this gesture for its proper moment. When that moment came he would approach Detective Inspector Turpin, touch him on the shoulder in the manner of a policeman making an arrest and say: 'Look here, my dear sir. I really am getting a little sick of all this conjecture touching the murder of that little girl Sonia Sabbatani. As a topic of conversation it's becoming a bore. Anything rather than a bore, don't you think? Let's face it. I did it.'

Taking a fresh glass from one of the waiters, he swallowed two or three more mouthfuls, turning the matter over in his mind.

Might it not be better simply, apropos of nothing, taking advantage of a blank space in the conversation, to say in a world-weary way: 'Oh, look here, I'm the man who killed Sonia Sabbatani.'

Again, it might be better to wait until the talk, inevitably, got around to the murder and then say: 'Oh, that? I did that.'

It needed working out. His head was swimming.

While his eyes were open it seemed actually to be swimming – striking out clumsily to keep itself above a sort of sticky, turbid pool in which he felt that he was immersed. As soon as he closed his eyes they seemed to roll up and backwards until they looked into the dome of his skull. Then he saw something indescribable – a kaleidoscope seen through something like an opal. Wretched little pieces of tinfoil, broken glass, crockery, metal and paper spun between mirrors and came to rest in queer and beautiful patterns – and as soon as The Murderer settled down to admire these patterns there was a whirr and a buzz and everything dispersed. It twirled away and came to rest in a fresh pattern.

Someone said: 'You're dreaming.'

He replied: 'Yes, yes... I'm afraid I am...'

Then he opened his eyes and saw the elegant, old-fashioned room, full of cigarette smoke, at the edge of which Asta Thundersley, red and damp as an autumnal dawn, was bullying the barman: 'Mix, you idle man, mix! What did I hire you for? To get drunk?'

The barman began to laugh like a man who is being tickled under the arms. His eyes were unnaturally bright, and his face had become mottled.

Meanwhile, Sinclair Wensday was flirting conspicuously with Catchy, occasionally darting venomous glances in the direction of his wife Avril, who, looking at him with the eyes of an angry cat, deliberately rested her head on the shoulder of the young man called Roget. Five or six glasses had reduced him to the self-revelatory stage of intoxication.

'You know,' he was saying, 'I'm good for nothing. I'm good for nothing at all. Some people, I mean, find happiness. Not me. I don't know what it feels like to be happy. I'm not a man, I'm a slave. A slave,' he repeated, while two maudlin tears trickled down his vacant face. 'Yes, that's all I am, a slave, a slave to pity.'

'You poor dear!'

'You understand me. Pity, that's what it is, pity! I'm too soft. I hate to hurt people's feelings. I'd rather kill a man than hurt his feelings – do you know that? And it's all my mother's fault. I hate my mother. I suppose you think that's a terrible thing to say, don't you?'

'I see you have the courage of your convictions,' said Avril.

'No, I haven't. I haven't got the courage of anything. I haven't got the courage... of... of... a daffodil. A daffodil fights for its bit of hold in the soil. But could I fight for anything? No. And it's all my mother's fault. Did she ever treat me as a human being? I tell you, dear sweet Avril, she always treated me like a dog, a dog!'

'There, there, don't cry.'

'How can I help crying if my mother treats me like a dog? How can I help it? If I had had a father things might have been different, but I never had a father. He died in the war, at Ypres. There was an explosion, and he was missing. The next time we meet, you kind, sweet, beautiful woman, I'll bring you his photograph. He sits on that little chair like a man on a throne. Why did he have to die? Tell me, why did he have to leave me all alone with my horrible mother? Why?'

'I don't know.'

'She was afraid of losing me,' said Roget, weeping. 'She lost him, and she didn't want to lose me. She wouldn't let me play football in case I got kicked, and she wouldn't let me play cricket in case somebody hit me with a bat. And she wouldn't let me let off fireworks on Guy Fawkes Day in case I burned my fingers, and she wouldn't let me go and play with other boys in case one of them knocked me down and I fractured my skull on the pavement, and she wouldn't let me cross the road, and she wouldn't let me climb trees. She wouldn't let me do anything. She kept me on a lead; she turned me into a dog, a dog, a dog! She wouldn't let me talk to any girls in case they led me astray or gave me diseases. You don't know what I've had to go through! Everybody else had a pony. Not me, oh no, not little me. I might have fallen off, or it might have bitten me or kicked me. She reads all the filthy newspapers, damn her, and she keeps a big book full of little bits she cuts out all about little boys who've had horrible accidents. Little boys and little girls. Sometimes they've been to a circus, and they go home and try and do a trapeze act and hang their bloody little selves. Or sometimes they blow up a toy balloon, and it goes the wrong way, and they choke themselves. So she never let me go to a circus, so she never let me have a toy balloon, so she filleted every bit of fish because once in some paper or other she saw something about some nauseating brat who swallowed a bone in a bit of fried cod. She never let me do anything. I wanted to be a writer, but she read somewhere, in some idiotic book, that writers are all womanisers and drunkards, and she didn't want me to go into business because she read somewhere in a paper about a businessman who defaulted and blew his brains out. And here I am, here I am!'

'Then why don't you simply put on your hat and walk out?'

Roget cried like a child, wrinkling up his face, and said: 'It's pity! Pity is the ruin of me. She'd be so brokenhearted if I went away. She'd die. She told me so. I'm all she has, and you don't know – you'll never know – you couldn't possibly know – how that woman has suffered. Oh my God, how I hate that woman! But she's sick, very sick. Or at least, she pretends she is, and one of these days...'

'– One of these days you'll come into her money and go on the loose, I suppose?'

'You've said it exactly. How well you understand me! One of these days... Listen, I'm going to tell you something.'

He paused. Avril said: 'Well?'

But Roget apparently had thought better of it. He looked as if he was going to be sick, but Avril's eyes were elsewhere. Her husband had moved from Catchy to Oonagh Scripture, and Mothmar Acord had taken his place. That leering, sinister man approached Catchy with frank, open lustfulness, putting a hand on the back of her neck, which in those days was cool and round and fine of texture; a famous neck, solid-looking as ivory. He said: 'You're a very good-looking girl, aren't you?'

'Do you think so?'

'I do. You can see I do. I want you to tell me something.'

'What would you like me to tell you?'

'Are you a masochist, by any chance?'

'Why do you ask?' said Catchy in an uncertain voice.

Mothmar Acord replied: 'There's something about you that invites violence.'

At this, a pleasurable tremor passed from the base of Catchy's skull to the base of her spine, and she felt her heart beating and her toes curling inwards. They exchanged glances. Asta Thundersley, who had approached with a couple of full glasses, heard the end of the conversation and observed the interchange of looks.

She remembered this later.

36

It seemed to Asta that her foolish, futile party had been limping on since the beginning of last week. She began to jeer – not to laugh but to jeer at herself for having organised it. Sir Storrington approached her and said: 'My God, Asta, what the devil have you given us? My dear good lady, these are knockout drops. I'd give a good deal to know what you put in it.'

Instantly Schiff, who appeared to be listening to everything in a dozen places at the same time, popped out with a dishevelled head and said: 'This is my *Formule*. It is I who have invented this. What do you mean by "a good deal"? I'm always ready, baronet, to make a deal.'

At this Sir Storrington Thirst gave him the look that he kept for his creditors, but then, stung by an idea, he took Schiff aside and said that his estate was somewhat embarrassed but the name of Sir Storrington Thirst was a good name – at least it sounded remarkably good – and was available, for a consideration, as a name to print on a label. Schiff made a note of this in a notebook with a transparent cover bound with wire. When Sir Storrington said: 'That's a clever sort of idea, that little book of yours,' Schiff told him that he could get them wholesale at 72/- a gross.

'There's a lady who has found herself a friend,' he concluded with a wink, pointing in the direction of Cigarette.

Shocket The Bloodsucker was sitting, half asleep, in a spidery-legged little chair. Nearby, Cigarette and Titch Whitbread were gazing into each other's eyes.

Although The Murderer had been involving himself with almost feverish gaiety in conversations to the left and the right of him, he had not let Detective Inspector Turpin slip out of his range of vision. He was a punctilious man. He liked everything in his life to be carefully timed. He agreed with the preacher – to everything there was a season and a time for every purpose under heaven. There was a time to save, and a time to cast away. He was on the lookout for an effective moment. Detective Inspector Turpin was now making distant yet friendly conversation with Cigarette and Muriel. Asta Thundersley was pressing a drink into his hand, and Turpin was refusing. The Murderer watched the detective inspector's face. He saw the twinkle of the watchful eyes and the little, quick smile of the pallid, disciplined lips. Turpin was refusing. Asta was insisting. Then, with a brusque gesture, Turpin surrendered. He took the glass. This pleased Asta Thundersley, who drank his health. Turpin raised his glass to his lips, tilted his head backwards and made his Adam's apple move up and down. One would have sworn that he was drinking, but The Murderer could see that the level of the orange-coloured liquid in the glass had not sunk. Asta had taken a great gulp; Muriel and Cigarette had emptied their glasses. But Turpin was keeping his wits about him, and that was exactly what The Murderer wanted.

He rose. There was a queer sensation, reminiscent of warm cotton wool, under the soles of his feet, and his head felt like a gum into which a dentist, before a difficult drilling, has injected an anaesthetic. He pinched himself under the left eye. His thumb and forefinger might have come together a yard away; he felt nothing, only well-being.

This was going to be good. This was going to be sensational. Given the right moment – one of those little chasms of silence that inevitably crack open any uproar – he would tell the world in general, and Detective Inspector Turpin in particular, the whole truth of the matter.

Muriel was saying: 'Oh, Mr Turpin! Cigarette just told me you're a detective. Are there any women detectives?'

Turpin said: 'I suppose so', and looked at his watch.

'How do you get that sort of job, Mr Turpin?' asked Muriel. 'I think I'd be good at that sort of job – don't you, darling?' she said to The Murderer, who had come, swaying, to join them.

'I should make enquiries if I were you,' said Turpin.

At this The Murderer, taken by a fit of laughter in the middle of a gulp of drink, was seized with a fit of coughing. It was merely a matter of a mouthful going the wrong way, yet it sounded so awful that two or three people came to bang him on the back, and for two or three seconds conversation stopped while everyone looked towards him.

He looked around and saw himself as the centre of a little crowd. Thea Olivia was offering him a tumblerful of soda water, and this, somehow, was irresistibly funny. In five seconds this dear little old lady, smelling of lavender and dressed in lavender, would recoil from him as from a decaying corpse in a cellar… in a cellar soiled with coal dust under the basement of a condemned house… a condemned house in a fog…

Now was the time to say it. Now was the time to say: 'Look here, Detective Inspector Turpin, has it never occurred to you that I – who don't eat sweets – went to Geogharty's sweetshop three days before the murder and bought three Pierrot Gourmand lollipops? Has it ever occurred to you, copper, to wonder exactly why I bought those? Did it ever occur to you, my good fool, to wonder why there was one of these in Sonia Sabbatani's pocket? Do you realise that the other two of the three I bought are in my room? Are you aware, Turpin, that I am offering you a rope with which to hang me? Let us make this perfectly clear – I killed Sonia Sabbatani.'

He drew a deep breath, moistened his lips and began: 'Listen to me just for a moment! I want to tell you something.'

'Well?' said Turpin.

'I want you all to listen,' said The Murderer. 'I have something important – most important–'

Then there was a disturbance.

Shocket The Bloodsucker and Mr Schiff came to blows. They had been discussing the relative merits of the Austrians and the English.

Schiff had said: 'The Austrians have, if you will allow me to say so, vivacity.'

'Listen, I agree with you – or may I be struck down dead this minute,' said Shocket.

'Yet the English have a certain something – a confidence, a solidness.'

'I should live so sure, you've hit the nail on the head.'

'Yet, allow me to say so, your Viennese has more life in him than your Londoner.'

'More life? You should live so sure! What's the matter with England?'

'I swear to you, most solemnly, that I was saying not a word against England. Your Englishman, indeed, is a better man than your Viennese.'

'You should live so sure! What's the matter with the Viennese? My father, God rest his soul, came from Vienna. What's the matter with that?'

'I beg you to be reasonable.'

'He begs me to be reasonable,' said Shocket, looking at the ceiling with one anguished eye and keeping the other on Schiff. 'That's as much as to say that I'm unreasonable.' Then Shocket struck Schiff on the shoulder, and Schiff pushed Shocket away.

Titch Whitbread bounded forward and separated them, saying: 'Break it up, break it up, Bloodsucker. Ladies present! Break it up.'

Then Asta, throwing an arm about Titch's shoulders and calling him a good boy, told Shocket to behave himself. Everybody laughed. The silence was broken.

Looking again at his watch, Turpin said: 'Well, it's been a very pleasant evening, but –'

'Please don't go yet. There's something very important I want to say to you,' said The Murderer. Turpin looked at him. He saw a man of indeterminate age and colour, whose average body was wrapped in the kind of clothes to which no witness could satisfactorily swear in a court of law. The man was a little drunk, somewhat exalted. His face had gone loose.

'Well, go ahead then,' said Turpin.

37

There was a pause.

'It's only ten o'clock. You can't possibly go yet,' said Asta.

'I'm a married man,' said Turpin. 'My good lady'll be waiting with a rolling-pin.'

In the six or seven seconds that passed while they exchanged these few words, The Murderer had more visions. He had drawn a deep breath and looked down at his hands, gathering himself. Now the world was to know that these soft-looking, ill-shaped hands were weapons of atrocious murder. He winked back at an asterisk of reflected electric light on his right thumbnail, and this fascinated him. It appeared to throb like a heart, spin like a Catherine wheel and finally throw out a great cone of blue-white light like a cinema projector. On a shaky screen between his eyes and the back of his head, then there flickered a spasmodically moving picture in mauve, grey-green and yellowish pink. A bell was tolling. He could hear it, and he knew that it was striking eight. There were grey-green tears upon the yellowish-pink cheeks of the priest. But he was smiling. A mauve and yellowish-pink jailer shook his head in grudging admiration... There was the grey-green prison yard... He felt wood under his feet. Something soft was slipped over his head. Everything became grey-mauve. A slippery roughness touched his neck. *I won't hurt you*, said a businesslike voice – and then the world fell away from beneath him, and there was a stab of light and an abominable jolt.

The Murderer hiccupped.

'Go on, go ahead,' said Detective Inspector Turpin.

'My heart leaps up when I behold a rainbow in the sky,' said The Murderer.

'And how right you are,' said Turpin. 'Well, thank you very much, Miss Thundersley, for a very pleasant evening.'

'Allow me, at least, to shake you by the hand,' said The Murderer.

Turpin gripped his hand and let it fall.

'You think I'm weak in the hands, perhaps?' said The Murderer. 'Then wait a minute!'

'Strong as a lion. Give all I possess for a grip like yours,' said Turpin. 'Good-night, miss. Good-night all.'

'Ah-ah-ah! You silly man!' cried Thea Olivia, stooping to pick a burning cigarette end out of The Murderer's trouser cuff. 'Do you want to burn your nice suit?'

'Oh no, no! Dear lady! Not on your knees before me!'

She had thrown the cigarette end into an ashtray and was making a great to-do over the brushing away of the ashes. Thea Olivia used handkerchiefs of the finest cambric, so exquisite that only she could wash them. In her excitement she had whisked out one of these to dust The Murderer's trouser cuff.

'You need a nurse, you silly man,' she said.

'I am a baby,' he confessed and added, with a lowering look, 'if you prefer to think of me in that way.'

Catchy laid a hand on his arm. 'Don't you think –' she began.

'It might surprise you to know what I think,' he replied.

Thea Olivia, looking from face to face in the crowd that surrounded her, was bewildered and a little frightened.

'You know, *I* think –' she said, making a decorous little bow.

At this the groups began to disintegrate. Asta looked glum and sullen but said little. She heard Cigarette saying to Mothmar Acord: 'Do I go home with you or do you come home with me?'

Acord seemed to go into a little sleep while he made calculations.

Then he pointed a forefinger at Catchy and said: '*You* are coming home with *me*.'

Catchy nodded, and they linked arms.

'Nobody loves me,' said Cigarette, more tragically than she had wanted to sound.

'Oh, but I do,' said Wensday, stroking her neck. Then he saw that Avril, who had been watching him, was hooking her chin over the shoulder of Tobit Osbert, who was drowsily drunk. 'But I'm a respectable married man,' Wensday added, going to the side of his wife and taking her hand in a grip which was meant to appear affectionate and intended to hurt.

Hate had got into the atmosphere. Everyone wanted to go away and, in quiet quarrels, say unforgivable things to near and dear ones. Mothmar Acord gave Asta a hand like a rubber glove full of cold water. Cigarette insisted on kissing her. Mrs Scripture caught at her hand and then dropped it as if she had picked up somebody else's soiled handkerchief. Titch Whitbread, still smiling with pure delight, cautiously squeezed her fingers in his gentle, mighty hand and swore eternal friendship. Soon, everyone was gone but Schiff. He was always the first to arrive and the last to leave.

'Your friend Amy Dory,' he said in a throaty whisper. 'So another boyfriend! Also Hemmeridge; also Osbert; also Soskin; also Roget; also Milton Catt; also Strindberg; also Mothmar Acord. Ha-ha! No more Tobit Osbert, eh?'

'Oh, go away!' said Asta Thundersley.

'A good sedative, take,' said Schiff.

'Go to hell, Schiff – be a good fellow.'

'Why not? Good-night till now.'

'Good-*night*, Schiff!'

'You will be seeing me.'

He left the house. Asta kicked the sitting-room door shut and turned and looked about her. Everywhere there floated and sank dust and ashes in the dregs of sticky glasses, and the place was disgusting with stale tobacco smoke. Two cigarettes had burned themselves out on the mantelpiece. Another had been surrep-titiously extinguished upon an oval silver frame that surrounded a photograph of Thea Olivia when she was young and pretty. One of the guests had pocketed a leaf-shaped jade ashtray. The ashtray was worth less than ten shillings, yet Asta was deeply and bitterly hurt. If whoever it was had said 'I like it' she would have replied: 'Do, please, take it.' But, no. People must pilfer – guests, invited in good faith!

She was sick to death of everybody in the world; sick and tired.

Asta took hold of a blue-and-white Chinese vase and raised it high, intending to throw it with a great smash into the fireplace. Two cigarette ends and a shower of ashes came out of the neck of it and ran into her armpit. At the same time something sizzled behind the sofa. She put down the vase and looked for the source of the noise. Mr Pink was asleep on the floor.

She looked at him in a white rage, grasped the vase again and, after a little deliberation, angrily put a soft cushion under his head and, with a whispered 'damn and blast', covered him with a tiger-skin rug.

The rain was pouring down.

'God, what am I to do?' said Asta Thundersley.

But if, at that moment, the Voice Of God had answered *'What are you to do about what, my daughter?'* she would have found nothing to say in reply – only that she was unhappy because of the badness of men and women and that her heart was sore at the imperfection of this rough, unfinished world.

Thea Olivia came in elegant and decorous in a pink-flowered black dressing-gown that covered her from white throat to rose-embroidered slippers.

'*Good*-night, my dear,' she began to say but stopped with a gasp in the middle of the second word, shocked by the spectacle of big red Asta weeping as noisily as a dog drinks into a little blue handkerchief.

'Darling! What is it?'

'Leave me alone, Tot – do leave me alone. I've got the miseries.'

'Let me get you –'

'I ask you… leave me alone,' said Asta, crying like a schoolboy.

Thea Olivia went to her bedroom.

38

It was her habit punctiliously to wash her handkerchief before she went to bed and to hang it up to dry for a meticulous ironing next day or the day after. She was worried about her handkerchief. What a fool she had been to give way to impulse and use it as a duster on the turn-up of a trouser leg! Thea Olivia let warm water run into the handbasin in her bedroom and cautiously opened her handkerchief.

She was horrified and disgusted.

In the folds of the cambric was a gritty blackness.

Exploring this grit with her delicate fingertips, and smelling it with one fine nostril, she recognised it.

It was coal dust.

Such stuff was ruin to cambric, destruction to delicate fabric of any kind. What madness had taken possession of her that she had gone down with only one handkerchief – a Good Handkerchief designed for dabbing instead of a Bad Handkerchief into which one might blow?

She bathed, rather than rinsed, that handkerchief. The blackness trickled away. The cambric, held against the light, was unpunctured.

Thea Olivia was profoundly relieved. She squeezed the handkerchief very tenderly and hung it to dry on the towel rail. There were not many squares of cambric like that left in this cottony, shoddy world. Thea Olivia loved little, exquisite things, and the more fragile they were the better she loved them. It was impossible for her to go to sleep if she had not first arranged, by the side of her bed, one flower in a precious vase of Chinese porcelain which a hearty sneeze might have blown to fragments. Also, she carried with her an extra-special tea set. It was over a hundred years old. You would have been reluctant to pick up the saucer: it looked as though it might bruise like the petal of a camellia. It was possible, in the right light and at the right angle, to read a newspaper through the side of the cup. Cup, saucer, diminutive plate, tiny teapot, hot-water pot, milk jug (which you might have fitted into your left ear) and sugar basin, all stood in order upon a silver tray as thin as paper. Cities had been demolished, great grey stone cathedrals had been cracked like hazelnuts, an empire had fallen, and still Tot's little tea set remained, unchipped, uncracked, serenely preserved like her virginity. When she travelled she wrapped it in so many layers of wadding and tissue paper that – together with her little tortoiseshell tea caddy and miniature silver kettle and spirit lamp – it occupied twelve cubic feet of space.

Before she could think of composing herself for sleep, everything had to be in its right place.

Thea Olivia took off part of the crowning glory that was her hair, shook it out, brushed it and put it carefully aside. A patterned vase on the mantelpiece offended her – it had been turned so that the visible part of the pattern did not match that of the vase on the other side. She readjusted this. A little rug was disarranged. She rearranged it. She did not touch the window, because she was convinced that she would find dust on the frame. The fire, she reassured herself, had settled down to a respectable dying glow, and the room was comfortably warm. Thea Olivia looked once more towards the jewellery she had taken off before she washed her handkerchief. She never moved a mile without a quaint little pale porcelain hand, mounted in a whimsical porcelain saucer: on the fingers of this little hand she always hung her rings, arranging her bracelets and brooches below.

She felt the bed. It was dry and warm. A pillow was patted down, another pillow was shaken up, and everything was ready, except the night-light – a squat cylinder of wax in a rose-coloured saucer of water. She lit this with a very small match out of a tiny box tucked into a silver container, assured herself that it was burning, then turned out the main light, took off her clothes, put on a pale-blue nightdress and went to bed, settling down with a sigh of pleasure.

Thea Olivia always said her prayers when she was comfortably arranged in her deep, warm bed. She did not like kneeling; it hurt her knees and distracted her. It was her contention that a prayer is more effective, goes quicker to God, if one can put one's whole heart and soul into it. It was necessary to detach the mind from the body – and how could you do that if your knees ached? No, better to be comfortable, discard the body in a good feather bed, and then give all of your untroubled mind to asking the Lord to preserve you from the perils and the dangers of the coming night, throwing in a good word for your relatives and friends.

Thea Olivia was not displeased with her evening. She had met all sorts of new people who would provide her with much to dream about. Yet she was not entirely happy.

There was something wrong with Asta, poor Asta, dear Asta – sweet silly Asta who took upon her big shoulders all the troubles of the world. She felt tenderly towards Asta and was grieved at having seen her broken down and wretched. And because of what? This murder of the little girl with the Russian or Italian name. How like Asta that was! As long as Thea Olivia could remember, Asta had always made a fool of herself, involving herself in affairs that were none of her business. Nice, foolish Asta had wasted her strength, her time and her money on things that were the business of the Approved Societies, the National Institutions and even the Police; and there Asta was, crying downstairs in a smoky sitting-room between two vases of dying chrysanthemums into which ill-bred men and not unquestionable women had surreptitiously popped cigarette ends. Dear Asta, good kind Asta – Asta was always on the go. Always sure of herself, always shouting at the top of her voice, making herself conspicuous, and in the end discrediting herself. Who but Asta would be so hot-headed, so crazily ambitious, as to butt her way into a murder case? Who but Asta would have been out, plodding about in dirty cellars when she might have been at home by a good clear fire reading an interesting or even an instructive book? Who but big-hearted, foolish Asta would take somebody else's business so terribly to heart that she could weep noisily and without restraint into a sixpenny handkerchief – and a bright-blue handkerchief at that?

How different we are, thought Thea Olivia drowsily. We might almost be strangers. We are as different as kitten and bulldog. Poor Asta. Wild horses couldn't drag her to Hartnell for something fit to wear. Poor Asta. I can picture her rushing into Barkers like a whirlwind: 'Give me a suit, quick! …What suit? Any suit! None of your frills and fal-lals, girl! Just a suit. Something durable. There, that'll do, that hairy check tweed thing over there. Take it off the hook. Wrap it up. Quick, where's the shoe department? … Hey, you! Give me a good solid pair of brogues, size 7½ – get a move on! Very wide-fitting – plenty of room in them – good heavy soles –'

Then, in the middle of a little affectionate laugh, Thea Olivia thought of something so horrible that she cried aloud and sat bolt upright with one fluttering hand over her fluttering heart.

She remembered Asta's shoes that afternoon when she had come in, sick and angry at the atrocity in the coal-cellar.

She remembered the gritty, black grains she had washed out of the cambric handkerchief that was drying on the towel rail. She felt as if a cold, clammy hand had suddenly clutched at the base of her spine. It occurred to Thea Olivia that she, with her cambric handkerchief, had dusted away damning evidence from the trousers of a rapist and a child-murderer.

She got out of bed, pushed her slender little feet into her pretty slippers and put on her dressing-gown. Her impulse was to run downstairs to Asta and tell her everything. That man, that man in the grey suit – she had forgotten his name – it would come back – that well-spoken, rather dreamy man – he ought to be questioned. The cuff of his trouser leg was full of coal dust. The police ought to be informed! There was no time to waste!

She switched on the light and paused while she looked in the mirror and patted her hair and arranged her dressing-gown so that it covered her throat. She was tremulous and very pale: she hated the idea of being seen in that state, so she gave herself a minute or two in which to compose herself.

She soon became calm, and then she began to wonder…

39

Downstairs in the stale-smelling sitting-room, Asta Thundersley, hot-eyed and melancholy, wrestled with shadows.

She felt now that if a bit of grit flew into her eye she would have to argue with herself before she found it worthwhile to blink. She felt that if she sat on a pin she would not start up but shrug her shoulders; that if her worst enemy spat in her face she would quietly beg him for the loan of his handkerchief. She was in the no-man's-land between light and dark. She felt like a long-forsaken house in late autumn, under a grey sky with a wet wind blowing while the night comes down and somewhere a broken gate lugubriously flaps. To her the lamp was only something that uncovered an emptiness. One last tarry bit of coal caught fire and shot out a spearhead of flame; and this, to Asta, was only another sharp white tooth in the closing jaws of the cold outer Dark. She was, she thought, a coffin in which there softly rattled the colourless dust that had been Asta Thundersley. She felt like the cooling cinders of a fire that is going out; like a hilt without a sword, a cracked pot, a gouged eye, a relic. There was no more life in her than there is poetry in an inkpot.

Once again she was revealed to herself as a crazy, helpless woman at whom Satan laughed; a stumpy maypole set up for the diversion of all the dancing devils of hell.

Midnight struck.

Asta dozed, and in a second of sleep, between two nods, she had a vivid dream of something she had seen many years before at the end of a happy birthday, when the world was as fresh as an apple. Her father had taken her to a music hall, and there was a juggler who filled Asta's soul with wonder and delight. Standing in a beam of light, twinkling like a skyful of stars in his spangled tights, the juggler did new and marvellous things. Last and best of all, turning off the applause with a twist of one supple hand, he took a piece of fine tissue-paper and balanced it on the end of his nose. The paper wanted to fly away on every current of air in the darkened, draughty theatre, but the juggler made it stand. He remained, a strong man straining all his muscles to balance this flimsy bit of paper, for about ten seconds. Then he struck a match and set fire to the upper end of the balanced tissue-paper. It burned down until the flame touched his nose and went out. The ash remained, miraculously balanced, for another ten seconds. Then the juggler jerked his head and the ash, floating down, disintegrated in the sizzling spotlight.

You know how, in a dream, you touch new heights and become aware of unexpected profundities in the most trivial of memories. You dream that you are untying a shoelace, and with the pleasant little jolt of the undone knot there comes into your mind a certain sensation of lightness and of power, as if you had done something great and wonderful. Or you may be dreaming that you are rocking on your heels on a window-ledge fifty storeys above a misty pavement; and you know that you cannot keep your balance, and are afraid. Sometimes, by God's grace, you have time to get an aide-de-camp to the vedettes of a reserve of courage that waits – that is always waiting for a signal – on one of your flanks at the edge of the nightmare. Courage charges in, like the Greys and the Gordons in the old battle print; you are rallied; you hurl yourself right into the darkest, dirtiest part of the dream and cut your way through.

Instead of falling you are flying.

The memory of that bit of burnt paper, coming back into Asta's mind in that brief dream, made her laugh. She did not laugh as one laughs heartily at a good joke. She did not laugh at the end of her teeth in anger or in scorn. She laughed, in her little sleep, as a child laughs when you show it the solution to an exceptionally mystifying yet simple trick.

The sound of this laugh awoke her. She felt a great deal better. Mrs Kipling, who had an eye on the heeltaps in the bottles and the dregs of the glasses, was loitering about the place with a hypocritical air of anxiety to be of service to her mistress.

'Kipling, put out all the lights and go to bed,' said Asta, going upstairs.

After two or three great clumping strides she remembered that her sister Tot had gone to bed and was probably asleep, so she took off her shoes, went on her way cautiously and at last got to bed with as little noise as she was capable of making.

Then Mrs Kipling and The Tiger Fitzpatrick slunk out to talk of old times over what the guests had left of the liquor.

40

Asta was awake, as usual, by seven o'clock in the morning, but she made less noise than usual while she dressed. She was almost tone deaf, yet she sang Russian drinking songs in her bath when she was alone in the house. But she would not for any consideration disturb the dangerous old lady whom she described as her 'little sister'. After a silent, unsatisfactory bath, she got into her loose tweed suit, knotted about her bullock throat a yellow-dotted tie and went (quietly for her) down to breakfast.

She was astonished to find Thea Olivia downstairs before her, dressed in a becoming garment of pink and grey and seated in a Queen Anne chair with a high back. Mrs Kipling was dancing attendance, as she always did when Thea Olivia paid a visit.

'What are you doing up so early, Tot?' said Asta.

'Good morning, Asta dear.'

'Good morning. What are you doing up so early? What's the matter with you? Couldn't you sleep? Since when did you get out of bed before nine o'clock?'

Thea Olivia said: 'Dear Asta!'

'Look at her! Bags under her eyes!' said Asta. 'What happened? I know. That idiot Kipling. If I've told her once I've told her a thousand times to give you a hot-water bottle. Two bottles. I didn't have time to see to it myself. I know, I know you, I know you to the heart and soul, Tot – you'd suffer on the rack rather than complain, but I know. Kipling!'

'No, please. Everything was just as it should be, Asta dear, I assure you.'

'What are you so angry about? I was only asking. I've never known you to be visible before nine or ten o'clock before.'

'I think your party excited me.'

'All the better. You need exciting, Tot. You know,' said Asta, half defiantly, 'you know I live my own kind of life here. Breakfast is breakfast. What are you going to have? Kidneys? Bacon? Eggs? Kippers? Finnan haddie? Say the word. Have an egg and haddock.'

Thea Olivia, to Asta's astonishment, said: 'I only want a cup of tea.'

For the first time in living memory Asta Thundersley was quiet at the breakfast table. She was marvelling at her sister's presence; and her sister was amazed at her silence.

They looked at each other. There was suspicion on both sides. Asta was full of a desire to slap her sister on the back, take hold of her with her enormous red hands, pick her up and swing her round and whirl her off her feet. Asta wanted to make conversation, to talk about people.

'What did you think of the party?' she asked. 'It struck me as being a complete failure. Didn't it you?'

'Do you mean as a party?'

'Yes, Tot darling, as a party. As anything. A failure. Socially or otherwise – not a success. How did it strike you? Be honest. D'you know what? Before I went to bed I found Pink asleep on the floor – fast asleep on the floor. I've often wondered whether that man was one of God's holy innocents or just another common drunk. What's your impression, Tot darling?'

'Mr Pink. That's the little gentleman who keeps talking about God, isn't it? Well, I don't think he's just a common drunk. I think he's a good sort of man, don't you?'

'Look here, Tot, I insist on your having at least an egg. Come now, a lightly boiled egg in a cup. Then you can put little bits of bread into it like you used to.'

'I couldn't face an egg,' said Thea Olivia almost in agony. 'I only want… I'll have some toast, some toast and some marmalade; some of that dark-brown marmalade. On the whole, Asta, I think it was a very good party.'

'You seemed to make quite a hit.'

'No, you don't really mean that? I didn't do a thing. I just kept still. Who were all those young men that kept talking to me?'

'Why, Tot darling, everybody was talking to you all the time. Which young men do you mean? There was young Hemmeridge, and there was Mothmar Acord. There was –'

'That young man in the grey suit.'

'Oh, you mean Tobit Osbert.'

'The one that got so drunk.'

'They were all drunk, Tot my sweet. And lots of them were wearing grey suits. You mean Tobit Osbert, do you? Why, I do believe you've fallen in love with him. Now what on earth for? You're old enough to be his mother.'

'Oh dear Asta, my dear Asta – can't I just make ordinary conversation without your assuming all kinds of things? Tobit Osbert, that's the man. He promised to get in touch with me about… a book I wanted to borrow. There's a book he has, and he said he'd lend it to me.'

'What sort of book?'

'A book about the Crusaders.'

'I've got his address somewhere in my little black book,' said Asta, referring to her address book. 'I'll get it for you later. Or do you want it now?'

'Oh no, not now. Any time will do.'

After breakfast Asta remembered that she had an appointment with a certain Mr Partridge, who was telling her something about a scandal concerning the adoption of illegitimate children. She went out at nine o'clock. As soon as the door had slammed behind Asta, and the sound of her big, heavy heeled feet had ceased to ring and snap between the front door and the end of the street, Thea Olivia went to the long, old-fashioned, untidy walnut desk in the room described as 'the study' and looked for a black book. She found several. One of them was like a digest of *Who's Who*; another resembled the notebook of somebody who has had to study *Whitaker's Almanack*. A third contained some queer record of letters that had been sent to a secretary of state. The fourth was full of addresses and telephone numbers. The numbers were written down, together with the exchanges, tolerably clearly. But the names were represented generally by initial letters, so that Thea Olivia had to apologise to Theodore Oxford, Ted Oliver, Timothy Ogden, Timothy O'Brien and Tudor Owen before she got an 'I'll see if he's in' from a woman who sounded like a landlady. Then she heard feet coming down creaking stairs, and her heart thumped as a gentle little voice said: 'Tobit Osbert speaking. Who is that, please?'

'This is Miss Thea Olivia Thundersley. I hope you will excuse me for disturbing you so early, but I wanted – if it's perfectly convenient – to have a word with you. It's rather urgent. I'd be so glad if we could meet fairly soon. Can we?'

'Why, whenever you like, of course. Where shall we meet? At the – I was going to say at the Savoy, but it's always so full of a certain sort of... you know what I mean? Shall I come along to your place?'

'No, I think it might be better if I came to yours. May I?'

'Why, yes, of course it would. Only I feel I ought to warn you. I live in a bed-sitting-room. It isn't much of a place.'

'Can I come along now?'

'By all means, if you like. But I ought to tell you that I have an appointment in about three-quarters of an hour from now – if that's all right.'

'I'm coming now.'

'Righty-ho.'

41

Osbert lived in a square not far from Mornington Crescent. His landlady was a thin, scowling woman with ferocious eyebrows and terrified eyes. She told Thea Olivia where to go, and so she found herself in a bed-sitting-room – remarkably neat considering that it was occupied by a man – overlooking a sodden and neglected garden, behind which was visible part of a zinc roof, sooty, striated with rain.

She said: 'Mr Osbert. Last night I washed my hankie.'

She paused, gulping back her heart, which had crept up into the back of her throat.

'Could I offer you a cup of tea?'

'No, I don't want a cup of tea. I mean, thank you so much. But I really couldn't. I've already had... Mr Osbert. I don't know if you remember last night. We were all very happy and merry and bright together, and... I don't know if you remember... You dropped a lighted cigarette. Do you remember? Do tell me, do you remember?'

Osbert looked at her steadily for a moment and then said: 'Why no, I can't say that I do.'

'Mr Osbert,' said Thea Olivia, breathing with a hissing noise, 'you were on the point of saying something – I don't know what – and then you let your cigarette fall, and it fell into the turned-up part of your trousers, and I took it out and brushed the place where it had fallen. Or don't you remember that?'

'My dear good lady, how could I possibly remember? The drinks Asta gave us last night were so tremendous – how could anyone remember anything?'

'I was saying, I took the cigarette end out of your trousers and wiped the ash and all that away with my handkerchief.'

'Are you quite sure I can't get you a cup of tea? Or else there's some milk...'

Almost suffocated with emotion Thea Olivia went on: 'I was going to tell you about my hankie. I have – at least I used to have – three or four dozen cambric handkerchiefs, very old ones; very fine ones. And you know – at least any woman knows – you know you use them only for dabbing, just once. I suppose you know?'

'Of course I know.'

'I used one of my handkerchiefs on the turn-up of your trousers last night. I'm in the habit of rinsing my cambric handkerchiefs every night before I go to bed. I did so last night. And what do you think I found in it?'

'Should I know?'

'Coal dust.'

She watched Tobit Osbert's face, but he only smiled and said: 'And so?'

Thea Olivia paused again, not knowing what to say, and felt a sense of impending defeat: 'You didn't talk like that last night,' she said.

'Didn't I?'

'I want you to tell me where you got that coal dust.'

'Why?'

'I suppose you know that the poor little girl everybody's so sorry for was killed in a place where there was coal dust?'

'Was she?'

'Yes, she was. I know somebody who was there.'

'Perhaps your somebody did it.'

Thea Olivia looked from the gas fire to the table covered with papers, and thence to the face – the calm, confident, firm yet dreamy face of Tobit Osbert, and she felt that nothing she could say might ever make a point.

'Do please let me offer you just one little cup of tea,' said Osbert.

Feeling that she needed to play for time, Thea Olivia said: 'Thank you very much. I think I'd like a cup of tea.'

The gas ring gasped and roared as the little tin kettle clanked down. Looking at his expressionless, fixed face, she detected the beginning of a sidelong look and a suppressed smile.

'Or perhaps you'd rather come out with me to some place or other, Miss Thundersley?'

'No, thank you very much. I'd rather... chat with you here, if I may, Mr Osbert.'

His smile stopped trying to suppress itself and spread. The corners of his eyes wrinkled. Last night he had appeared to be a gentle, amiable young man; even a desirable young man. But now he appeared to Thea Olivia as sly, mocking and indefinably repulsive. He reminded her of a painting she had seen in an exhibition: it depicted a man in a black suit and, from a distance of about three yards, looked almost like a tinted photograph. The man in the picture was, at this distance, altogether nondescript. He was standing in a self-conscious attitude against a vaguely familiar background of trees and fields, such as photographers used to hang in their studios; and one of his hands was awkwardly poised on the tip of a sawn-off tree trunk flagrantly made of papier mâché, while the other held a bowler hat. But when Thea Olivia took two little ladylike steps forward, this seemingly inoffensive picture became so horrible that she actually let out a little genteel shriek. In the folds of the respectable jacket, waistcoat and trousers, there were things that should have been elsewhere – small pale worms, which had passed at first as highlights upon a shabby but presentable surface. The five teeth exposed by the prim smile were toenails. Queer little things with wicked black eyes were coming out of his scalp and peeping through the parting in his hair; one of the buttons of his shirt was a gorged and bloated bug; and in place of eyes he had purplish-blue, bruise-coloured fingerprints. She had been told that this was Super Realism and that it represented a Suburb. She was astonished, later, to hear that an American had bought this picture for a large sum of money: it would have given her nightmares – and did, for several nights, until she got it out of her mind.

Tobit Osbert, on close inspection – now that her suspicions were aroused – was like that picture. He appeared to Thea Olivia as sick, a product of corruption. She thought that his eyes were twisted so that they made her look in two directions at once: they were eyes into which she found it impossible to look while she talked to him, and she hated that. Also, she saw, or thought that she saw, a certain loathsome wetness in his smile, and the smile itself was creepy, mean and cunning, yet at the same time odiously confident and detestably familiar. Somewhere she had seen it all before.

Today Mr Osbert was working. He was wearing a pair of seedy flannel trousers, slippers and a short-sleeved shirt, which left uncovered his white, wiry arms. He begged pardon for this and, while the gas roared under the kettle, put on an exhausted old blue blazer, upon the breast pocket of which a shield-shaped patch of darker blue marked the place where a badge had once been sewn. She could not stop looking at his hands. They were, of course, hands like any other hands, only something behind them had made them kill, and take pleasure in killing, the child named Sonia Sabbatani.

He said: 'My dear Miss Thundersley, I wonder what in the world makes you think I have anything to do with that horrible business!'

'I didn't say you had, Mr Osbert. I only said that after I had dusted the turned-up parts of your... your trousers,' said Thea Olivia, blushing, 'I found some coal dust. And I wanted to ask you where you had got it.'

'And what if I tell you that I might have got it putting coal on the fire?' said Tobit Osbert playfully.

'What fire? You have a gas fire,' said Thea Olivia, who felt her heart bouncing like a punchball in an echoing gymnasium.

'Why, of course I have a gas fire, Miss Thundersley. Who said I hadn't? But I'm only at home to work and sleep. I pay lots of visits. Lots of my friends have coal fires, and I often build them up. Actually I'm a homely sort of man, Miss Thundersley. I like making myself useful about the place. Do you know what? I can even cook. Only the other day I cooked dinner at a friend's house. And there, by the by, I had to put coal in the kitchen stove. Now you mention it, there you are. Coal. Goodness knows why you drag me into this business, Miss Thundersley. Ah-ah! Kettle's boiling! Do you like it strong or weak?'

'Anything at all, thank you. It doesn't matter a bit.'

'Milk of course?'

'Well, thank you, yes... No, thank you very much, no sugar.'

'I hope this is drinkable. But I beg your pardon. You were saying, Miss Thundersley?'

Thea Olivia no longer knew exactly what she had been saying. The virtue had gone out of her. Still, like an exhausted captain in a retreat, she rallied one last staggering platoon of words and said: 'Quite simply... There was, as I was saying, coal dust. To put it plainly, there was coal dust. Coal dust which you can account for, of course, but all the same... coal dust. I believe... I mean, I have been told, I have seen it on the pictures, it is common knowledge, that the police can find out all kinds of things from dust. I mean, there are all sorts of coal. I mean, nowadays, with microscopes and all that sort of thing, they can identify... well, they can identify practically anything they like. They can look through a microscope and tell you, let us say, where such and such a kind of wool came from – just looking at dust – or whether this, that or the other sort of dust came from this or that street... I don't think I'm making myself quite clear, but perhaps you understand what I mean, Mr Osbert?'

'Oh, perfectly, my dear Miss Thundersley. Is your tea all right?'

'Thank you, yes. Yes, thank you very much. What was I saying? Now you've put me off. No, no, I've got it.' Thea Olivia Thundersley made her last desperate charge. She said: 'All that coal dust in your... your trousers. You say you must have got it in one of your friends' houses, perhaps cooking dinners or something. If you say so, I must believe you. I have no reason to disbelieve you, Mr Osbert. Why should you tell me stories? I believe that what you say is true.'

'But I haven't said anything, Miss Thundersley.'

'I believe that what you say is true, Mr Osbert. But to set my mind at rest... I will gladly defray any incidental expenses, if I may say so without giving you offence... Would you, for instance, allow those garments to be examined under microscopes et cetera by, for example, Scotland Yard?'

'I do hope that tea's all right. I'm not much of a hand at tea. I'm no good at this sort of thing. Do excuse me.'

'I thought you said you cooked your friends' dinners.'

'Oh, but I do! I do indeed, Miss Thundersley, but as you no doubt know – anyone can cook a dinner, whereas there is an art in making a good cup of tea.'

'No, but would you?'

'I beg your pardon, would I what?'

'I'm sure you can't have forgotten what I was saying,' said Thea Olivia, almost in tears. 'I was asking you, and I believe that you remember as well as I do, I was asking you whether you would let the Scotland Yard people examine your trousers.'

Tobit Osbert nodded and, making a little astonished gesture, said: 'Why, of course!'

Struggling with her instinctive reticence and hacking it away tentacle by tentacle, Thea Olivia managed to say: 'I understand (you understand, Mr Osbert), I understand that I have no legal right to speak to you like this. In fact, no right at all. As a matter of fact, I believe, in point of fact, that I am wasting your time and mine – not that my time is of any value to me, but I'm sure your time is very valuable to you. What I mean to say is, if I may be allowed to say so without offence – I'd gladly recompense you (because I know that you are a literary gentleman and might have been earning the Lord knows how many pounds while I've been taking up your time) – glad, I mean, to, to, to…'

She wanted to say that she would pay twenty pounds to Tobit Osbert if he would let the police put a microscope on his trousers, but she could not say it.

He, however, guessed it and said: 'I do wish I had some biscuits to offer you. Or could you eat a little bread and butter? I can cut it quite thin… No? Well, you know best, Miss Thundersley. Do forgive me. I'm afraid I sidetracked you. I may be wrong, but I somehow seemed to gather that you wanted to have my clothes examined by – it seems funny – the police?'

'Yes,' said Thea Olivia, and now she could get it out. 'That's right. And I'd gladly recompense you for any trouble –'

'I'd be only too happy,' said Tobit Osbert.

In a flat, disillusioned tone, Thea Olivia said: 'I'm very glad to hear it.' It occurred to her that she was making as big a fool of herself as her sister Asta.

'I should be only too delighted,' said Osbert, 'only…'

'Only what?' asked Thea Olivia, almost hopefully.

'It would give me all the pleasure in the world, my dear Miss Thundersley,' said Osbert with a theatrical sort of deliberation, 'but I sent that suit to be dry-cleaned and pressed this morning. You don't know what pleasure it would have given me to be able to do what you asked of me, but there it is. I can't.'

'It may not be too late,' said Thea Olivia. 'You can't have sent it off very long ago. You can call it back, surely?'

There was a silence. Then Osbert said: 'You're not drinking

your tea. I'm afraid it isn't much good. Shall I make you a fresh cup? If only you'd tell me just how you like it…'

'I know I'm a silly old woman – very silly and very old – but won't you get that suit back, Mr Osbert? I know I've wasted most of your valuable morning. Don't be offended – you are a professional man – let me pay you, say, twenty-five guineas for wasting your morning if you get that suit back. Say I'm a little bit crazy like my sis – I mean, humour me in this, it is merely a fancy. Will you do it for me?'

Tobit Osbert looked at her steadily. His face had been politely serious. Now it changed. One tiny smile altered it as an impalpable corrugation changes a reflection in a mirror.

'No,' he said.

'No?'

With severity in his voice and derision at the corner of his mouth, Tobit Osbert said: 'My dear madam, I'm afraid you don't quite realise that you are talking to a gentleman. We had a delightful evening last night, and I'll always remember it. But I don't think you can be quite yourself this morning. Do you realise that you have come into my room, more or less accused me of a very horrible murder and actually offered me money to demonstrate to you whether or no I have committed it? Do you seriously, I ask you in all seriousness, do you seriously, my dear madam, expect me to accept money in such circumstances? For what do you take me? I don't think I understand you.'

Thea Olivia looked at the shabby rug and the downtrodden linoleum; raised her eyes to the flaky ceiling and at last looked into the eyes of Tobit Osbert, and she saw that he was laughing at her.

She rose.

'I do beg your pardon. That tea couldn't have been any good,' he said.

'One last thing, Mr Osbert. Will you tell me to whom you sent your suit to be cleaned and pressed?'

'Since you put it that way, madam, no, I won't.'

'Then I can only say good day.'

'I'm sorry you have to go so soon.'

Thea Olivia went back to Asta's house, full of frustration.

42

The Murderer sat down to write. He had sent his suit to be cleaned by Sam Sabbatani, who gave his dyeing and cleaning to the great Goldberg Dye Works, which takes in half the dirty clothes in London every morning at nine o'clock. The firm of Goldberg makes a speciality of what they call 'mourning orders' and will dye anything funereally black within twenty-four hours.

Tobit Osbert found a certain refined pleasure in the contemplation of the fact that Sam Sabbatani, still red-eyed and thunderstruck with grief, was washing away evidence which might possibly have convicted the murderer of his daughter for three-and-sixpence – on the slate, at that.

Tobit Osbert checked himself on the edge of one of his day-dreams. No, there must be no daydreaming now, discipline above all things, self-control. He had an article to write for *The Theoretician,* which would be paid for on delivery. He needed the six guineas, and, as it happened, he really wanted to write the article, which was a critical one on the subject of books for the young. In this, too, there was to be found a certain refined pleasure, a titillation, an indefinable thrill, half intellectual and half voluptuous. So he saved his little daydream for later and settled down to a survey of the works of Beatrix Potter. In a little while he would make a name for himself. Meanwhile there was enough to do to keep him occupied for three or four days – which was just as well, since his only presentable suit was at the cleaners. But by next week he would be able to buy himself a new suit. There was a tailor near Cambridge Circus who produced an excellent suit for five pounds. Tobit Osbert had his eye on a piece of gentlemanly drab cloth with the faintest, discreetest block check, which he planned to have made up – single-breasted, perhaps, with two intriguing little slits in the tail of the jacket. Dare he have very narrow trousers without turn-ups? That might convey an impression of elegant nonchalance. In such a get-up one might lounge about with a gay little scarf around the neck and introduce oneself to anybody, with a free-and-easy sportsmanlike looseness in one's manner of approach.

But enough! Discipline! No daydreams! To work!

All the same, he thought as he dipped his pen into the inkpot, the world is full of pleasures for a man who knows how to appreciate things. He would have gone to Sam Sabbatani for his new suit, but the fact of the matter was that he owed Sam a little money and was going to owe him three-and-sixpence more in forty-eight hours.

And in this, too, there was refined pleasure.

43

Angry with herself and with all the world, Thea Olivia went back to Asta's house in Frame Place by the river. She wanted to smash things and to kick people, herself first of all. She was a fool like her sister, she decided. She, Thea Olivia, the only sane girl in the family, had involved herself in something that was none of her business. She walked part of the way because she wanted to get the smell of Osbert's room out of her nostrils. It was not that the room had a characteristic odour – far from it – but the air of the place, sucked dry by the gas fire, seemed to have got into the back of her nose, so that she was glad to draw deep breaths of the wet and smoky air of the streets. She had no doubt that Osbert had committed that murder. For one mad minute she toyed with the idea of going to the police and telling them what she knew. But then she asked herself: 'What do I know?'

Everything; she knew everything, but she could prove nothing. Thea Olivia had read many crime stories – she had little to do but read – she realised that there was nothing to say and shuddered at the thought of an interrogation in a cold green-painted waiting-room. She could not even mention the affair to Asta. Asta would fly into a fury and rush everywhere in all directions at once, shouting at the top of her voice, raising scandal and making the most appalling scenes. If one gave Asta the merest sniff of suspicion she (so to speak) threw up her trunk and stuck out her ears and charged, screaming, like an elephant. It did not matter to Asta if she was proved to be wrong: she never admitted it and, even if forced to an admission, did not care. As a matter of fact Asta loved a commotion for its own sake.

But the end of it would be that Thea Olivia would be dragged into this filthy affair; jostled into the witness-box, hauled into the Old Bailey and made to stand up to be cross-examined by some such deadly counsel as Norman Birkett. And for what? A false alarm. It was not for nothing that she read the writings of the best-informed authors of detective stories.

Now, if she went and told Asta, the whole world would be turned upside down before lunchtime. Apart from everything else, who knew what Scotland Yard had up its sleeve?

She was surprised to see that she had reached the Embankment. The grubby grey river slid away to the sea. She saw, through the heavy wet air that hung like damp gauze, the spidery outlines of a gasworks and of two enormous cranes on the other side. Several seagulls, driven inland by the bad weather, were wheeling, screeching, over the dirty water. Thea Olivia decided, suddenly, that she wanted to go away. She wanted to visit Cousin Oxford Thundersley in Hampshire. She wanted to make friends with her grand-niece Olivia, who had been named after her because somebody had an eye on her money, and invite the girl to come with her on a long holiday, preferably to the south of France.

Thea Olivia hurried back to Asta's house and found that her sister had gone out. She asked Mrs Kipling to help her with her packing; gave The Tiger Fitzpatrick a pound note and told him to bring her luggage downstairs.

Then she picked up the cambric handkerchief, carried it at arm's length to the fireplace and dropped it into the fire. It was still damp so it hissed like a snake, then writhed, shrivelled, caught fire, and in a second or two burned away to a flake of ash, which the draft whisked up the chimney and out into the heavy, threatening air of the sad, dripping city.

Then she sat at one of the little tables and wrote a note. In this note she said that she did not feel very well, because the unexpectedly damp weather was bringing on an attack of bronchitis, and so she was going away. No doubt it seemed strange to leave so abruptly, but Asta would, she was sure, understand and sympathise. She was leaving because she did not want to impose herself on Asta as a sick woman – Asta had so many demands on her already. With a couple of blessings and many expressions of affection Thea Olivia signed her name with a couple of Xs for kisses, put the note in an envelope and, in a taxi loaded with luggage, went off to Waterloo Station.

Asta came home at about four o'clock, read her sister's note and fell into what was, for her, a state of abstraction – she kicked a little table across the room, poked the fire until a great lump of blazing coal fell out, which she picked up with a pair of tongs that were too short, so that she burned her fingers and threw the tongs across the room. She felt uneasy. She was convinced that Thea Olivia had been offended by the unconventional nature of the cocktail party of the previous evening. 'If you don't like it, lump it! If it doesn't suit you, you can go to the dickens!' she shouted in the empty room and sat down to write an acrimonious letter which began:

My dearest Tot,
I quite understand that I am not good enough for you and that my way of living is offensive to your very refined tastes, so-called.
But

'Oh, to hell with it,' she said, tore the sheet of paper into little pieces, squeezed the pieces into a ball and threw it into the fire.

After that, irritated and depressed, she went to the Bar Bacchus to have a drink and a chat, and there she met Osbert's girlfriend, Catchy, who was slouching at the bar looking tired and defiant – which meant that she was ashamed of herself.

At the end of the bar, by the wall, the stool next to the one on which Catchy was sitting was vacant. Asta Thundersley, squeezing past, laid a hand between the shoulders of Catchy, who started away with a cry of pain and a sickly smile and said: 'Oh-oh! No touchy!'

'What the hell's the matter with you?' asked Asta.

Obviously it hurt Catchy to move her shoulders, so she shrugged one side of her face – hitched up her right cheek and let it drop – and said: 'Oh, he-men, he-men…'

Gonger the barman had mixed Asta's usual Tom Collins. She swallowed a mouthful of it and then what Catchy had said seemed to tick in her head like a time bomb. She remembered all that Detective Inspector Turpin had said to her one morning: *'Somebody who gets a thrill out of suffering: it might be a woman, it might be a man. Up comes the willing victim, which is all that this shy torturer, as you might call him, this murderer who is afraid to commit his murder – this willing victim is all that he needs to make him feel powerful.'*

And then Asta knew that the submissive Catchy, who said that she only wanted to make men happy, made happy only those men that needed victims, willing victims. She gave strength and confidence and comfort only to Evil. She was a back to be beaten, a backside to be lashed, a pair of wrists and a pair of ankles to be tied up – she was a training depot for murderers.

Asta Thundersley's big red face grew larger and redder. She got off her stool, drew herself up and shouted: 'Damn you! Take that!' – and, bringing up her right hand, slapped Catchy's face, adding: 'You destroy the world! You are filth! You are the Devil! I hate you!'

Then Asta walked out of the Bar Bacchus.

It was regarded as really extraordinary that, for the first time in living memory, Asta Thundersley had left a drink unfinished.

Catchy went into hysterics.

44

And so it comes to pass that Asta Thundersley is the one human being in the whole world of whom Catchy speaks with acrimony, even after all these years – all these dreary and terrible years, during which so many good men have died, so many strong men have got tired, so many soft hearts have hardened and so many beloved ones have been blown to dust.

Catchy could easily have forgotten that slap in the face, in spite of the fact that a slap in the face from Asta was something not easily forgotten. But, somehow, the words that had gone before the blow stuck in her mind. They touched a spring in her head, and somewhere a little door opened. Between Catchy and her pleasures, thereafter, there intruded nasty little visions of dead children.

All the same, she has not fundamentally changed. Not fundamentally. Now, if and when she is required to assist in the reinforcement of someone's dirty self-esteem, she collaborates willingly. But she cries afterwards.

There is, she feels, a great deal to cry for. She feels, especially in the dim hours before half past eleven in the morning, that nobody loves her, everybody hates her and life is not what it used to be in the good old gay days when the Bar Bacchus was full of life and everyone was sweet and kind to her.

From time to time she says, with a look of wild incredulity, that she simply cannot believe that so many people can have changed so much in such a little time. It is true that things have happened. The Sonia Sabbatani affair became a bore. Franco jostled it away into the lower right-hand corners of the newspapers when he began to poke his Moorish spearhead into the guts of Spain. Hitler, to whose name we still prefixed a polite *Herr,* was getting ready to take Czechoslovakia. Things were happening in the world, and things – very terrible things – have happened, compared with which the murder of the Sabbatani girl is nothing but a flea bite.

Yet, as Mr Pink never tires of reiterating: 'It is all the same sort of thing. Maidanek, Belsen, Auschwitz, Sonia Sabbatani – the difference is only a matter of scale and legality.'

He is still around. God knows what has happened to most of the rest. Gonger has retired. Mrs Sabbatani, living in misery with her sister-in-law Sarah, is drifting to bankruptcy. Sam is dead and is prayed for every year on the anniversary of his death. The Tiger

Fitzpatrick and Mrs Kipling are going downhill as fast as they can possibly go; Turpin has become chief inspector; Schiff has made money by marketing a mixture of cheap gin and horseradish which is called *Ish*; Shocket The Bloodsucker fell dead of a stroke, and nobody mourns him; Titch Whitbread, having lost the sight of one eye, makes a good living whistling for taxis outside a West End restaurant; Hemmeridge, to everyone's astonishment, died like a proper man in the Western Desert; Goggs the butcher went to jail for black-market operations and then seemed to evaporate. All the others have simply gone away, and no one even thinks of them. Thea Olivia continues to visit members of her family. Generally, she is received with hypocritical shrieks of false delight: she has fifty thousand pounds to leave when she dies. Her patchwork quilt is six feet long and five feet wide and still unfinished; she wants to add, and add, and add to it – she will see to it that the work lasts as long as her eyesight. She is an exquisite needlewoman, and her quilt keeps her happy. God knows what she thinks of as the fine, gold-eyed needle goes in and out. She has washed Tobit Osbert out of her mind.

45

He has got into Public Relations and is doing tolerably well.

There is no doubt about it – the man has charm. He still takes his nieces to the circus, and the joke still holds good – that he does not take the children, but they take him. Now, as ever, he gasps at the whip-crack and laughs until he cries at the clowns, the Joeys and the Alphonses as they tumble in.

It was always the same with Uncle Toby. He always sucked in an anxious breath while the lion-tamers cowed the tawny, snarling big cats. When the wire-walker, who pretended to be drunk, climbed up the pylon to the high wire and, reeling and stumbling, seemed about to fall, he half rose with sweat on his face. The little girls laughed at their silly uncle. Did he not realise that it was all an act? Didn't he know that in a circus such things were done every day, year in and year out? Silly uncle, nice uncle! Simple-minded uncle!

The children could not be expected to know that he went to the circus as he went to musical reviews, half hoping that something unexpected might happen.

The equestrienne might fall off the great white horse. The leopard that watched, crouching, lashing its tail, might spring and rend. There was one chance in a million that the intoxicated-looking man on the high wire might just for that once really be drunk and fall; and, oh, the soft wicked thud of the body in the sawdust!

There was the woman who hung by the chin on the edge of a sabre; and there were the Flying Foxes, three men and a girl. One of them always pretended, on the high trapeze, to miss his cue. There was a moment of frightful tension. Say, just say, that he had been up a little too late the night before and for one split second lost confidence? The Murderer knew how easily, in a split second, a man can lose confidence. Or say that the girl, who fascinated and terrified the whole world with her triple somersaults, underestimated or overestimated her take-off by the merest mote of time, so that the big man missed? He could see the madly clutching fingers grasping nothing; hear the screams of the spectators… The big man swung himself back to his platform, but before he reached it the girl was bouncing on the sawdust, while everyone stood up, stretched taut with horror.

Meanwhile, to the left and the right of him, his nieces squealed with delight.

Then there were the sideshows. There were midgets, bearded ladies, living skeletons, The Ugliest Woman In The World and The Limbless Wonder. This last-named freak had a beautiful head and an indeterminate torso without arms or legs. She painted in watercolour, holding the brush between her teeth. He could watch her for hours.

Also he liked the midgets that lived in dolls' houses – men and women of mature age; the biggest was no taller than a four-year-old child. How nice to be with such people, the strongest of whom he could pick up with one hand!

After these exhibitions, there were always things to do. One spieler invited him to 'smash up the happy home'. At the end of a brightly lit blind-alley stood a representation of a peaceful kitchen – a table set with plates, cups and dishes and a dresser full of plates and cups and saucers. You bought the right to smash everything – seven balls cost a shilling. You took careful aim and threw. A tea-cup flew to fragments; a dinner plate dropped to shards. Crash! – and a soup plate tinkled down. Respectable husbands of wives and fathers of families slapped down their shillings and hurled their wooden balls at 'The Happy Home'.

And the shooting galleries, too, had clay figures of men and animals which, when hit with a little lead bullet, burst asunder like Judas Iscariot. Or there was a tired-looking little old man in a high silk hat. You could see him in his entirety, but he was protected up to the crown of his head by a wire fence. Only the hat was vulnerable, and you knocked that off – with wooden balls again. The nieces shrieked with glee and congratulated their uncle on his skill.

There was a softer side to this idealist: he loved to amuse the children.

Above everything – the crack of little rifles, the spank of wooden balls against skittles, the smash of broken crockery and the twang of the wire fence that guarded the man in the silk hat – there was the gay scream of the calliope and the shrieks of the young ladies coming out of the 'Haunted House'. Here, passing down dark passages made comically horrible by dancing skeletons and uncertain floors, you arrived at a chute. It let you down with a rush. Scores of young men jostled one another at the bottom of the chute. As the girls slid down, kicking and shrieking, the watchful spectators could rely upon a glimpse of underwear and sometimes that which it was supposed to conceal.

Having taken his nieces home, he generally went back to the funfair alone.

46

Asta, as I write, is being talked into militancy on the side of August Lang Fowler, who claims to have recorded the thin, high, agonised cry of cut flowers.

Only Catchy goes regularly to the Bar Bacchus nowadays – and about her there clings, always, an atmosphere of guilt, of maudlin grief, stale liquor and decay that makes you long for a good high wind to blow her and her kind from the face of the earth, the fly-blown face of the exhausted earth.

LONDON BOOKS

FLYING THE FLAG FOR
FREE-THINKING LITERATURE

www.london-books.co.uk

London Classics

The Angel And The Cuckoo *Gerald Kersh*
Doctor Of The Lost *Simon Blumenfeld*
The Gilt Kid *James Curtis*
It Always Rains On Sunday *Arthur La Bern*
Jew Boy *Simon Blumenfeld*
May Day *John Sommerfield*
Night And The City *Gerald Kersh*
Prelude To A Certain Midnight *Gerald Kersh*
A Start In Life *Alan Sillitoe*
There Ain't No Justice *James Curtis*
They Drive By Night *James Curtis*
Wide Boys Never Work *Robert Westerby*

LONDON CLASSICS

NIGHT AND THE CITY

GERALD KERSH

Harry Fabian is a cockney wide boy who will do anything for
a pound note; a storyteller who craves recognition, his endless
lies hiding a deeper, inner weakness. He is also a ponce, and
one who is walking on the edge. It is only a matter of time
before he topples over the side.

Set in 1930s London, against a fluorescent West End backdrop,
Night And The City brings the Soho of legend to life, the streets
a tangle of drinking dens and night-clubs, author Gerald Kersh's
characters flamboyant creations who add a cosmopolitan edge to
the book's journey into the darker shades of human nature.

Twice filmed, *Night And The City* remains a 'lowlife' classic,
and comes with an introduction by John King, author of
The Football Factory and *Human Punk*.

London Books
£11.99 hardback
ISBN 978-0-9551851-3-7

London Classics

THE ANGEL AND THE CUCKOO

GERALD KERSH

Paul Auster, Ian McEwan and Don DeLillo all know that the city is a place of absurdity, and each of them have played with the form of their novels to accentuate and clarify the absurdities that city-dwellers face on a daily basis. Yet before any of them had their first novel published Gerald Kersh had written his last masterpiece *The Angel And The Cuckoo*. This is a novel of London that cuts back and forth in time through the Depression years between the two world wars, following artists, criminals, lovers, singers, conmen, film producers, writers and other lowlifes as they each follow their singular obsessions.

There are three love stories, all connected by Steve Zobrany, proprietor of The Angel And The Cuckoo, a café in a hidden courtyard at one end of Carnaby Street. Through Zobrany we meet film producer Gèza Cseh, the sublime Alma, artist without an art Tom Henceforth, omnipotent criminal mastermind Perp and many others. Kersh shows that each of them carries the seeds of corruption, and what they do with these desires will define them for the rest of their lives. All this, and the book is as funny as hell.

Comes with an in-depth introduction by Paul Duncan, author of *Alfred Hitchcock* and *Stanley Kubrick*, and editor of *The Charlie Chaplin Archives* and *The James Bond Archives*. He is currently preparing a biography on Gerald Kersh.

London Books
£11.99 hardback
ISBN 978-0-9568155-0-7

London Classics

IT ALWAYS RAINS ON SUNDAY

ARTHUR LA BERN

Set over a single day in 1939, *It Always Rains On Sunday* captures the East End of London shortly before the start of the Second World War. The book is centred around the residents of Coronet Grove, its focus the Sandigate family. People go about their lives, heading to the local church and pub, while those looking for excitement are drawn to the bright lights of Whitechapel. Rose – a former barmaid in The Two Compasses – is married to George Sandigate, twenty years her senior, the thrill of her time with villain Tommy Swann firmly in the past. Church bells ring as small-time crooks plot in the pub, a newspaper headline telling Rose that Swann has escaped from Dartmoor.

It Always Rains On Sunday is the atmospheric debut novel of Arthur La Bern and features a large, colourful cast of characters. Dreams and reality clash as arguments rage, gangsters lurk, madness simmers, violence is threatened. Sex and death hang heavy in the air. Described as a predecessor to Alan Sillitoe's *Saturday Night And Sunday Morning*, the film adaptation was a great success and *It Always Rains On Sunday* remains a classic of British cinema. The book and its author were likewise lauded, and La Bern would go on to write a series of largely London-based, working-class gems.

London Books
£11.99
ISBN 978-0-9568155-5-2

London Classics

MAY DAY

JOHN SOMMERFIELD

Set across a three-day period in 1930s London, *May Day* follows
the fortunes of a wide range of characters as working-class anger
bubbles over in the East End and spills towards the West End on
May 1st. Idealism, exploitation and police violence all play a part
in the journey from cockney London to moneyed London,
the climactic demonstration highlighting a period of
heightened social awareness in the capital.

First published in 1936, *May Day* is an imaginative, fast-paced
book that rejects stereotypes as it searches for the common
humanity in every individual. From the hardships and dreams of
factory workers to the privilege and regrets of the wealthy, author
John Sommerfield brings a whole society into the spotlight.
Sommerfield was a politically active man who fought in the
Spanish Civil War and on the streets of London, and his writing
reflects both his beliefs and his own positive nature.

London Books
£11.99 hardback
ISBN 978-0-9551851-8-2

LONDON CLASSICS

A START IN LIFE

ALAN SILLITOE

Alan Sillitoe's first novel, *Saturday Night And Sunday Morning*, was published in 1958, *The Loneliness Of The Long-Distance Runner* arriving the following year. Both were hits and led to high-profile films, which in turn cemented his reputation. Tagged an 'Angry Young Man' by the media, Sillitoe's ability to record and interpret the lives of ordinary people was nothing short of revolutionary. He wrote prolifically right up to his death in 2010, his stature as one of England's greatest post-war authors remaining unchallenged

A Start In Life tells the story of Michael Cullen, who abandons his pregnant girlfriend and heads 'to the lollipop-metropolis of London in the 1960s'. Cullen is, in theory, leaving his problems behind, but he is 'the Devil on two sticks' and becomes involved in a smuggling ring with Moggerhanger, a man who believes 'that you must get anything you want no matter at what cost to others'. Cullen is an optimist, with an eye for the ladies, but his new swinging lifestyle is soon under threat.

London Books
£11.99 hardback
ISBN 978-0-9551851-1-3

LONDON CLASSICS

THE GILT KID

JAMES CURTIS

The Gilt Kid is fresh out of prison, a burglar with communist sympathies who isn't thinking about rehabilitation. Society is unfair and he wants some cash in his pocket and a place to live, and he quickly lines up a couple of burglaries in the London suburbs. But complications arise, and he finds himself dodging the police, checking the newspapers and looking over his shoulder, fearing the ultimate punishment for a crime he hasn't committed. He remains defiant throughout, right up until the book's final, ironic conclusion.

James Curtis recreates the excitement of 1930s London as he delves into the sleazy glamour of the underworld mindset; a world of low-level criminals and prostitutes. His vibrant use of slang is as snappy as anything around today, his dialogue cosh-like as the Gilt Kid moves through the pubs and clubs and caffs of Soho. Curtis knew his subject matter, and this cult novel doubles as a powerful social observation.

This new edition comes with an introduction by Paul Willetts, author of *Fear And Loathing In Fitzrovia*, the best-selling biography of author Julian Maclaren-Ross, and an interview with Curtis's daughter, Nicolette Edwards.

London Books
£11.99 hardback
ISBN 978-0-9551851-2-0

LONDON CLASSICS

THEY DRIVE BY NIGHT

JAMES CURTIS

When he discovers the body of a murdered girlfriend, former
convict and small-time crook Shorty Mathews panics and heads
for the Great North Road, leaving London behind as he enters
a world of bustling transport caffs, canny lorry drivers and
happy-go-lucky tarts. A manhunt is soon launched, Shorty
hitching rides as he tries to stay ahead of the police, along the
way saving a travelling girl from being raped. Decency and
romance are alive and well, while back in London the real
murderer is busy prowling the streets of the West End,
his mental ramblings promising further killings.

They Drive By Night is a fast-paced, slang-sharp,
socially aware novel that sees author James Curtis developing
themes previously explored in his first London Classics
release *The Gilt Kid*. Curtis captures both the vibrancy and
realities of the lorry-driving world and life on the streets of
1930s London, while at the same time highlighting the
murderous contempt some people felt towards those
they considered below them in society's pecking order.

London Books
£11.99 hardback
ISBN 978-0-9551851-4-4

London Classics

THERE AIN'T NO JUSTICE

JAMES CURTIS

Tommy Mutch is a working-class lad from the slums of West London, eager to escape the mean streets of Notting Dale. Boxing is in its heyday and, like many in his position, Tommy sees it as an escape route from poverty. As a 'preliminary' boy on the verge of making the breakthrough this is more than just a dream, but he hasn't bargained for the obstacles he has to face outside the ring – crooked promoters, hucksters, pimps, small-time gangsters. Tommy has strong morals and a fierce sense of justice, but these are about to be put to the test.

In one respect, *There Ain't No Justice* is an exposé of boxing in the 1930s, but as with all of James Curtis' fiction there is another level to the book. While he captures the blood, sweat and tears of the sport, he also questions the dream – if it is right this should be the only way Tommy can emerge from the ranks of the downtrodden. Tommy's inherent decency runs through the narrative, but he has been sucked into a world where losers are winners, and winners often lose out. Turned into a successful film, *There Ain't No Justice* is raw, sad and exciting, but ultimately the uplifting story of a good family man battling hard times in pre-war London.

This edition includes an introduction by Martin Knight, author of books such as *Common People* and *Battersea Girl*, as well as biographies on the bare-knuckle fighters Jimmy Stockins and Joe Smith.

London Books
£11.99 hardback
ISBN 978-0-9568155-3-8

LONDON CLASSICS

WIDE BOYS NEVER WORK

ROBERT WESTERBY

Young Jim Bankley yearns to leave behind the production line in a provincial town when he chances on a London razor-gang at a local dog track. Seduced by the opportunity to live life on the edge, he follows them back to London. He is thrown into a milieu of bruisers, brasses, car dealers and con-merchants. Drenched in sleaze and brutality, he begins to wonder if the simple life is so bad after all.

Robert Westerby's 1937 novel provoked a stir at the time, authentically lifting the lid on an underworld metropolis that many pretended did not exist. It has lost none of its punch in the ensuing seventy years – and slang historians generally credit Westerby with coining the term wide boy. The book was filmed in 1956 under the name *Soho Incident*.

This new edition boasts a penetrative introduction from leading London author and broadcaster Iain Sinclair, whose work includes *London Orbital* and *London, City of Disappearances*. He is a long-time champion of often overlooked vintage London writers such as Westerby, James Curtis and Gerald Kersh.

London Books
£11.99 hardback
ISBN 978-0-9551851-5-1

JEW BOY

SIMON BLUMENFELD

Jew Boy is a novel about poverty and politics in the tumultuous world of London's Jewish East End in the 1930s, where boxers mixed with anarchists and communists, and Yiddish actors and poets rubbed shoulders with gamblers and gangsters. All were united in their hatred of fascism, and were prepared to fight it when necessary. Yet of equal interest is the novel's exploration of the personal lives and thwarted aspirations of young people at this time, both Jewish and non-Jewish. Class means as much to the main protagonists as the older ties of religion and race.

Author Simon Blumenfeld – born in Whitechapel, working its markets as a young man – brings to life the reality of sweatshops and sweated labour, vividly portraying the exhaustion produced by long hours, unforgiving deadlines and cut-throat competition. But this is a story driven by hope, a desire for change, and his descriptions of the exciting culture that existed beyond the workplace help produce a testimony to a unique time and place now firmly embedded in London's volatile history. *Jew Boy* is nothing less than the founding work of what went on to become a unique body of fiction, autobiography and drama – the literature of the twentieth-century Jewish East End.

Ken Worpole, who introduces the novel, is the author of *Dockers And Detectives*, and has played a major part in reviving public interest in the work of Simon Blumenfeld and other Jewish writers from the pre-war East End.

London Books
£11.99 hardback
ISBN 978-0-9568155-1-4

DOCTOR OF THE LOST

SIMON BLUMENFELD

When young Thomas Barnardo arrived in London in 1866, he planned to study at the London Hospital before venturing abroad to work as a missionary. The conditions he found in the East End stopped him in his tracks. Unemployment, poverty, overcrowding, alcoholism and deathly diseases were bad enough, but seeing thousands of half-starved children living on the streets broke his heart. Inside a year Dr Barnardo had opened the ragged-school Hope Place and by 1870 the first of his eponymous homes was in operation. His work continues to this day. *Doctor Of The Lost* is the fictionalised story of Tom Barnardo's early years in East London.

Author Simon Blumenfeld grew up in the same streets, his cult 1935 novel *Jew Boy* capturing the magic of the Jewish East End of the 1930s, and *Doctor Of The Lost* (1938) recreates the area in Dr Barnardo's day. Drawing on a friendship with his widow, Blumenfeld brings Barnardo vividly to life, showing the struggles he faced and the battles won. *Doctor Of The Lost* is set in a London of rampant industrialisation, when the few became rich at the expense of the many, and yet this was also a period of charity and good works, when idealists such as Thomas Barnardo were prepared to stand tall and fight back.

London Books
£11.99 hardback
ISBN 978-0-9568155-2-1

New British Fiction

MALAYAN SWING

PETE HAYNES

Aidan is different. He is small, awkward and often silent, an easy
man to ignore, mock or exploit, yet on the inside he is intelligent
and thoughtful. He speaks to the reader in a way he can't manage
in everyday life, reflecting on the world around him with great
insight and an almost childlike honesty. This is the internal
life of an outsider.

We meet Aidan not long after he has moved into a room in a
shared flat, forced from the home in which he felt secure by a policy
labelled 'care in the community'. But the community is dismissive
and threatening. He becomes lonely and scared, his best friend
the radio he carries everywhere. An old shed offers a hideaway
during the day, while his evenings are often spent in the local pubs.

Aidan's physical and mental state starts to deteriorate, and when
he bumps into Joey from the home he comes to the notice of some
bad people. He wanders the streets and is attacked, his life quickly
spiralling out of control. The story ends in dramatic fashion, but it is
Aidan's decency and a sense of escape that remain with the reader.
Malayan Swing is a moving novel, a testament to those living on the
margins of society, and as such is a brave and important work.

London Books
£8.99 paperback
ISBN 978-0-9551851-6-8

NEW BRITISH FICTION

BARRY DESMOND IS A WANKER

MARTIN KNIGHT

Barry Desmond is an only child. He's had a sheltered upbringing by ageing parents distrustful of the outside world. This leaves him ill-equipped to deal with the savagery of school, the trials of adolescence and the reality and politics of the workplace.

At school he is a figure of fun, excluded and picked on. At home he struggles with the eccentricities of his parents and is alarmed and confused as his hormones spring into life. He finds guilty pleasure in self-relief. Later, he follows his father into a career with the Empire Bank, a throwback organisation doomed to become extinct. In middle age, and following the death of his parents and redundancy, Barry ventures out into the wider world determined to live his life and strike up relationships. Unlike his parents Barry believes that people are fundamentally decent.
Will he find the fulfilment and interaction he craves?
Will society repay Barry's trust?

This novel from Martin Knight, author of *Battersea Girl* and *Common People*, explores and illuminates 21st-century suburban loneliness and the grim reality of having a face that doesn't fit. *Barry Desmond Is A Wanker* is a seductive and surprising book, laced with humour, shot through with poignancy and sensitivity.

London Books
£8.99 paperback
ISBN 978-0-9551851-9-9

New British Fiction

THE LIBERAL POLITICS OF ADOLF HITLER

JOHN KING

It is sometime in the future and the individual nations of Europe no longer exist, with power centralised in a United State Of Europe (USE). This corporate-driven, closet dictatorship promotes New Democracy, its true nature hidden behind wide smiles, easy debt and lots of empty liberal rhetoric. With the major cities run by Good Europeans, locals live as second-class citizens. Across the continent, resistance groups fight back. Britain is no different.

In London, an ambitious young bureaucrat uses Suspicion software to identify threats to the USE, stumbling across a shocking murder just as a high-ranking Controller is about to arrive from Brussels. At the same time, a member of GB45 leaves one of the Free English towns in Wessex and heads towards the capital. Despite the efforts of special police unit Cool and the threat of Hardcore paramilitaries, these three men are set on a collision course.

The Liberal Politics Of Adolf Hitler imagines a world where doublespeak meets baby-talk; the internet has morphed into propaganda/surveillance tool InterZone; correctness and a denied censorship crushes expression; physical copies of books, audio and film are illegal; the people's culture is consistently stolen and sold back to them in distorted forms; and enforced digitisation has seen history edited, deleted and rewritten. In the USE, even the most wicked of individuals can be reinvented.

London Books
£9.99 paperback
ISBN 978-0-9568155-8-3